Mildred Downey Broxon

Too Long a Sacrifice

Futura
Macdonald & Co
London & Sydney

An Orbit Book

First published in Great Britain in 1983
by Futura Publications, a Division of
Macdonald & Co (Publishers) Ltd
London & Sydney

68307761

ISBN 0 7088 8096 7

Made and printed in Great Britain by
Hazell Watson & Viney Ltd, Aylesbury, Bucks

NELSON

Futura Publications
A Division of
Macdonald & Co (Publishers) Ltd
Maxwell House
74 Worship Street
London EC2A 2EN

THIS WAS NOT THE TIME FOR LAMENTS, BUT FOR VENGEANCE . . .

He had witnessed a deed that called for cursing such as he had never done. He stood in the sunshine beside the three corpses and struck a note on his harp, that all who dwelt in the air and under the earth might hear:

Those who ride the wind, dwellers in the ancient mounds, soldiers slain in honest battle, hear the call of Tadhg MacNiall, the bard, for vengeance for my fallen friends. May the Poet's Curse lie long on those who did this thing. May their land be black and blighted as their hearts; may their barren wives mock them as the cause; may their bastard children revile their names. May they wish to die long before their time, and when they perish, may they wander cold and in torment, shunned by those on the earth and under the earth alike. I, Tadhg MacNiall, call this curse on them, and will that it be so.

To my father,
who spoke to me of Ireland

TOO LONG A SACRIFICE

MILDRED DOWNEY BROXON

"Too long a sacrifice
Can make a stone of the heart.
O when may it suffice?
That is Heaven's part . . ."

W. B. Yeats: "Easter 1916"

Map of Ireland

ULSTER

CONNAUGHT

LEINSTER

MUNSTER

N

1. Lough Neagh
2. Antrim
3. Belfast
4. Dundalk
5. Newry
6. River Boyne
7. Hill of Tara
8. Dublin
9. Rathcrogan
10. River Shannon
11. The Border of
    the Six Counties
12. Achill Island

- BASSILVERGORAN -

INTRODUCTION

The Irish use of the English language involves some non-English constructions, or Gaelicisms. I have tried to reproduce this speech pattern.

As the novel is set in Ireland, various Irish words appear in the text. Gaelic spelling is anything but phonetic. Those who find it difficult to read words they cannot pronounce may be interested in the following; others may skip this section. PRONUNCIATION: Concerning character names, Maire is pronounced *May*-ruh. Tadhg is Tahg. Conn Sléaghéar's name is rendered Conn *Shlay*-year and means Sharpspear. Fionn equals Finn. Padraig is pronounced *Pad*-rig. Sean is Shawn. Eoin is equivalent to the English "Owen"; Ciara, his sister's name, is *Key*-arra. Diancecht, the Irish god of healing, is pronounced *Dee*-an-ket. And King Laoghaire, who was buried standing up, is the ancient equivalent of "Leary." The Tuatha Dé Danann, the ancient gods of Ireland, are pronounced *Too*-aha *Day Dan*-nann. And the Sídhe are pronounced shee. Ceili is a music festival: *kay*-lee.

As to festivals, Bealtaine (bahl-*tay*-nya) is May first; Samhain (Sow-*ween*) is October thirty-first.

The Taín Bo Cuailnge, an Irish epic, is pronounced Toyn Boe Coo-*lee*-nya. The tribe to which Tadhg and Maire belonged, the Cruthini, is pronounced Croo-*hee*-nee. Lough Neagh is pronounced Lah Nay, and Cruachan, Maeve's palace, is *Croo*-ah-han. And finally, a *geas* (an injunction laid on one, usually by supernatural means) is pronounced gaysh.

Other words are close enough to phonetic that finer points of pronunciation may be disregarded.

ACKNOWLEDGEMENTS: A number of persons have been generous with their time. I would like to take this opportunity to thank you. The Harvey Powder Company and John Neiswanger provided me with specialized information I could not have otherwise obtained.

William D. Broxon, my husband, was with me almost every step of the way (I did *not* take him to Ulster!). Many elements in the book originated with him.

Poul and Karen Anderson, F. M. and Elinor Busby, Dr. and Mrs. Thomas E. Downey, Donald Bensen, and James Frenkel all went through the original manuscript with care. Their comments were valid and extremely valuable.

None of the above, of course, are to be blamed for any errors or infelicities. For those I claim full credit.

Lastly, I would like to thank the people of Northern Ireland. They remain warm, human, and hospitable under intolerable conditions. They took kindly care of a lone, frightened American who had never before lived in a war zone.

The first two chapters are based on an earlier work, "The Antrim Hills," published in *Aurora: Beyond Equality*, edited by Vonda N. McIntyre and Susan Janice Anderson, Fawcett–Gold Medal, 1976. These chapters have been completely rewritten and bear only historical resemblance to their original form.

CHAPTER ONE

On the shores of deep, dreaming Lough Neagh, in the Kingdom of Ulaídh, when Conn Sléaghéar was King of the Cruthini, Tadhg MacNiall and his wife Maire ní Donnall dwelt together in peace. Comely they both were, and young. The folk of the countryside liked them well, for Tadhg was a harpist, and Maire had skill as a healer.

As was the custom with noble families, Tadhg's birth parents fostered him in his youth to others of their clan, that he might learn a young man's skills, and that the ties between families grow strong. His foster-father was a harpist, and Tadhg soon took up that instrument himself. His foster-brother, Fionn, the son of the house, was a merry lad. He and Tadhg played many a boyish prank together.

When Tadhg grew older, he was sent to study with a bard, for he had far surpassed his foster-father in skill. Tadhg was away for some time.

At Lugnasad, Tadhg returned to his foster-home singing. He swung his harp beside him as he strode through the summer forest. Overhead, birds joined his song, the sky was blue and cloudless, and sunshafts smote through rustling boughs. Lough Neagh glimmered in the distance, and the air hung sweet with the smells of leaf and grass and earth.

His foster-parents' *rath* was a large fortification, its earth wall topped with a palisade of sharpened stakes. Inside were thatched dwellings, cattle pens, storerooms, houses for spinning and churning and weaving, a cook hut, and the Great Hall whose wooden pillars, carved and painted, gleamed in the early sunlight. At this hour few folk were about, save those who tended the dairy.

All the better, thought Tadhg, *I can greet them with the sun.* He rubbed his chin, thinking. He was proud of the soft new down. He lifted his harp and struck a chord.

> *Hello to the household*
> *For homeward has come*
> *Your far-faring harpist,*
> *Your own foster-son!*

At that the door opened, and Tadhg's foster-mother stepped forth. She embraced him, stood back to marvel at how tall he'd grown, and told him welcome. She was richly dressed as usual, in embroidered linen and golden bangles, but her face was lined and sad. *She's grown old.*

"At least," she said, "I've one son left to me."

He would have asked what she meant, but then Fionn shambled forth, and he saw. The two boys were of an age, and Fionn too had grown tall and gangly, with a first shadow of beard; but while Tadhg was bright-eyed with the joy of life, Fionn's gaze focused on something beyond. He smiled at empty air. Only then did he greet Tadhg.

"Welcome, foster-brother." His tone was flat, and he held his head to one side, as if he heard something out of human ken. He struck Tadhg's harp and laughed. "Brass strings! Brass, to play the moonlight!"

Tadhg wondered if Fionn were drunk, so early in the day; but no, he sensed an otherness about him. His foster-mother shook her head and led the boys inside.

Fionn had been this way for months, she explained, and slipped daily farther from the ways of men. He slept but little. When he spoke his words were strange. Tadhg's foster-father sat by the hearth, staring at the coals. He'd kept mostly silent.

"He was never a changeling, he was a normal boy, you and he would play . . ." his foster-mother wept, and Tadhg lay a clumsy hand on her shoulder. Across the room Fionn stared into darkness. A faint smile curved his lips.

"Have you sent for a healer?" Tadhg said.

"I did. She lives not far from here. She came and brought her fosterling—a comely lass. Nothing they did was any use, and at last they went home in sorrow. Fionn looks at me so strangely, as if at times he did not know his own mother."

Fionn smote the wall, rose, and stalked out. Tadhg excused himself and followed.

Moonlight silvered the treetops and glimmered the wavelets on Lough Neagh; a wind soughed through the forest. Fionn walked toward the crest of a hill and stood looking down into a depression. Stars gleamed on the bog-water where reeds shivered.

"What is it, Fionn?" Tadhg came close, but did not touch him.

"Eyes." Fionn gestured at the starry bog. "Eyes, pulling me, promising—" he turned and spat. "You, with all your studies—how can the druids teach you the magic of a bard? You will be a harpist, a reciter of old tales and genealogies, that is all. You cannot *learn* the power to blight crops, to raise boils on a man's face, to strike women barren—no matter how many years you study, Tadhg, you will never grasp magic! Magic has touched me. It cannot be learned. Let me be!" His voice held flat hate, and he raised an arm as if to strike.

Tadhg stepped back, reining in his anger. He had no wish to fight his brother. Best he withdraw. "Very well."

Back home, Tadhg slept ill, and his dreams were troubled. A horned man shook a spear, and laughed. Tadgh woke sweating. There was nothing but night, and his brother's wakeful breathing. But why fear the Horned One?

Nonetheless, he left home to resume his studies long before Lugnasad festivities were over. By autumn word came that Fionn had been found drowned in the bog. No mark was on his body. Self-murder, it was whispered. Folk spoke no more of the shame, nor did Tadhg ever say his foster-brother's name again.

So Tadhg MacNiall grew to manhood. He committed the great legends to memory, and became a favorite of the king, Conn Sléaghéar. For his poems folk gave him arm-rings, bright mantles, cattle, and goods of every sort. Never mind what Fionn had said, Tadhg was a bard. Magic lay in his words, the power to bless and to curse. When his foster-parents died, their *rath* came to him, for they had no living children.

Maire ní Donnall, the healer's foster-daughter, grew woman-tall, and she and Tadhg looked on each other with gladness. One feast of Imbolc, on a chill foggy morning, they walked toward each other past the fire, and were handfasted for a year. When that year passed, they did not walk apart; so time went on in peace.

*   *   *

Months slid around to the warm season. Winter blasts shivered to silence; sun called life from the earth, and things awoke. It was time for the great change, the handing over of the year.

He and She faced each other, He on His gaunt, hard-ridden steed. Its mane was wind, its hooves hail. She was sleepy yet, and unfurled Her arms like tender shoots. He nodded. "The year is yours," He said. "I will reclaim it at Samhain." He rode slowly off.

On Bealtaine Eve the household bustled with preparations. Nonetheless, when an old beggarman brought news that Brigid's newborn did not thrive, Maire ní Donnall left the day's instructions to her bondfolk, packed her bag of herbs, and walked from the cool house. She passed through the gate in the outer defensive wall and set off down the road afoot. Dust and gravel gritted beneath her sandals, and her mantle swirled behind her. The morning was already warm.

Maire had scant liking for Brigid, nor for Brigid's husband Seamus. They might, in courtesy, have brought the child to her, rather than send summons. But she was by profession a healer, and she had attended Brigid at the birth. Thus she was honor-bound. A fine day for walking: Goddess-weather, it was. The scent of flowers and grass lay thick in the air, and the sun glowed her skin. She made note of medicinal herbs she might pick tomorrow, when they'd be strengthened by the holy day.

As she walked, her resentment cooled. It was the child that needed her, after all, and the poor suckling should not be scorned for his parents' sloth. Had he been of noble birth he might hope to be fostered out in later years, but in his lowborn condition he would soon grow as slovenly as his mother and father, for lack of better example.

It was no great distance to the small sod-walled

hut. The refuse heap outside buzzed with flies. Maire's nostrils flared at the stench.

Brigid slouched in the doorway. Her once-saffron dress was stained brown at the hem where it dragged in the dirt, and the front was streaked with food. She was enormously fat, nigh as great in girth as she'd been when carrying the child. Her long hair hung in tangles, and her skin was smeared with soot. She grunted and stepped aside; Maire followed her into the hut.

At first she was blinded by darkness. She stumbled over refuse on the packed earthen floor. In the corner she heard a cry. As her eyes adjusted to dim light she saw the infant, naked on a crusted sheepskin.

"He will not nurse," said Brigid, "and he thrashes so—" Even as she spoke a spasm shook the baby. He arched his back and forced out a bleat. His fists clenched and his eyes rolled back in his head. For a few moments he stopped breathing, then gasped.

Hands on hips, Brigid confronted Maire. "My others never did so, even those who died."

Maire looked down at the emaciated form. True, this birth had been much longer than usual for Brigid, who bore with the ease of a cow. Maire had feared, at the start, that the child would never breathe, but at last he did, and he'd then seemed brisk enough. Now, a brief nine days later—no, none of Brigid's other get had been like this. Sickness had claimed six, yes, but three others roared and played outside in the muck. She could hear the din of them now.

She set down her bag of herbs and touched the child. He was too warm, even for such a day, and instead of filling out, as a newborn should, he was thin, his skin dry and loose. This thing was imperfect, a twisted mockery of humankind. The child she had helped deliver was not the child that lay before her now. Sickness gagged her as she spoke: "I fear your son has been Taken, and you nurse a changeling, Brigid."

The woman screamed and flew at her. Maire grasped the fat wrists, held the clawing nails from her face, until Brigid collapsed into sobs. "It's old I'm getting, this one may be the last, why would They—why would They—Seamus will be saying I should have had him Christened, as the monks advise. But no, you with your fine airs and graces and special studies, *you* said to pay them no heed. Seamus will leave me now, he will—" She changed, quick as wind over water, from grief back to rage. "I curse you, Maire ní Donnall, with the mother's curse, and may the Goddess hear! You who cannot heal my son, you who envied me my children, may you be struck barren. You who live in your fine house with your husband the bard, may he wander far and may you seek him down the years."

Maire held both of Brigid's wrists in one strong hand and slapped the puffy face. "Mind what you summon! It's your grief that drives you mad, else you'd crawl for that. I cannot bring back a changeling; no healer could. Be kind to him, and know your own son is safe in Faerie."

The other woman collapsed again in grief. "But the child was mine, I carried him. They had no right—"

"The Old Ones *need* no right," said Maire. "Guard your tongue. As for the poor little thing here, you might wash it, and give it a mead-soaked rag to suck. That will quiet it, at least, and may stop the fits. Now I'll be going, and forgetting what else you said." She turned toward the door; behind her she heard only sobs.

The day had gone grey, and it seemed the sky sat heavy on the land. On her walk home she noticed clumps of feverfew and liverwort that she might gather on the morrow, but her heart was not disposed

toward healing. The 'child preyed on her mind, more
so than Brigid's curse; for what power, save that of a
mother, did Brigid wield? *But the power of a mother
will never be mine*; then, lest she ill-speak herself: *or
at least such power has not yet been granted me.*

Once she'd almost had a child of her body, and the
father was Tadhg. After the long months, she, the
healer, must at the last be tended by lesser women.
She knew, then, why mothers screamed. Even she
could not help shrieking as the pains came closer and
more intense—but they kept on, kept on, until one of
the women, desperate, reached in with dirty hands
and turned the child to bring it forth.

It did not cry. *It must be slapped, doused in cold
water, anything to make it cry.* But Maire was too
weak; when she tried to rise, the women held her
down. Bloody from childbed she fought them off and
reached her infant, but it lay blue and still. A boy, it
was; she would have named him after Tadhg.

The women murmured the usual consolations:
whatever soul the little one possessed had not been
ready to return; she was young, she would have more
children—all the meaningless phrases. Maire stood,
bleeding, and wept, then collapsed. They made her
drink brews she'd prepared, so that she slept for a
time. But in the night when none watched, her
aching breasts woke her, and she crept from the
house, down to the lakeshore.

Tadhg found her there, crawling toward the water,
trying to reach it and drown. He caught her, sang to
her, and carried her home.

Maire shivered. Ill it was to think of that time. She
had now so much to joy in. Tadhg was a good man,
and never had she regretted their decision at Imbolc,
four years past. Nor had they parted since their hand-
fasting, though others at times joyed their beds, as
was right for freefolk. But never since their first child
had Maire conceived.

She thought of Brigid, who yearly whelped to her dull husband. *Goddess, You give where You will, I should not question.* She hastened homeward.

She passed through the gate of her earth-walled *rath,* acknowledged the greeting of servants and bond-folk, and entered her long, cool, many-pillared house. She set down her bag of herbs and, grateful for the coolness, strode into the long hall.

Tadhg sat before the fireless hearth. In this heat he wore no woolen mantle. His bright linen tunic hung in folds; his long brown hair was combed, and his beard was trimmed. Gold circled his neck and wrists, and about his waist he wore an amber-studded belt.

He struck a chord upon his harp. Proud he was of that instrument, for he had fashioned it himself. From cutting, curing, and carving the willow to the final stringing with brass wire, it was uniquely his. He rose as she entered, set down the harp, and clasped her close. "Maire! They told me Brigid's child fared ill—"

Maire buried her face against his shoulder. "Changeling. Naught I could do." She felt him flinch, and did not add, *the mother cursed me.*

Tadhg drew a deep breath. "Festivities tomorrow, and great feasting tonight." His arms were muscular, his body hard. He smiled down at her. "Have we time, then, to close off our chamber?"

Maire smelled his clean man-scent, the sunny odor of new-washed linen. She felt his fine strong hands about her waist. *Tadhg will never leave me, it matters not Brigid's curse.*

They told the servants they would not be disturbed, went to the master chamber, and pulled the curtains.

"More beautiful are you, almost, than music," said Tadhg, "and more substantial, entirely." He raised on one elbow and regarded her.

Their narrow bedchamber was dark, the shutters

closed. Linen sheets draped the feather mattress, and woolen blankets heaped the shelves.

Maire kissed Tadhg on the chest and ran her hand down the length of his body. "Did time permit," she tickled him, "and had you any strength left"—he seized her in mock fury—"but we must be off down the road if we're to reach the royal *rath* by sunset."

"Conn Sléaghéar may wield his sharp spear tonight," Tadhg chuckled. "For I've seen his eye on you."

"As well he might. And I doubt not Queen Deirdre smiles on you."

Tadhg winced. Maire regretted her words. It was Tadhg who'd sung courage to the warriors before the very battle in which Deirdre—fighting beside her husband—had been scarred. No matter how carefully Maire had stitched the wounds, the Queen's cheek and breast yet bore white sword-tracks. She'd suckle no more children. Conn had brought his Queen the enemy's head. She kept it near her, preserved in oil.

"Cold it may be, this night." Tadhg took, from an overhead shelf, a fine green mantle. Maire herself had woven it.

"Chariot, or horse?" said Maire. "Shall we return together or separately?"

"Chariot," said Tadhg. "It's an ill night to fare alone." They dressed, combed their hair, and told the servants to harness the team.

Before sundown, the cattle-herds were driven between the two sacred Bealtaine fires, to purify them for the coming year. When light faded, the company entered the great hall of Conn Sléaghéar, King of the Cruthini. Firelight flickered off carved wooden pillars, and folk sat according to rank.

Bright were the garments, brilliant the ornaments, and lively the talk and jest. Conn proposed a toast to summer, to the handing over of the year from the

Horned God to the Goddess; then Tadhg, who as
bard sat in a place of honor, rose and sang:

Bealtaine: the hillsides bear burdens of blossoms;
The Goddess gives grace to the year.
Begone now, the black blasts! No more the dark
      powers
Wield winter, and weeping, and fear.

It is not so, of course, thought Maire. Goddess or
no, death and suffering struck in summer as well as in
winter. But enough gloom! This was a feast. She
lifted her cup as the company shouted and drank to
Tadhg. He smiled, but then looked down and
plucked at his harp. The dark mood was on him
again. It struck always without warning, and he
would strum his harp, try to draw forth more than
music, strive toward something only he knew. *The
changeling,* Maire thought, *I should have said
nothing.*

Tadhg set down his harp and picked up a silver
goblet. He drank deep, and waited while a cupbearer
refilled it.

Before the song, the King had been smiling at
Maire, and she had been smiling back. A fine man he
was, merry and handsome. She found him attractive,
but now she met his gaze, frowned, and bent her head
toward Tadhg. Conn looked puzzled for a moment,
then nodded. Well he knew the grey moods of his
bard. He rose and lifted his glass. "To Tadhg Mac-
Niall, who brings magic with his music!" He stripped
off a thick golden bracelet and handed it over. "Mere
gold cannot compare with song, but gold is all I
have." Tadhg rose, bowed, and slipped the bracelet
onto his arm.

"Thank you for the praise. Had I true magic in
music—but I am merely human." He sat again, picked
up his harp, and sang an ancient and rather bawdy

song about Maeve of Connaught and her *true* interest
in the Brown Bull of Cuailnge. The company roared,
and Tadhg hewed off another chunk of roast pork.
Yet Maire watched him. His grey moods did not lift
so quickly, and his was a longlived pain herbs could
not heal.

The feasting and drinking went late; most of the
company planned to spend the night, but Tadhg
wanted to go home. As they took their leave, Conn
kissed Maire and said, "Another time, then, when
your man's not troubled and 'twould cause no hurt?"

She smiled. "I'll do my best to cheer him, and that
quickly." She bowed her head to the Queen, wincing
inside at the sight of the scarred, once-beautiful face.
"Your husband's in a rare mood tonight, my lady."

Deirdre laughed. "With him, such moods are not so
rare." She slid her arm about his waist and smiled up
at him.

At least the scar is only on her skin, Maire thought,
*and Conn is man enough it does not trouble him. A
lesser man might have rejected her, even if it's the
King, not the Queen, who must reign unblemished.*
She wished her surgery had more skill, but for deep
cuts, what could be done? To close the wound, she
had needed to stitch; on the face, that left marks.
The Queen was lucky that the cuts were clean. When
she healed she'd given Maire her mirror: Polished
bronze, ornamented on the back with silver swirls.
Maire had accepted it with thanks, but it pained her
to know why the Queen no longer wished to see her
own face. *I'll be sinking into my own grey mood
soon, and Tadhg and me together will be too much.*
She made her other farewells, and she and Tadhg left
the hall.

Tadhg, on the drive home, was silent. He reined
the horses as they passed the low-lying area where
mist gleamed in the moonlight. Maire knew what he

was thinking, and wrapped her mantle close. *He is besieged by the thought of Fionn, he will go there some night and I cannot stop him. He is a free man. But the danger, the danger! Yet his greyness is a danger too.*

When they reached home, the servants had strewn the doorway with flowers. All seemed ready for Bealtaine. Maire would have stayed up with Tadhg, but she was weary, and her eyes kept closing. Tadhg sat silent by the banked hearth, playing the same melody over and again. Finally Maire kissed his forehead. "I must to bed. Morning comes early and there's the first well-water to fetch. If you've any notions when you retire, I'd not mind being roused." Tadhg smiled, but his fingers strayed again to the harpstrings.

Clatter and talk woke Maire well past first light. She must haste to fetch water, lest the household luck be stolen. She reached out for Tadhg, then sat up in terror. The blankets on his side of the bed lay undisturbed. She threw on the linen dress she'd worn the night before and stumbled into the hall. Tadhg was not there. She asked the servants, but when they had risen he was nowhere in sight; they'd thought him yet abed, after the feast. Some looked puzzled at her panic. *They think he is with a woman. Would that he were.* She feared where his greyness had led him.

Sungilt green hills sheltered misty valleys, but Maire was blind to beauty. Barefoot and uncombed, she ran from the house. Stones bruised her feet. Nettles stung her ankles. *He has been Taken, for last night he went to hear the music of the Sidhe.*

She took the path by the boggy lowland, where mist always hovered even on the hottest days. Those who ventured here on moonlit nights claimed to see gaunt armies of barrow-folk creep from their graves. They spoke of the gleam of bronze weapons as legions met in silent battle. No weapons clashed, no wounded screamed, and the horror was greater for that. At dawn the dead crawled home again to sleep.

Turf-cutters once had found a golden collar in the bog, but those who handled it soon died, and it was cast back into sticky blackness. No one worked in that haunted place.

This morning the air was sweet-sharp with the smell of peat. The sun glanced silver off the sheet of mist; the ground beneath was veiled. One fog-tendril crept up the nearest hill. As Maire reached its top she paused. Never before had the mist spread like this. The dead were reaching out, and the cold whiteness filled the next hollow as well. The faerie-mound with its single hawthorn tree stood above the haze.

She felt herself go pale. She'd expected, nay, dreaded this—but now she knew it true. On the mound lay Tadhg, his green mantle spread about him, his harp by his side. One ear was pressed to the earth, as if he listened. Maire hesitated, then stepped down to the mist, trying not to think of what might grab her ankles and drag her under. Tadhg had heard Their music.

She knelt on the wet grass and touched his cheek. His skin was cool, not like the flesh of a living man. She shook him; he did not respond. She shook him again, roughly. He opened his eyes.

His eyes.

Blue they once had been, and bright, but now they were milky as the eyes of the old or blind. He did not see her. With one smooth boneless motion he sat up. His fingers dug into the ground, his knuckles twined with the roots of the hawthorn tree.

Maire let go his shoulder. Her hand burned cold. "Tadhg?" She expected, and received, no answer.

Bewildered, he looked at her out of old-new eyes. He sat a moment as if listening for something, then picked up his harp. Maire led him home.

* * *

She fed him bloodwort, and burned bunches of remember-me, but no steams, no tea, no potions did him any good. Leechcraft could not restore a changeling. Diancecht the Physician himself would not have helped, for was he not one of the Tuatha Dé Danann? Through sleepless nights she watched Tadhg as he lay cold and dreaming. Never once did he reach out for her. She wept, soundless.

Through the month of Bealtaine, while springtime woke the sleeping land, Tadhg huddled by the fire. He spoke with no travellers, nor joined the hunt; neither gave he orders to his cattle-men, though it was past time the herds should have sought summer pasture. Day and night he shook with chill and plucked strange melodies on his brass-stringed harp. His fingernails broke, and his hands were cut and bleeding, but yet he clawed at the music.

Maire watched Tadhg's pale shadow in despair. She could not call on his people, or hers, for help; what could they do? He was lost, as lost as she had been in that terrible time after their child was stillborn.

For a time, then, all she'd known was darkness, dim dreams and walking nightmares. But Tadhg had sung to her, called her back from the grey land with his songs. He spoke best with his harp. When she grew strong again in body, he had walked the hills with her, in sunlight and in storm, until at last the violence of wind and rain left her at peace, and she could speak again, even laugh, and once more think of healing others.

But that Tadhg was not this thing that shivered by the fire on the warmest summer days, his strange eyes vacant. He had brought her back; could she do less for him? She remembered Brigid's curse: *May he wander far, and may you seek him down the years.*

She did not know where to search, but she knew where to begin.

The Christians now claimed the holy pool by Lough Neagh; they said a saint dwelt there, whatever sort of god a saint might be. Maire had not visited the spot in a year or more. She wondered if the sacred trout were safe.

She need not have feared. The pool lay clear and calm, though the path to it had narrowed, choked by crowding grass. Narrow or not, the way was worn by centuries of pilgrim feet, and a few tokens still fluttered on the tree. Among them was the strip from her best mantle she'd hung there when begging for another child. The red wool was tattered now, faded by sun and wind and rain. And yet she had no answer. Children came, or did not; it was not hers to question. She tried not to think of Brigid's curse. She knelt beside the pool.

But this I challenge! Tadhg is Taken beyond all healing, and this last is too much to bear.

The pool was small; white stones gleamed on the bottom. Through interlacing branches Maire watched a wind ruffle the lake, though the pool itself lay calm. Across its surface an insect's hairlike feet dimpled the water. A shadow rose, and the insect disappeared.

Maire leaned forward. She had never seen the sacred trout in all the times she had come here. It turned sideways; its eye was not the flat black-and-silver of a fish. It glowed amber, unafraid.

Soundless, it spoke. "You would be Maire ní Donnall?"

"I am she."

"You search for Tadhg MacNiall, your husband." The trout hung in the water, effortless, its gills opening and closing, its fins rippling.

"It seems he is mine no longer," Maire said. "He slept on the faerie-mound to hear the music of the

Sídhe. Since then he has changed, and in no way can I heal him."

"He played for Conn, King of the Cruthini, and wished to play for the High King at Emain Macha," spoke the trout, "but now he plays for the ruler of the Sídhe, while another wears his shape. The Queen of the Sídhe is very beautiful; perhaps in the palace beneath the lake, your man has forgotten you."

"Four years we had together, tears and laughter. For beauty alone he would not be forgetting me." Maire grew angry. Was Tadhg a man, or a bull to be captured by a goddess-Queen? "I will go after him."

"Return here, then," said the trout. "Bring your changeling with you, if you can." It flicked in a circle, then disappeared. Maire could not see how it left, but the pool was empty.

She led Tadhg to bed that night—he never left the fire willingly—and lay awake beside her changeling-man. The night was warm. Through the open shutter she saw silvered treetops shiver in the wind, the cloud wisps streak the sky. Tadhg would scarcely leave the fire; how could she lure him to the pool?

"There is a treasure of amber by the lakeshore," she whispered, thinking of the trout's eyes. "Come with me. I will show you."

Tadhg rolled on his side, away from her.

She watched the stars march overhead, pale and bright, as sleepless as she was. After a long time she said, thinking of the water, "I have heard music by the lakeshore. Come with me and hear it." Tadhg covered his ears and slept on.

When the sky paled toward dawn, Maire said, "Those who sleep beneath the hills ask that you play for them. Their night is long and dreamless. Sing them dreams."

Only then did Tadhg rise from their bed. He stood

pale and naked in the grey morning light. He let her dress him.

Maire led him by the hand, for he cringed from sunlight and always sought the shade. His pale eyes blinked until he closed them and allowed himself to be guided like a blind man. He could not have known where they were going, but still he clutched his harp in one bleeding hand.

Something of Tadhg yet dwelt in him, unless the faerie-change had been a harpist too.

Tree-ghosts loomed in mist as Maire and Tadhg neared the pool. The trout waited.

"Well-done, Maire ní Donnall," it said. Tadhg sat on the ground, his eyes blank. "I can guide you now to the palace in the lake, if you would go."

"Others have seen things under the lake, but not I. I lack the special sight," said Maire.

"The palace is there, nonetheless, and there also dwells your husband. But if you go, eat and drink nothing, or you must stay forever." The trout's amber eyes gleamed.

"If I go beneath Lough Neagh I may well stay forever, drowned." Maire said. "Trout clan or no, I can scarcely breathe water."

"Death and age never enter the crystal palace." The trout flicked in an impatient circle. "Come now, or go home."

Maire hesitated, thinking of the Tadhg-changeling. "What of him? He is like a child, and I brought him here by trickery."

"Follow me," said the trout, and vanished.

Maire stared for a long time at the empty pool, and then at Tadhg. She could not abandon him. The form of Tadhg lay on this thing, and something of Tadhg still lived in him. She took him by the hand and led him to where a boat was beached on the lakeshore. Seating him in the shade of a boulder, she pointed to the nearby hills and said, "The sleepers wish you to play dreams for them. Play now, while I go out on the lake."

He took up his harp, striking the strange melody she had heard so often in the last month. Somehow, hearing it strengthened her resolve.

The boat was heavy, hewn from a single log. It smelled of fish, and iridescent scales littered the rough wood bottom. Its length was half again Maire's height; she dragged it to the water somehow. Once water-borne it bobbed, light and at home. She waded out and climbed aboard.

She looked back once to where Tadhg sat playing the same melody over and over again. Already he was fading into the rock. She took the oars and rowed.

Through the shallow water she could see pebbles gleam on the brown lake-bottom; a few rotting logs lay massive and dead, but there was nothing she'd not seen in other lakes and streams, though Lough Neagh was the greatest lake in Ireland. She drew away from shore, and the bottom disappeared. She rowed, and watched, and saw nothing.

She was far from land. The sun was scorching her face and hands, when she heard a splash and saw a silver trout flash into the air. Not *a* trout: *the* trout, for its eyes were amber. It swam to the side of the boat.

"Look toward shore, Maire. What do you see?"

She looked. "Naught but stones and weeds," she said, "and a harp gleaming in the sun."

The Tadhg-changeling was faded and gone.

"What do you hear, Maire?"

"Naught but wind in the trees, lapping water, and the music of a harp."

The music stayed.

"Look into the lake, Maire," said the trout. "What see you there?"

She looked. Beneath her, in the depths, the palace shone through the water.

"Go to your husband, Maire," said the trout. "Go find him in the palace under the lake."

Sorry am I, fisherman, to leave your boat adrift. Her mantle would burden her. She removed it and folded it on the carved-block seat. Atop it she set her belt and knife. *What will they think when they find my things? That I drowned myself for shame?* She removed her heavy gold bracelets—Tadhg had given them to her, and the memory brought pain. She should not be afraid; was she not of the trout clan? She plunged into the lake.

As the cold greenness covered her she choked and thrashed, for she could not swim. The trout returned. "Do not struggle," it said. "Flow with the water, until the water is no more to you than air."

Maire had already sunk too deep to reach the surface. Overhead the world of air gleamed far away. She gasped, and lakewater burned her lungs. She tried to cough, but the trout hung before her, motionless, its gills waving. Maire looked down to the lake-bottom, to where the palace lay, and of a sudden she was a drifting snowflake, a feather. She no longer needed breath.

Slowly she sank through the water; slowly the structure became more distinct. The walls were like glass—not the wavy white streaked glass of Conn Sléaghéar's best goblet, but as clear as the small patches through which one could glimpse the wine.

The palace walls gleamed green and red and yellow. From nearby, golden-haired folk in embroidered garments looked at Maire and laughed. Their laughter was sharp and clear as bells.

She came to rest beside the palace wall; behind her was the lake-bottom of stones and weeds and logs. She struggled for footing. Her hair drifted upward in an unruly cloud. Here, beneath the lake, her dress was drab, and she herself felt plain and clumsy, though on land she was deemed fair. But she was only human, and those who dwelt here were not her kin. Ageless, unchanging, immortal: Their pale faces framed eyes of milky blue, and their forms were clothed in mist and moonlight. She dared not look at them too closely, lest their beauty make her forget her purpose, even who she was. Eyes downcast, she approached the palace.

In all the host of Faerie she did not see Tadhg; nor saw she any old folk to tell tales by the fire, or children to hear them. All were aged the same. Their age was timeless.

Maire stood on golden pavement. Green towers soared to faerie-bells which chimed upon their tops. The music caught her heart. She knew, now, how Tadhg had been trapped. Through small windows, clouds of fish swam in and out. The palace had no door; the faerie-folk melted through its walls like ice in water.

As the last of the Sídhe entered, Maire tried to step through, but the wall was solid. She stepped back, rubbing her nose. *Will they then refuse a guest?* She knocked. Her hand was slowed by water, and the sound was muffled, but in the wall a green-glass door swung open to a pearl-lined room, a giant musselshell. In one wall a streak of silver shone. Fish glittered overhead, and on the walls blue-lighted torches gleamed. Maire stepped inside, and the door swung shut and vanished. She stood within the curving shell-like room; a silver door opened to her touch. She stepped through it to a silver room, whose torches shone silver. Set in the farthest wall, a carved golden door beckoned. Maire thought the carving might be words, but it was not the edge-notches of Ogham script; this writing writhed across the golden surface as currents flow in water. Maire studied it and felt dizzy.

She woke with an effort. "Enough," she said. "Far have I travelled to be guested so. Is this the Good Folk's hospitality?" After she spoke she was afraid, for the golden door swung open to a green-lit hall, and in it sat the Sídhe.

CHAPTER TWO

Clear and green, the Great Hall's roof arched overhead, but it did not dwarf those who sat feasting. All the pale faces turned toward Maire. She was more chilled now than when she had first plunged into the water; she feared to look on them, but look she must.

Tables laden with crystal fruits and glowing wine stretched back into the gloom, toward a green-flamed, cold-crackling fire. At the table's head sat two whose star-crowns dimmed the flames: a man and a woman. About the neck of each hung a gold collar—faerie-gold, bog-gold. Maire shivered. Behind them, crouched, was—

The Queen rose, her eyes blue and terrible as a storm. Her gown was moonlight, her hair the color of the sky before sunrise. "What do you want here, woman? Why have you come?"

Laughter rippled round the table, but no one smiled. Maire spoke: "Queen of the Sídhe, I come in search of my husband, the bard Tadhg MacNiall."

The Queen set down her golden cup. Beside her, the King leaned back in his chair. The Queen's eyes were scalding milk, but her voice was honey.

"Woman," she said, "is this your man?" She sat and gestured toward the green fire.

He who sat near it, Maire saw, wore Tadhg's face. He began to play:

They rest after battle, cold silver in moonlight
The bright hills guard all of the bold ancient
dreams.
They will sleep through the ages, until, in the dark
night
They stir, for their slumber is not as it seems.

It was Tadhg's own voice, and Tadhg's own playing. The Sídhe listened in silence.

"A fine harpist," said the Queen. "He serves me well." She smiled, now; her teeth were like frostspears on grass. "Come sit for a time and enjoy the music."

Laughter once again rippled round the table. Maire bowed and walked down the room. Her saffron dress was streaked with mud, and she, human, felt coarse in such company; but she had come too far, risked too much for shame.

"Sit by me," said the Queen. She gestured: A bench appeared. With one slim hand she drew aside her gown, lest Maire's nearness muddy it. Maire sat and looked at Tadhg.

From the bard's place of honor, he played for the faerie court. When the song finished he looked at her, his eyes sleepy.

"Will you have a cup of wine, child?" said the Queen. As she spoke Tadhg turned toward her; Maire saw in his face how it was between them. The Queen glanced at her, smiled, and poured wine into a silver cup. She proffered it to Maire.

Maire reached for it; at that moment Tadhg's harp crashed to the floor. "NO!" Tadhg leapt forward and dashed the cup from Maire's hand. The wine bled crimson on the tablecloth. The Queen laughed again, too quickly. Tadhg turned to his wife. "Go, Maire, while there is yet time." Even as he spoke his gaze sought the Queen, who looked at her dress; the wine had not touched it. The King remained silent.

Go, and leave Tadhg enslaved? "If I will not go, what then?"

"Then," said Tadhg, "you are bound here forever, as am I." He looked into the distance at the lofty walls, then at the floor, but at last his gaze returned to the Queen.

The Queen smiled at Maire.

"My Lady, forgive me, but my wine seems to have spilled." Maire held out her cup, but it was the King, not the Queen, who filled it. She raised it to her lips. She looked at no one until she had drunk it all. When she set the goblet down, she had nothing left to fear.

"Play, harpist," sighed the Queen. Tadhg sang of moonglow on the hills and starshimmer on waves, and the company fell silent. Then, like the moon in clouds, they vanished, leaving only the green fire in the Great Hall. Maire and Tadhg stood alone. The tables had vanished as well, and the hall was gloomy, cavernous and cold.

"They come and go as the wind," said Tadhg. "Something caught their fancy, and they were off to enjoy it. Who knows why they go or stay?" He set his harp on the floor, but did not face Maire. "Ill was the night I heard their music, and ill it was when you came after me. Why did you drink their wine? Now you too must remain." He picked up his harp again and stroked its strings. Music always soothed him.

"Should I then have stayed on land without you," Maire said, "wed to the poor mad changeling they left in your place? Or should I have divorced you, and you never knowing it?"

"You could have made a new life," said Tadhg.

"But you are trapped here now, and you have offended the Queen." His voice caressed the last word.

For a time Maire made no reply. She might have found him, but he was no longer hers. "I would like to see this place," she said at last, "if I must live here."

Tadhg smiled, though not at her. "Come then. It is all beauty."

As they walked through the gleaming rooms, Maire saw that nothing here was twice the same. If she looked where she had passed, the colors and shapes had shifted. The palace had no more permanence than rippling water or drifting clouds. She shivered. In such a place it would be easy to get lost.

"How long has it been?" said Tadhg. They stood in a green-glass room; amber, amethyst, and garnet ripples chased each other across the walls. Windows and doors appeared and melted, and the floor was now silver, now pearl, now carnelian.

"It was a month past Bealtaine when I came," Maire said. "But here"—she looked at the wavering walls—"here, who knows how time passes?"

"There are no days or nights, no months or years," Tadhg said. "The sun and stars do not shine. Before the banquets, no one is hungry; after them, no one is filled. Neither do these folk sleep, for they need no dreams."

Bells rang high overhead, and a song drifted down. "Their music," said Tadhg. His voice was sick with longing. "If I had their gifts—"

"But they admire your playing," Maire said. Then, because she was hurt, "or the Queen does."

"Perhaps they laugh at me."

Maire thought of the still, white faces and the silence round the board. "No," she said, "you speak to them." She knew that somehow it was true; Tadhg's music moved even the Sidhe.

"I wonder, then, what I say." The bells rang again, closer. Tadhg looked upward, his eyes alight. They were returning. He hurried back to the Great Hall.

Pale and slim they stood, the great lords and ladies alike silver-garbed, their golden tresses drifting in the currents. They stood as if listening, their blue-white eyes unfocused, their slender, bloodless hands clasped before them. There was no merriment in the company now, nor wild abandon; instead, a tinge of sadness.

The Queen moved first; she paced the length of the hall and threw herself down on her throne. "Play, harpist!" she called, her voice unnecessarily loud. "Fill the hall with music!" She looked toward the ceiling a moment, then shook her head and poured a glass of wine.

Was it Maire's imagination or had the light somehow dimmed?

Tadhg stepped forward and played—played well—but the company was slow to respond, and the Queen, from time to time, let the smile slip from her face. At those moments she looked old and griefstruck. The King stood halfway down the hall, amid the company, motionless; Maire became aware that he was looking at her. She dared not meet his gaze.

"Play something merrier," the Queen commanded, and rose to dance. The company followed her; around the chamber they spun, rising from the floor, whirling near the ceiling, as Tadhg played faster and faster, until the frenzied circle broke and, like thistledown, all drifted toward their places, and the banquet proceeded as before.

Or almost as before. The Queen sat gripping the arms of her throne; she held herself rigid, as if she were in pain. The King, beside her now, ate and drank but little; from time to time, he too glanced upward, then quickly down again.

Maire also ate, though the food had no taste and

the wine lacked warmth. Two by two the shining company drifted away until the hall was empty of all save Tadhg, Maire, and the rulers of the Sídhe.

Then did the Queen rise, and hold out her hand to Tadhg. To the King and Maire she said, "Leave us."

Maire looked toward Tadhg; he would not meet her gaze, but stared only at the Queen. He rose and knelt before the throne. Maire turned and fled through the nearest door, bound she knew not where.

She stood in a chamber whose walls pulsed scarlet with her heartbeat. *If I were on land I would have soldiers to fight beside me, soldiers from my mother's training school, and I could meet her in honest battle. But here I stand against her weapons, clanless, without even Tadhg.* Her anger cooled; the walls slowly faded to violet, and were still. *He is enchanted and cannot help himself, nor can I help him.* She wished, briefly, she had never come to find him. *I am a skilled healer, I own a good herd of cattle; I could have divorced him, and many another would be glad to wed me. But I could not love another. I want Tadhg.*

She stumbled blindly through a series of shifting rooms. She stood, for a moment, in what looked like the pearl anteroom, the entrance to the palace, but no doorway pierced its walls. When she had drunk the wine she had made her decision, and for her there was no way home.

She went back through the two doors, the silver and the golden, until she stood once more in the Great Hall. All was gone now, thrones and tables and faerie-folk. Naught remained but the pale green fire. Somewhere in the palace, even now, Tadhg was with the Queen.

Maire ran through chambers of garnet and amethyst until at last she found a doorway that led, not to another part of the palace, but to a walled garden.

The plants that bloomed there chimed like bells;

their flowers were crystalline. Bright clouds of fish darted through the knifelike leaves. She sat on a carven bench and watched the palace walls waver—or might it be water-currents that shifted? In the green light all seemed dim and unreal. She looked toward where the lake surface must be, but saw only darkness. Had it been this dark before?

Across the garden she saw a glowing man-tall shape. As it drew nearer she recognized the King. She stood, respectful, for he was a great lord. But even the King stared at the overhead darkness.

Taller far was he than Tadhg, and his hair and beard were pale. His crown of stars glowed through the dusk, and the silver garments swirled about his body. He stood quiet, looking upward, his thin hands clenched.

When finally he glanced at Maire, his blue-white eyes held sadness. "You have travelled far, woman." His voice was like wind through the trees: soft, it bent all before it. "Too far, to be left alone, and you so bold." He touched her shoulder.

She was aware of nothing but his hand, cold, yet burning through her dress. Did the Lord of the Sídhe mock her?

He towered over her. From his eyes of mist and moonlight came a fog across her mind. "You come from the mortal world." He glanced upward once more. "Why do you wish to return . . . to *that?*" His face twisted, then grew calm once more. "You always wish to go home, all of you Taken ones. Why?"

Maire could not speak; when she tried, she could not remember Tadhg's face. The Lord of the Sídhe stood before her, and she could see nothing else. Around his neck he wore the golden collar of the barrow-folk. She shivered. He held her close.

His flesh was not cold as she had feared, but warm; her body sang with joy. Long had it been, since she'd known the touch of a man—*but this was no man!* His cool white hands ran through her hair, and his slender fingers caressed her face and lips; he kissed her eyelids, and she forgot the darkness overhead. He released her a moment and twisted the collar from his neck, placing it about hers. *Cold, dead,* part of her cried, then shuddered into silence. His arms closed about her again, and he laid her on the ground. The brittle blades of grass did not harm her, and when she brushed a flower, it was soft and alive. All was beauty, joy, and light. She lay in his arms and forgot who she was, or what she had come to seek.

When Maire rejoined the company, though she walked garbed in moonlight as the women of the Sídhe, she was not one of them. Her gossamer garments made her mortal flesh seem dull. She flinched when the Queen stared at her golden collar, but the faerie-woman said nothing.

✗She could not join their dances, nor dared presume to sit beside the King; grateful she was to crouch at his feet. She was no bard, to have a place of honor, and these immortal folk had no need of a healer. Here she was nothing.

When the ghostly company, bent on other revels, left Maire and Tadhg alone, they sat in the Great Hall, each immersed in private dreams. Tadhg plucked at his harp and sang:

> *The hills of this kingdom will bear no more battles*
> *Nor will the old rivers run red to the sea*
> *For the folk of the loughs and the hills lie a-sleep-*
> *ing;*
> *A-dream in the arms of the Sídhe.*

Maire wondered, for a moment, of what Tadhg sang. The two of them once had dwelt on land—why had she been living with the Queen's harpist? For a brief sharp moment she remembered love, and pain. There had almost been a child. After the loss this man had walked the hills with her, sung to her, brought her back from darkness into sunlight. The palace walls grew dim. Maire tried to think of her faerie-lover, the King; for one cold moment she could not recall his face. Tadhg too looked stunned, as if half-awakened.

"Maire, how long has it been?" he whispered.

She shook her head; she did not know. Tinkling bells and merry voices signaled the faerie-host's return.

"And what comes with you now to claim the year?" The voice was sharp silver, and frost glittered the leaves of Her crown.

"A follower of mine," He said. He sat astride His giant steed. Lightning flashed in its eyes, and its hooves smoked cold. "A creature of wildness, that has grown in the land."

"It is none of mine," She said.

"Which is why it follows me." He rode forward and held out His hand, demanding. She was weary. Her hair was streaked with grey, and Her breasts sagged empty.

"Take it, then." She opened Her arms in surrender. Behind the Horned One, the beast snarled. Its eyes were red. She sank down to the earth.

Maire found the child sitting in the garden. He wore the rags of black pantaloons and a white shirt. His legs and feet were bare; his hair hung tangled. He sat with his hands clasped and his feet close together. His face was pinched. His large blue eyes followed every wall-ripple, each fish-flash.

Like a mouse, afraid to move. Maire circled into his field of vision, not wishing to startle him. He cringed and put his hands up to shield his face. His fingers were blistered and his knuckles were red.

"A greeting to you," said Maire, and smiled. Even ensorcelled as she was, a part of her yet remembered children, and this boy looked no older than seven. The terror in his eyes, though, was ancient.

"You are not one of them," he cried.

His speech was odd; Maire wondered if she might be forgetting human language. "No, I am not of the Sídhe." Her heart was sore within her. "I will gladly take you to them, if you wish. What are you called, and how came you here?"

The child looked suspicious. "Would you be a Scot, then? You do not talk like me."

"No, I am born of this very land," said Maire, "though in ancient times my people settled Scotland. If we speak slowly we might understand each other."

"Then would you be a Protestant?" The boy began to edge away.

The fear in his face was real; what was happening ashore? "Child," Maire said, as gently as she could, "I am not understanding half your words."

"Can there be anyone," he said, "that has not heard of the killing and burning and shooting done by Cromwell's men?"

Maire shook her head, "I came in time of peace. Are the Cruthini attacked? Is Conn Sléaghéar, our King, dead? Where are your people?"

The child began to cry. "There is no king in Ireland. My mother starved on the roads after my father was slain. I have no people."

"Come," said Maire, "I will lead you to the folk of the palace."

The boy stood, but would not take her hand. "What sort of flower would this be?" He touched one of the crystal blooms; it shattered, cutting his fingers. A curl of blood eddied into the green twilight. He watched it in silence.

Maire led him into the palace of dreams, to the Great Hall, where the Queen welcomed him. He ran toward her and buried his head in her lap. "After my mother died, the trout told me to come here, and I did. Will you be my mother?"

The Queen ruffled his hair. "That I will, child."

The Sídhe, Maire remembered, always wanted human children. But when she asked them what his earlier words had meant, no one would answer.

The boy sat at the Queen's side and was made much over. Dressed in silver, garlanded in crystal blooms—they no longer cut him, now that he was faerie-fostered—he seemed to forget his human birth. When he was left behind while the Sídhe danced through the air, he would sit, small and lost, until their return. Then he would run to the Queen.

Maire envied her; she too had wanted a child.

Time passed unmarked by days or years, and the green twilight faded toward darkness. The Sídhe went less often, now, to the lands of mortal men; when they did go they returned, not star-drenched as before, but somehow dimmed. Maire realized that time and change were passing overhead, and the change was for ill.

It happened at last when the company sat in the Great Hall, and Tadhg was playing the harp. The ever-encroaching darkness thickened, until the strange green fire gave the only light. Maire looked up and gasped: a thin crimson tendril curled through a window and twisted across the ceiling. Harpsong died. The Sídhe covered their ears as if to block out screams.

The Queen's fingers snapped the stem of her golden goblet. Though the metal sprang together mended, its shape was now distorted, its shining surface marred. The company froze, watching more tendrils writhe into the hall. Maire threw herself to the floor in front of the King. "What is it, Lord?"

He stared upward. When he looked down his misty eyes were blank. "It is the blood of the land."

The child cried and ran to the Queen's lap; she stroked him and watched the stains spread across the crystal ceiling. As it neared the clouds of fish they shuddered away.

Maire studied the inhuman faces. Was it fear she saw in them, or sorrow, or some nameless alien emotion? Their milky eyes were wide, and their gleaming features had become pale masks. Enchantment was fading, and they with it.

Maire and Tadhg stared at each other. Tadhg spoke first. "What is happening?" His eyes were no longer dreamy. He sprang to his feet, and his golden harp fell soundless to the floor.

Maire stood. Why should she lie prostrate? She looked at him who sat the throne, he who now was pale and faded. The company was shadowy as ghosts. Where was their merriment, their endless joy?

Tadhg spoke. "It was no dream, then. The stories were true. I was—I have been Taken." He turned toward the throne where the Queen sat frozen, the child huddled in her lap. "I loved—*you!*"

Maire felt the King's collar on her neck, heavy and cold. *Barrow-treasure!*

Tadhg and Maire touched; their hands were warm human flesh. "All is fading," said Tadhg, "and only we are left."

From the throne the King spoke. His voice was weak. "This is the end of all we knew. Hatred has poisoned the land, and magic dies."

The ceiling was bloodier now, and tendrils were descending. "Is there then nothing you can do?" Maire's flesh stayed solid, as did that of Tadhg and the child. "You are fading, but we humans remain. Return us to our world and our own people."

"Your people have been dead these many years,"

said the Queen, "and your world is greatly changed. You would not recognize it."

"Nevertheless, it is *our* world. Would you have us die here, helpless under *that*?" Tadhg pointed to the spreading stain. "Whatever else has happened, surely music lives."

"And humans still need healing." Maire's hands had hung idle far too long. Freed now from enchantment, she longed for toil, even honest weariness. "Let us go."

The faces of the King and Queen were sad. "The humans are more brave than we, husband, if they can face what walks the land. You are both free, then." The Queen held the child, then glanced upward again and shuddered. The King touched her hand; for the first time in aeons, their fingers interlaced.

"What is done cannot be undone," the King said, "but you may return to whatever you find up there." He paused. Then, to the Queen, "The boy is human too. Free him as well."

"No," said the Queen fiercely, "let him decide. He came to us for refuge." She smoothed his hair and said, "Open your eyes, little one. Which do you choose—the human world, or ours?"

"You can come home with us," Maire said.

The child shook his head. "I have seen the human world. I have no home but here, no family but these."

"If you stay, child," said the King, "here beneath the lake we cannot know what will happen." He looked up again at the spreading darkness, then covered his ears. His hands were near-transparent. "The land screams in torment. Surely you can hear! How can you humans live, knowing always that you will die? I perish now, I who was immortal. Even so, child, you belong with your people."

The boy clung to the Queen. "*You* are my people. I will never go back."

"He has made his decision," said the Queen. Then, to Tadhg and Maire, "We cannot hold you here; yet if we return you to the land above"—she shook her head. "The years, the very cycles have shifted. I know not how you will survive." She beckoned to Tadhg, who approached slowly. "What few gifts I yet have, I will give you." She touched his eyes. "I give you Sight, that you may see the meanings of things and understand what is strange and hidden." She then touched his lips. "Men's language has changed, so I give you the Speech, that you may understand and be understood by both the living and the dead." She gazed at him for a long time. "Last, I give you the power of invisibility, for in this new world you will need to hide. Music, your greatest gift, I cannot give you. That you always had."

Tadhg stepped away, and the King beckoned to Maire. "To you also would I give the Sight, the Speech, and invisibility. They may aid your work as a healer, for your land and its new people are sore in need of your art."

Maire stood for a few moments, then twisted the heavy gold collar from her neck. "I will return your other gift," she said, "for I have no further use for it." He did not reach out. She placed it on his lap and watched it sink through him as if he did not exist.

She stepped back beside her husband. "We are free to go?" The royal pair nodded, and Tadhg and Maire walked swiftly from the hall. Maire looked back once; the Sídhe were pale shadows, and the human child sat in the gloom, his eyes tightly shut.

The Queen half-rose, clutching the child. "Tadhg—" she cried. Her voice was tarnished silver. "Tadhg—stay! I fear what waits for you!"

The King put his hand on her arm. She settled back. "Let them go," he said. "Let them both go.

They are called by those greater than we." Then all was silent. The company faded away.

"We can live again," Maire said to Tadhg. "We can laugh, and love, and have children." But she was troubled by the King's parting words.

Out they walked through the gold door into the silver room, and through the silver door into the pearl room, until the palace wall opened and they stepped outside. The pavement was tarnished, and the water surrounding them stung cold. The need for air clutched at Maire's throat. In the distance she saw a flash, and stepped toward it.

Tadhg hesitated. "My harp," he said. "I have forgotten my harp!" He turned back.

"Tadhg, no!" Maire cried. "There is no time!" It was as if a wall separated them. She could not move, and he seemed not to hear her. His shape wavered into distance. The flash came closer; it was the trout, its eyes glowing. "Wait," Maire begged. "My husband—" Heedless, the fish flicked toward the surface. Maire looked back into the gloom; there was no sign of Tadhg. She was under water, she could not breathe, she was drowning! The trout was almost gone from sight. In the darkness she could not find the surface of the lake. "Tadhg?" Choking, trying not to swallow water, she followed the trout. She did not know whether she approached the surface or not until, lungs bursting, she broke into a starless night.

Unable to swim, she splashed about. Where was Tadhg? She heard a sound far off, and thrashed toward where a dark shape showed low against the skygleam.

"Ho! Who's there?" Oars shivered the water. A brilliant light swept the surface like a wand and came to rest on her face. "What are you doing out here, Miss, so far from land?" a voice said. "Like to drown, you are. Here, grasp onto the side."

She clung to the wooden boat. "Let me help you in

now, Miss," the man said. He pulled Maire aboard. "You must be well-nigh frozen, in yer nightclothes." He took off a rough wool jacket and handed it to her. "Wha' happen, then? Swamp yer boat, or out swimming?" He skimmed the light along the lake surface. "If you had a boat, it's sunk by now. Lucky for you I came along."

Maire sat gasping.

"Quiet, aren't ya? Ah!" The man set down the light and reached for a pole propped under the seat; the end was bobbing and jerking. "Think I got somethin' at last. Besides a fool swimmer, that is." He reeled in the line. At the end of it, fighting for its life, was a trout—a silver fish whose eyes glowed amber in the dark. "Ah, a fine large one, too."

"No!" said Maire. "Let it live!" She reached out; her hands snapped the line, though the filament sliced her fingers. The trout vanished into the deep. "Fare you well, trout."

The fisherman stared at her. "So you're talkin' to fish, now? That one was the finest trout I've ever had on me line, and you cast away me lure and hook in the bargain!"

Maire did not answer. She looked across the darkened water and wished she could weep.

"Sore distressed you seem, Miss," the fisherman said. In the distance a dull-red flash was followed by a roar. The man flinched. "They're at it agin', the bloody IRA bastards." He picked up his oars, rowing with long, angry strokes. "Blew off me brother's leg, and him only going to post a letter. Fought all through the War, and then bought it on his own street with a car-bomb." He stopped rowing. "Where might you be from, Miss, and where headed?"

Maire cleared her throat. "Here." The word was strange on her tongue. "I've lived here a long time." She wondered how long.

"Have you people, then?"

Maire shook her head. She had no one now.

Far in the distance sounded a rattling noise. "It's shooting they are now," the man said. "Hope we hit more than they do." The boat scraped on stones. "It's been a bad week. They'll be needin' me at home. The wife takes fright, these days. Where will you be going?"

Maire helped him drag the boat ashore and stood at last on dry ground. The breeze was chill.

"Keep the jacket, Miss," the man said. "You need it." He hesitated. "Where be you headed?"

Maire stared into darkness. With her new Sight she knew why the Sídhe had grown pale. Over the land hung a dense red fog of hatred, blood, and anguish. The land itself cried out for release, but none save Maire could hear.

The fisherman looked at her strangely. "Are you all right, then, Miss?" Maire shook her head. She could not find words. "You've had a bit of a shock, I think," he said. "Best you come home to the missus, until we find your people."

I have no people, Maire thought. *All I knew is dead, Tadhg is gone, and I am alone.* Centuries of history weighed on the land. The living presence of the Sídhe, which had shimmered in streams and woodlands, was no more. The night was dust and ashes, save for the coals of hate.

"Come home with me, Miss," the fisherman repeated, and held out his hand as if to a child. Maire followed him; she knew nothing else to do.

Wind screamed overhead beneath stone-bright stars. Out of season, the Two met. One hissed and threw a thunder of birds across the moon. The Other bugled up a hammering hunt and a howling beast.

The forces clashed, and the land below dripped red. A sigh rose from grass and trees and tender plants, from fragile flying things, from swift deep fish and velvet mice.

And yet the Two fought. At last They looked down, down at the star-sheened lake, down at another Two. Then They smiled through fangs and vanished earthward.

The wind ran raw and wild beneath the stars.

CHAPTER THREE

My harp, Tadhg thought, *I cannot leave my harp.* In the distance he heard Maire calling, but could not see through the gloom. He hesitated, then was drawn back. *Only a moment—*

The palace wall wavered green and translucent. He ran his hand over the glassy surface, seeking a doorway. Beneath his fingers the palace vanished, and his hands grasped water. He was drowning on a muddy lake-bottom; instead of golden pavement he stood amid rocks and logs. Panic clutched him as his lungs cried for air. With all his will he forced himself not to breathe. He kicked upward.

His head broke the surface. Air caressed his face. He gulped it, smelling lakewater and various harsh scents from shore. He struggled to stay afloat. Not too far off, through the gloom, he saw a dark mass: land. He thrashed toward it, sputtering and swallowing water. At last his feet touched bottom. *Where was Maire?* He'd heard no sounds but his own. She had stood beside him only a moment past. Was she lost beneath the lake? But she had the trout to guide her. He could see only the faint glimmer of skygleam, and heard only lapping water. The night was hushed.

Then, at the limits of sound, he heard it: From the soil and rocks, from the very land itself rose cries and lamentations. Battle-screams mixed with widows' wailing, curses vied with helpless sobs—the voice of centuries. He shivered, but it was not the breeze that chilled him, it was that which rode the breeze. Nowhere in the night did living creatures stir. Who, then, suffered without ceasing? And where was Maire? None of the voices was hers.

His eyes were adjusting to the darkness. In the faint gleam from the overcast sky he could see some distance down the shore. Beside a large rock something gleamed; beside the gleam a pale shape shimmered.

He went forward to investigate. There lay his brass-stringed willow harp—not the golden instrument given him by the Queen of the Sídhe, but the one he himself had fashioned. And what stood beside it vanished—not before he saw it had worn his face.

Whatever time this was, his harp could not have lain on the lakeshore undisturbed; it must have been guarded. He picked it up and stroked the strings. They were badly out of tune. He made adjustments and looked out across the water, toward the submerged palace. Could any of the Old Folk hear him now? He spoke aloud: "Thank you, for without a harp—" He played a few notes. As he played the night grew silent. Murmurs ceased.

While weary long lifetimes lie scattered on hillsides
And, faded like phantoms, the Sídhe fare no more—

A shudder sighed across the land. No living person was near. Tadhg was cold and alone. Where had Maire gone? He searched the shore and called. Nothing answered, save the wind.

At last Tadhg stood, weary, his head bent, as if some burden weighed it down. Long had he searched, and found no trace of Maire. Inside him, a voice whispered: *Belfast.* He started and looked around, but saw no one. A place, Belfast must be; how to reach it? He stood a few more moments on the lakeshore. No, he would not yet sing Maire's lament.

He had no set direction, so took the widest path from the lakeshore. In the darkness he stumbled into a building; he put out his hand and felt the wall. It was neither stone nor wood. Smooth, the material was. The structure loomed as large as a great hall of Tadhg's day, yet no folk dwelt therein. Farther up the path he came upon what must surely be a road, though overlarge for chariot or foot travel. Its surface was hard and smooth; sharp, unpleasant smells clung to it. Any road must lead somewhere. He stepped forth.

Behind him the night roared, and a light glared. He leapt aside as something screamed past. The vile wind of its passing slapped his face. It rushed down the road; the last he saw was two red glows, like demon eyes. What walked the night? And had the monster seen him?

Again, a voice spoke, invisible. He was not alone. *That was no living creature. It is a chariot of these times. Though it moves itself, it is guided by mortals.*

When the next such device roared past, Tadhg flattened against the hedge, but forced himself to face it. It was fashioned of beaten metal, he saw, even as was a cauldron or shield, and inside it he did spy a human. Devoured? But the man showed no distress.

More of them thundered by; Tadhg grew bold, and stopped cringing. At last one vehicle halted. Its side opened and a man called out, "Would you be wanting a lift?" Though the words were strange, Tadhg understood the meaning.

"Thank you." He puzzled a moment, wondering

how to get in; the driver leaned across the front seat and opened the left-hand side.

"Where are you bound, then?" The stranger seemed an ordinary-enough person, though he wore some device in front of his eyes—glass and metal, it seemed—and his clothes were of a duller hue than Tadhg preferred. But his garb was patterned on standard peasant attire, jacket and trews. His footgear was heavier, and perhaps more durable, than Tadhg's sandals. *I must look odd to him, in my linen robe.*

Indeed the man was regarding him with a certain amazement. "You're soaking wet, man! Fall in the lake?"

Tadhg nodded.

"Wearing only your nightshirt? You must have a tale to tell! Here, I've some things in the boot, you'll catch your death like that. There's a cold breeze tonight, it's October, after all. You might as well wear something dry." He climbed out, rummaged in back, and returned with an armload of garments. Tadhg stood by the side of the road and put them on; the fastenings were tricky. His sandals, at least, would serve as footgear, though his feet were cold.

"So, where are you bound?" the driver repeated, when Tadhg climbed in.

"I have no—" Tadhg started, then he remembered. "Belfast."

"Ah, you're in luck, for it's there I'm heading myself. And where are you from, wandering about in your nightshirt falling into lakes?"

Tadhg shrugged. "Like as not you've never heard of the place. I'm grateful indeed for the clothing." The garments were this man's own. In silence they spoke to Tadhg: The man worked for others, for wages. A creamery—something to do with milk and butter, but no cows. He lived in a tiny room, crowded next to other rooms and houses. No wife dwelt with him, but there was an impression of a woman—she did something with manuscripts? A scribe? No art was involved. All was jumbled and difficult to sort.

"It's purely silent you are," the driver remarked.

"I am that," said Tadhg, "and sore confused."

"As are we all," the driver said, "as are we all." He slowed the vehicle. "Drenched as you were, I'll be hoping you rescued your identification. We've come to a checkpoint." He rolled down the window and stopped.

A frightened pimple-faced lad stood outside. He was dressed, like his several companions, in a loose-fitting garment patterned in shades of green and brown.

The driver proffered a card; the youth scanned it and nodded. "And your passenger?" He shifted from one foot to another, impatient.

The driver turned to Tadhg. "On with it, we're holding up the queue. It's a fair long drive to Belfast."

Tadhg flinched. He had no "identification," nor knew even what it was. The soldier frowned and raised what must be a weapon.

I give you invisibility. The Queen's voice. Tadhg took a deep breath; the soldier's face grew blank and he released the chain. "Proceed." The driver went on in silence, nor did he glance toward Tadhg again.

How had he escaped notice? He looked down; he could not see his body. He stretched out his hand and saw only air. So the Queen had spoken truth. *You will need to hide.*

The car sped onward through the night. Tadhg had never travelled so fast. The darkness held countryside, with fields and cattle, but spots of brightness showed clumps of houses. The stench and press of humanity was offensive. How could folk live so huddled? Tadhg could sense the interiors of the houses, hear the people's thoughts: fears, vague yearnings, anger. Money, telly, rent, the dole, the Troubles, taxes, Saturday's match, the price of a pint—Tadhg felt lost and alien.

What called him to Belfast? What might he seek there? Could he find Maire? Best to try first among his own, if folk still needed songs and stories.

At the next checkpoint Tadhg, yet invisible, slipped from the car and watched it drive away. The driver would, no doubt, wonder how several hours of travel had vanished. Tadhg still wore the man's clothing, and he'd taken a favor when he had no means to repay; he was ashamed.

The young soldiers, pale-faced, watched the passing cars. Their fear and tension were almost visible. Any dark corner might hide an assailant. Tadhg stood near the checkpoint, observing the sentries and those who were stopped.

Bloody Tommies, bet they don't search the Prots half this well . . . Didn't something move in the alley, Sergeant? . . . Look at them there with their rifles; one good fire-bomb would . . .

This street corner was not the place he sought. Tadhg shouldered his harp and set out down amid huddled rows of houses. For whatever reason, he had reached Belfast.

He knew the place he sought when he saw it: a guesting-house, but here they called it a pub. The door swung wide. Tadhg stepped into light and clatter. The air was thick with smoke, beer, wet wool, and strong drink. Voices and laughter mixed with music; in one corner, on an elevated platform, three young men played a guitar, an accordion, and a fiddle.

Tadhg wondered how he knew the names of the instruments: he had seen none of them before. The music was strange, but the rhythm pleased him. Unnoticed, he surveyed the scene.

Bottles glittered on the wall behind a long, high

sideboard. So much glass! He marvelled. The room was jammed with young folk, men and women alike, crowded around tiny tables, talking or listening to the music. Their clothing was frayed at the elbows, their features coarse—how different they were from the elegant Sídhe! But the Sídhe were faded now. These drab, strong mortals had outlasted them.

Tadhg chose a seat near the musicians. Folk noticed him and frowned. *Never seen him before. What's he carrying there? . . . Only a harp . . . They don't make bombs to look like harps yet, do they? . . . He's an odd one, see the expression on him . . .*

The song ended. One of the musicians, a short, pale young man with black hair and blue eyes, moved near. He wore a brown leather jacket and coarse blue breeches. He crouched at the edge of the stage and gestured toward Tadhg's harp. "A charming instrument. Would it be of old design?"

"It would," Tadhg admitted.

"I've seen the Brian Ború harp in Trinity College Library, of course," the man continued—Tadhg knew not whereof he spoke—"and O'Carolan's in the National Museum, but such a harp as yours I've never seen. Did you make it yourself?"

"That I did," said Tadhg, not without pride. "Cured and carved the wood, as well."

"My name is Padraig Byrne," said the young man, "and these are my group, the Three Bards."

"Bards, now," Tadhg said. He smiled. Some things had not changed. "I am Tadhg MacNiall."

One of the other musicians came forward. "I am Thomas O'Brien," he said. "We've not seen you before, have we?"

"I doubt you could have," said Tadhg, "for I am not from these parts at all."

"Are you up from the Republic, then?" asked Padraig.

"I come from Lough Neagh." Tadhg did not elaborate.

"Oh, County Antrim. Terrible troubles they had there earlier this evening, I hear." Some of the onlookers smiled; Tadhg saw red bursting flashes, heard screams—he shivered. Those who smiled seemed to approve the carnage. Perhaps they'd played a part in it.

The third musician, he with the guitar, introduced himself. "I'm Rory White, from Dublin, where I met up with these two farmboys from the West. Tom there, he with the fiddle, is from County Clare. He used to play at the castle banquets for the tourists, before he came to the city to seek his fortune. He's yet to find it. And Padraig, there, is from County-Mayo-God-Help-Us, where each year his father's farm raises a fine and bountiful crop of rocks."

"Ah, farming is honest work, but hard on the hands," said Padraig. "Like to have broke my mother's heart when I left, but it's been mended by the money I send home." He looked at the newcomer. "Here you are, now, Tadhg from Lough Neagh, with your old harp and your quiet ways; would you be having a drink with us and playing a tune?"

Tadhg nodded.

"Guinness, then?" A tall, heavy glass of foam-topped black liquid was pressed into his hand. "Smoke?" He looked at the proffered package, realized he had no idea what to do with it, and shook his head. "Come on up, then," said Padraig, holding out a steadying hand. Tadhg mounted the platform. Padraig motioned for quiet. "We have a friend tonight, from peaceful, blessed County Antrim"—the crowd's laughter was bitter—"who will play for us on his harp. Surely any who carries a harp is a friend of ours. Here he is, Tadhg MacNiall, from Lough Neagh!"

Tadhg looked out at the upturned faces. They were more friendly now. What sort of song would in-

terest these folk? A soothing song of love? A lullabye?
No; he sensed excitement, danger, and conflict here.
A battle-song, then, to bestow courage and fire the
blood. Conn Sléaghéar, King of the Cruthini, must be
dead these many years, perhaps even his kingdom forgotten, but in his time he had enjoyed Tadhg's songs.
He sang to Conn's memory, in Gaelic:

> *First in the fighting, our King thunders forward—*
> *His chariot thrusts to the thick of the fray.*
> *His gold-shielded army of valiant, wild warriors*
> *Will bear home the heads of our foemen today.*

He paused. The King had given Tadhg a gold
bracelet for that song. In the next battle many of
Tadhg's friends had fallen, and more were crippled;
the Queen herself had been sword-hacked. But one
never mentioned realities in battle-songs, only in laments.

Tadhg continued with tales of glory, though bitter-
ness and fear stuck in his throat. The crowd's excitement seemed somehow perverse. Few, he knew, could
understand his words; what moved them? He ended
the song.

Padraig was looking at him with curiosity. "I have
the Gaelic not only from school, but from collecting
folklore," he said, "and that would be a very old song
indeed. Where might you have learned it?"

Tadhg shrugged. "In my travels." He sipped his
drink. It was strong and bitter, but good. He sat
down and watched while the Three Bards played another song. The music was strange, repetitive, and the
words were stranger still. No doubt there were different types of music now. All else had changed.

The musicians stopped. "Time for a rest, and to
soothe our parched palates," Padraig annnounced. He
held his throat and rasped, "Dry as dust, and my
tongue cleaving like cotton to the roof of my mouth!"

Three brimming glasses immediately appeared; Padraig waved and stepped down from the stage, seized one, and drained it. He turned toward Tadhg. "You're new in town, then?"

Tadhg nodded. "I arrived tonight."

"Have you a place to stay?"

Tadhg shrugged.

"Well, man, you can't be wandering about the city past curfew. From the looks of you, you've precious little money for bed and breakfast. We've booked rooms, but the landlady's full up. Our van is parked nearby; you're welcome to sleep in back. Have you business to keep you here, or would you be driving down to Dublin with us tomorrow?"

Where was Dublin? Tadhg had no idea of distance or direction. He'd been told to come to Belfast, but here he could not feel Maire's presence. She must be dead. He would do as the fates decreed. And he had, in truth, nowhere to go. He nodded.

Padraig turned to his companions. "They should admire him at the ceili Saturday, with his harp and his old songs. I'd hate to leave this man in the Six Counties; there's an innocence about him."

His companions nodded. "Bring him along, if he'll come," said Tom. "Have you any gear?"

"The clothes I stand in, and my harp."

"Well, it's settled, then! Drink another pint, and we'll sing a few more songs." Padraig clapped him on the back, set another full mug before him, and leapt up on stage.

CHAPTER FOUR

Maire lay asleep beside Tadhg. Her breathing was quiet. He reached out to touch her shoulder, and his hand struck cold metal. He woke in a space crowded with boxes; outside he heard rumbling. Memory returned: he slept in a van in Belfast, and Maire was dead. He stared into darkness, listening to the city, then curled up and covered his face. When he slept again his dreams were jumbled shapes and colors: a green palace, grey buildings, water and smoke and yellow lights.

Soon after sunrise the van's interior grew stifling. Tadhg fumbled the door open. In daylight he saw his surroundings: grey walls pierced, here and there, by shattered windows and doors. His three friends were nowhere about.

On the street, cars rumbled, and a few early risers strolled the sidewalks. He rubbed his eyes and yawned, watching a large vehicle turn a corner. Something crashed from its rear and shattered on the pavement.

A man threw himself to the ground, and a woman screamed. Others cringed against walls. In the silence that followed he saw the source of the noise: a broken milk bottle. The folk brushed themselves off and went their separate ways, embarrassed.

Curious. What had they thought the noise might be? Tadhg was thirsty, and his mouth tasted foul. He needed food and drink, and would like to wash.

Around a corner came Padraig Byrne, carrying a parcel. "Ho, Tadhg! I'm up and about before those two slugabeds, and thought you might be hungry. Here's some bread and butter from breakfast, and a couple slices of bacon. I fear the egg wouldn't travel. How did you sleep?"

"Poorly," said Tadhg, yawning. He unwrapped the parcel. "Thank you for the food. I doubted I'd ever eat again." He gulped it down.

Padraig watched him. "You're cruelly low on money, then, as I thought."

"Indeed, I've none at all," said Tadhg. This much was true, for he did not know what money was. *Something to be exchanged for items of value*, his inner voice said.

"If you travel with us for a time you'll lack for nothing—we've not much but we're not poverty-stricken—and you should soon be earning your own way, though why you haven't before, the way you play, is past my ken. Lose it gambling? Ah, if you're wanting a drink of Guinness or, Lord forbid, water, we must have some back here." He rummaged in one of the boxes and pulled out a brown bottle and a battered metal flask. "Here, take your pick." Tadhg chose to drink the Guinness and wash his face and hands with water. Padraig laughed. "Ah, that's the spirit! We've some business here in town before we leave for Dublin; Tom and Rory should be along in a moment, as soon as they wipe the sleep from their eyes. You'd think them accustomed to a life of leisure, so loath are they to waken. Ah, here they come now!"

Pale-faced and disheveled, the missing two of the

Three Bards approached the van, and wearily slung their burdens in the back. "Anyone cheerful at such an unholy hour cannot be human," Rory mumbled.

"It's the getting up early on the farm to feed the rocks so accustomed him," Tom said. "I suppose we're off into the blinding sunrise."

"At this hour? Scarcely. Nearer the blinding noon. On with you now, we've information to pick up before we leave, as well you know. The sooner we're back in the Republic the safer I'll feel. Tom, you ride up front with me to help navigate and keep lookout. You'll need to stay awake for that."

Rory crawled into the back, wedged himself among boxes, and promptly fell asleep. Padraig sat behind the wheel, and Tom, grumbling, took the passenger's seat. "Why can't Tadhg navigate? He's wide awake."

"He's never been in the city before, and you can atone for your many sins." With a roar Padraig started the engine and the van lurched into the street.

In the daylight Tadhg was curious for a better look at the city, but could see little from the windowless rear of the van. He caught glimpses, through the windscreen, of long dismal rows of houses, huddled wall-to-wall, slogans in a strange script scrawled across their bricks; rolls of wire, fanged and dangerous, draped, shattered, board-bandaged wreckage. Amid all this disorder children played and men and women went about their business, but their glances were quick, their eyes wary, and the children carried sticks.

The van shuddered to a halt. Rory, in back, sat up. This neighborhood was the shabbiest yet; trash blew in the streets, and most buildings were boarded up. "Tadhg, you stay here"—Padraig hesitated—"and watch the van. If anyone asks, do not say where we have gone. We will return in a short time, fifteen minutes at most. Best you sit up front to show patrols the van is not abandoned."

Tadhg, as instructed, changed his place, and

Padraig, Tom, and Rory disappeared into one of the faceless buildings. Something in the atmosphere made Tadhg nervous: the anticipation of battle, without the excitement that banished fear. He watched the street and tried to make sense of the painted slogans. With his faerie-gifts he could read the lettering, but the references were obscure. What might *Join Provos* or *Up the IRA* mean?

The three returned. Padraig carried a large brown envelope. "In back with you again, Tadhg," he said, "and be quick. There's an army patrol due, and we don't want to be caught here in Falls. Rory, set this with the music—it's the last place anyone would look." He handed over the envelope and they were off.

Though Padraig drove rapidly southward, Tadhg could see that he took extra time to detour around certain areas.

"We'll be passing through Newry, crossing the Border, then stopping in dear Dundalk, where we've friends to meet. Have you ever been there, Tadhg?"

"No," he admitted, "I have not travelled much before today."

"But you carry identification? Ah, you could never have gotten this far—"

"I'll manage," said Tadhg, hoping this were true. In this strange time he had naught but his faerie-gifts, and he was unsure how they might be used.

The journey was long. As they left the outskirts of the city, the air cleared. The three relaxed and began to sing cheerful martial-sounding songs. Tadhg understood the references no better than he had the painted slogans, but the tunes were lively, and he was among his own kind.

From time to time they passsed through small towns, but most of the road traversed countryside, in which stone fences crisscrossed tiny fields. "We didn't want to spend another night in Belfast," Padraig explained. "We may perhaps stop over with our friends in Dundalk, then press onward come morning—or earlier, if the need is urgent. And there's the ceili in Dublin tomorrow."

Tadhg, still weary, held his harp close and tried to doze, but his mind was too full, and the van's jostling disturbed him. *Dublin. The Republic. Six Counties* . . . at last he slept. He half-woke at one point to hear Padraig say, "Here we are in Newry; seven miles to the border, and then a free road home, praise God."

Tadhg dozed again for a short time.

"Jesus, Mary, and Joseph!" Padraig exclaimed. It sounded like no prayer. "They wouldn't, in broad daylight, so close to the border! *Get down!* There's a Morris across the road, and it's no accident. I recognize one of the men. There's no way I can pass and the road's too narrow to turn."

Beside him, Tadhg heard Rory gasp, then saw him scramble among the boxes. "We shouldn't have hidden the pistols so deep."

"They're coming, now, three of them, all armed," Padraig said. "It must be us they were waiting for."

"Ah, Christ, there's cases piled all over—" Rory stopped tugging at the boxes as the rear door of the van was flung open. At the same time Padraig and Thomas were pulled from the front seat. Tadhg gasped; it seemed no one saw him. He stepped out and stood, clutching his harp.

Three men, holding what must be weapons, stood on the roadway. "Against the van, you! Hands on the roof, feet apart. Move!" One trained his weapon while another patted their clothing. The third entered the back of the van and began to toss articles out.

Tadhg did not understand what was happening; neither did he know what to do.

"We're only harmless players," Padraig said. "The

Three Bards. You may have heard of us. We'd an engagement in Belfast last night, and a ceili in Dublin tomorrow—"

"And tonight you stop in Dundalk, I've no doubt," one of their captors sneered.

A shout came from the back of the van. "It's as we thought. Three pistols, under the floorboards. Innocent musicians indeed!"

"Ah, but what else might they be carrying?" said the first who had spoken. "It's not arms you'd be running from the North; what else had you to protect?"

None of the musicians spoke. The man pushed Padraig, who fell to the roadway and slowly rose. He cuffed him across the mouth. "I said, what had you to protect?"

Padraig spat blood, then closed his mouth again.

"Troubles last night in Antrim, and here you all are with pistols in your van, scum from the Republic anyway. We'll not have your kind." Then, to the man in the back, "Can you find nothing else?"

Books and papers showered forth onto the roadway. "Only a pile of music and rubbish."

"Must have carried the information in your heads, then. Bloody rebel bastards!"

Tadhg stood transfixed. They were insulting bards— and the bards permitted it! The strangers carried no spears or bows, only metal sticks; how dared they touch a bard?

One of the men raised his weapon; it stuttered briefly. Tadhg could not see anything strike, but Thomas, Rory, and Padraig jolted and collapsed onto the road. The weapon stuttered again, longer this time. Bright blood spurted from the Three Bards' jackets and pooled on the roadway. Another burst, and they lay still. Blood trickled from Thomas' mouth, and there was something wrong with the back of Rory's head. What sort of weapon could do that?

They could not be dead, not so quickly—even an honest sword-cut took longer.

The leader pulled Rory's guitar case from the van. "Nothing here." He smashed the instrument with his heel, and followed with Thomas' fiddle. Padraig's accordion moaned as it collapsed on the road and was stamped into the dust.

Tadhg still clutched his harp. He had not moved. All had happened so fast. *Guns,* said his inner voice. *Lethal, and longer-range than arrows or spears. They are the chosen weapons of this time; you must learn about them.*

The three men kicked at the corpses' faces and walked to their car. They backed, turned it, and sped northward up the road, swinging past the van.

Tadhg knelt by the bodies. Life had fled while he stood powerless. He looked at the shattered instruments. Those brigands had murdered *bards!* Who would dare raise his hand to one who carried such an honor-price? Even to offend a bard risked a fearsome curse. Tadhg rolled Padraig's body onto its back. Sightless eyes stared skyward. The mouth lay open, and blood pooled behind the teeth. Tadhg swallowed. He felt sick, then anger gripped him.

This was not the time for laments, but for vengeance. He had witnessed a deed that called for cursing such as he had never done. He stood in the sunshine beside the three corpses and struck a note on his harp, that all who dwelt in the air and under the earth might hear. "Those who ride the wind, dwellers in the ancient mounds, soldiers slain in honest battle, hear the call of Tadhg MacNiall, the bard, for vengeance for my fallen friends. May the Poet's Curse lie long on those who did this thing. May their land be black and blighted as their hearts; may their barren wives mock them as the cause"—for a brief, sharp moment he remembered Maire—"may their bastard children revile their names, and may their ancestors rise from the grave to breathe on them. May they wish to die long before their time, and when they perish may they wander cold and in torment, shunned by those on the earth and under the earth alike. I, Tadhg MacNiall, call this curse on them, and will that it be so."

From the azure sky a cloud crept cold across the sun, and a small wind worried the hedgerows. With his faerie-senses Tadhg heard the dead stir in their sleep. *How many dead lay beneath this bloodsoaked land?* Rusty weapons clanked, and fleshless skulls rattled inside helmets. Tadhg felt a moment of panic; here, in the daylight, night-terrors caught him. What had he waked, when he disturbed the dead? *No*, a voice said, *this is your right and your sacred duty. Honor cries for vengeance*. But the voice was remote and cold.

"I will summon you when needed," Tadhg breathed. "Meantime stay on watch." The rustling subsided into sighs, and the breeze stilled. The day was again bright. A few late-autumn flies clustered on the blood.

His friends had mentioned Dundalk, and said they bore a message. The murderers had not found it. Might it be the papers Padraig had carried from that grim Belfast house? Tadhg rummaged among the scatter: song-sheets, for the most part—until he found the envelope. If his friends had given their lives to deliver it, then delivered it would be. And he could call their clan to bury their dead.

Tadhg shouldered his harp, stuffed the papers in his jacket, and set off down the road on foot. No use to bid farewell to those new-fallen; unlike the ancient dead, they did not heed his song.

Even in the bright sunlight, a cold shadow covered him. In the distance a bird began to sing, then stopped. This was an evil day for music.

*   *   *

He slipped unseen across the guarded border, past soldiers and more guns. This war, if such it was, was like no war he'd known. Conn and his foes were wont to match their forces, set a time and place, and then halt at sundown to feast and tend their wounds. But there was no honor in a land where not even bards were sacred.

The land—what had befallen it? He smelled the stench of history: Putrid blood and smoke mingled with the stink of crowding and oppression. Yet on the hillsides green grass gleamed, cattle grazed, and the autumn wind blew crisp.

Since his time so many folk had lived on this land, breathed this air, farmed and built and bred and fought and died—yet their life seemed no better, but rather worse. Tadhg was weary, and he had not been weary in—how long? Self-moving chariots, weapons that slew from afar, soldiers stalking amid huddled buildings, murdered bards—and Maire was lost. He stumbled, and his eyes would not focus. Too much had happened. He did not even know the month. He'd last trod earth on Bealtaine Eve, how many years ago? And Maire said 'twas some time later she'd come after him. *Maire*. Now the wind smelt of autumn. How many times had Samhain and Bealtaine divided the year? Was this Goddess-time, or did the Hunter ride?

To Tadhg's left a *boreen* drew aside from the main road. The scent of newness lay fainter there. He followed it.

He walked, unnoticed, through the grounds of a small guesting-house and up a hill. The going was steep; tired as he was, he kept on. Near the hilltop he sensed something familiar, though he'd never fared this way before.

Atop the hill, a grey dolmen loomed against the sky. Beyond it seethed the sea. In his own time, Tadhg had seen structures such as this, and then they were already ancient. Three huge lichen-splotched stones, capped by an even larger fourth, marked a door to Faerie. The stone stood rough, solid, and eternal. He bowed his head. Against his cheek the rock was warm. He held his breath, but heard no music.

No. The Sidhe are faded. He might be the last who remembered them, now that Maire was gone. He sank to the earth, leaning against one of the upright stones. Idly he plucked his harp, letting the notes seek their own company, as, his back to the sea, he faced the tortured land. Trees rustled, and trash scuttered across the gravel.

A few more notes rose from Tadhg's harp; the music soothed him, as did the whispering leaves and the soft wind. Heard he aught within the stone? He ceased his playing.

"Play on, harpist. Long has it been since we were graced with music." Shivers and clanks mingled with parched whispers. "Play, for the grave is dry and lonely; naught have we heard but each other, for far too many years."

Tadhg faced the monument. "Who are you? They call these entries to Faerie, but you speak not as do the Sidhe." *Who more than I should know how they speak?* He recalled their singing, and his grief was great.

"The Sidhe?" Grave-laughter echoed. "They told you *our tombs* were homes of the Sidhe? Play, harpist, play! Our only music is the sound of pebbles some wayfarers throw on the capstone for luck. No one sings to us, nor do any remember who we were."

"Who are you? Monuments like this were old even when I lived. Are you older than the Sidhe?"

"When *you* lived?" One querulous voice took charge. "You are yet alive. You walk the land, and make music. We are the dead, trapped in this house of stone, ancestors together with descendants, a jumble of family, clan, and bones. We know naught of Sídhe. We lived and died here, and were buried under monuments that we not be forgotten. One day each year, the Winter Solstice sun warms the chamber of our tomb; only thus can we mark the passage of time."

Bones clinked and voices clamored: "Remember me! I was mighty in battle, valiant in the hunt, until I fell and the healer took my leg. I lay then in torture until the gods gave me rest. My treacherous body was burned, and I am only bones and ashes. . . . I was the fairest any saw, and I wed the chief's son, but died birthing our firstborn. I was burned and buried with my dead child. In later years my husband joined me here, but after four other wives, he did not recall my name. . . . I, an old woman, bore twenty children, five of whom lived, and I reached thirty-six summers before my joints swelled and my teeth wore down to stumps. . . ."

As they spoke, Tadhg could see the young warrior, shorter and darker far than he; the young woman, almost a dwarf, and the old crone—she would not be thought old now, nor even in Tadhg's day. "When did you live?"

"When King . . . In the time of the great . . . Fish were scant, two winters . . ." From the cacophony of answers, Tadhg could tell that they knew not, or if they knew, had no way of telling him. "Know you, then, what time this is?"

"Dark-time, for the most. Strange sounds, when we wake."

"What know you of the conflict?"

"What conflict? There is always conflict." It was the voice of the old woman.

Tadhg strummed a few more notes on his harp and listened to the dead bones rustle back to sleep. To find peace. . . .

*   *   *

Sunlight slanted low, and warmed his face. With his eyes closed, Tadhg could see a red glow. Eyes open, he saw westlight through the trees. His muscles were stiff. He sat propped against a dolmen, his harp beside him. He should not sleep near dolmens—gateways to Faerie! Then he remembered. These were only burial-places of ancient, simple folk—and Faerie was faded.

Dundalk. He must get to Dundalk. He bore a message. He walked down to the main road, and headed south. Early spots of ground-fog pooled in the low places; he remembered the haunted mist back home. But he no longer feared the dead.

He walked briskly, to warm himself and to cover distance. Several cars passed him on the road; one driver offered him a lift, but he declined. He no longer knew whom to trust.

The outskirts of Dundalk lay golden in the slanted light. Small houses lined the streets. Dogs basked in the gutters, and, on a western window-ledge, an orange cat groomed herself. Blue turf-smoke trickled from the chimneys; the smell was familiar and home-like.

Tadhg wondered where to go. Nearby, a graveyard surrounded a large stone building; he entered the gate. Dead folk lay here, but these dead were much closer to this time. Tadhg stopped at a leaning stone. The inscription had worn almost smooth, and lichen blotched the surface. He struck a note on his harp and heard a sigh. "I am weary. Who calls me?" The voice was a woman's.

"I come from Faerie, and I do not know this time," said Tadhg. "Speak to me."

"A sad and dreadful time this is indeed." The voice was weak and far away. "The hunger lies upon the land, and folk starve on the road, trying to reach Cork for passage to America, but that costs dear. Those not dead of hunger take the plague. My man is gone, and I with two small children and a babe, with no food for us and no milk to nurse the wee one. Today I woke with fever, and could not rise—the babe beside me lies too still—WHERE AM I? AM I DEAD?" And then, a scream. "IT IS DARK. DID THE PRIESTS LIE?" The voice shrilled into keening.

Tadhg struck his harp again, with a song of sleeping. "Sleep, then, wake no more." The sobs faded. Tadhg stood looking at the sunken grave. Cruel it was to wake the dead. Best he seek his answers with the living.

He turned again toward the building; it must be a temple of some sort.

The doors opened and an old woman stepped forth. She was short and stooped; her frayed black skirt fell to mid-calf, and her shoes were scuffed. Across her head and shoulders she wore a black shawl, and she clutched a string of beads in her hand. She peered up at Tadhg.

"God bless you this evening," she said. Her face was sad.

Tadhg nodded in reply. "I am a stranger here, and would ask directions. I seek the friends of those who called themselves the Three Bards. Did you know them? Padraig Byrne, Thomas O'Brien, and Rory White?"

The old woman turned pale. "Jesus, Mary, and Joseph, you'll not be telling me something has happened to the lads?"

Tadhg nodded. "Sad am I to bear ill tidings."

The old woman raised her hands to the sky and wailed. "Oh, and such fine music they made, they were such merry lads. But they *would* get involved—'twas after Rory's brother was murdered at school, of a sudden they'd had enough." She stopped and looked at him. "What happened? When and where?"

"Earlier today, across the Border."

"And how would you be knowing? You, a stranger in these parts?"

"I travelled with them. They liked harpsong."

Her eyes narrowed. "How came it, then, that you escaped and they did not?"

Tadhg shrugged. "I do not know. I know only that I must tell of their death, so their kin may seek the honor-price."

The old woman's laugh was bitter. "A price there'll be indeed, and a high one! I've no dealings with the Provos myself, of course, with even the priests talking agin' them now, but I know some of the boys, and can take you to the ones you want." She peered at Tadhg. "You look fair famished. Did you walk all the way?"

Tadhg nodded.

"Come home with me, and I'll give you tea. Good boys, they were, a bit wild, but warmhearted. Oh, we'll be missing them! But you were their friend, and you've a message to deliver, so come home until dark—then I'll take you to the others."

Tadhg followed her down the street to her home; at last, in this time, he'd found a guide.

CHAPTER FIVE

The fisherman led Maire through the dark. The air burned her lungs, and in the distance she heard rumbles and whimpers of pain. Stumbling in shock, she was glad their goal was nearby. She followed the man into a small stone cottage, not unlike those of her own time; but once inside, instead of flickering firelight, the lamps glared brilliant as the sun. Coming from darkness, Maire was blinded. Toward the rear of the house she heard a door close.

"Is that you, then, Jack?" A woman entered the room, wiping her hands. She was plump, grey-haired, and wore a faded dress. Her forehead wrinkled. "I heard the explosion—a large bomb, this time, it sounded like." She stopped and stared at Maire, whose garments pooled water on the floor.

"I've brought home a waif," Jack said. "Rescued her from drowning; out in the middle of the lake, she was. I've no idea how she came to be there, and she has not said."

The woman peered more closely. "It's soaking wet you are, lass, and lightly clad. You could catch your death. October's a bit late to be out swimming." She waited.

The woman seemed kind; Maire felt she should explain. "I was not swimming—I had to follow the trout when the palace vanished. Then Tadhg went back, and I could not find him."

The woman glanced at her husband and shook her head. "The trout, and the palace? I'm not understanding. And who might Tadhg be?"

"Tadhg is my husband," said Maire. "He went to hear faerie-music, but he was Taken. I followed him to the palace. He could not leave, so I also stayed, and we two dwelt under the lake until the Sídhe—" The faded figures and the vanished palace were vivid again. "I loved the King." Maire hid her face. "They are gone, all of them, all the faerie-folk, and Tadhg."

"I'd best make you a cup of tea." The woman left the room, and the man followed. They whispered, but Maire could overhear.

"She's purely daft, Jack. Such wild talk!"

"I'm thinking she's suffered a great shock."

"Ah, there's shocks enough, these days. But what are we to do with her? Has she any people? Might she have escaped from a Home?"

"As I said, she has told me nothing. I brought her here because she was wandering lost, and I could not in charity leave her on the lakeshore, could I? Still, I've heard strange old stories of that lake."

"Ah, Jack, if you keep on you'll be sounding as daft as her. Those are tales to frighten children. Shame on you, a grown man!"

So, Maire thought, *they know nothing of the Sídhe, and think me mad. I might once have thought the same.* She wondered how the folk of this time cared for their strange ones. Could it be that the Sídhe no longer lived? *No,* an inner voice whispered, *they yet live, but they are very weak.* Maire flinched and covered her ears. Whose voice was that? Was she fey?

The couple reentered the room. The woman

handed Maire a steaming cup. "Here's your tea, Miss. What did you say your name was?"

Maire sipped and flinched. The drink was hot and bitter. "Maire ní Donnall, I am called." *By whom? No one here knows me.* Suddenly she was very tired, alone in a world she could not understand. She began to shake, and set down the cup.

"Are you all right, Miss?" The woman laid a hand on Maire's arm.

Maire shook her head. "Tadhg is likely dead, all the world has changed, and I hear the land keening. I've nowhere to go and know not a soul alive."

The woman patted Maire's shoulder. "There, there, it's a terrible time you've had for sure, whatever it may have been. Come on upstairs, and I'll put you to bed. A night's rest may set things right."

The bed was soft, and the house seemed safe, but each time Maire dozed, her body would arch and she gasped awake, clawing at the darkness. Eyes watched her, she was sure, and something weighted down her chest.

In the morning the woman fed and clothed her; Maire needed help with the new garments, and did not know how to use the house's facilities. The woman looked at her in sorrow. "I'll be taking you to the doctor now, Miss. No one will hurt you."

The local healer was a grey, quiet man with tired eyes. His workplace was full of objects whose function Maire could not imagine. He examined her, and pronounced her body healthy. He was surprised at her teeth. "Few folk these days lack cavities," he said. "It's the sweets, I suppose." But when he questioned Maire on her story, she could do nothing else but tell the truth: She herself was a healer. She spoke of Tadhg, and the faded Sídhe, and how Tadhg had vanished.

The healer nodded from time to time. "I'll not be

saying I understand your story, Miss, but I know how
you must feel. It's a fearsome world, and there's days
I myself would rather live quiet in a palace beneath
the lake." He rubbed his eyes. "Up all night, I was,
caring for casualties. Two died; nothing I could do,
or any man. When will it suffice?" He scribbled on a
thin parchment—Maire was fascinated, watching him
write—and passed the note to the fisherman's wife.
"They may be able to help her in Belfast. They see
enough of these, and they'll be wanting to look at
her, in any case. Can you take her safely to City Hospital?"

The woman nodded, and pocketed the note. "I'll
go with her on the train, poor thing."

Belfast. Maire had never heard the name before,
but knew that was where she was called. She rose and
bowed to the healer. "Thank you, and may your work
prosper. When I am able to repay—"

He smiled, and shook his head. "No need for that.
It's covered by the National Health."

The railway station was a cavern of seething steam
and smoke; the train itself shuddered and shrieked.
Maire cringed, sure it would devour her. She watched
the other people: Not even small children seemed
afraid. Another common horror of this time, then.
She forced herself to board. Such wonders these folk
dwelt with! She tried to reason: Despite its appear-
ance, this was merely a vehicle.

The train lurched into motion and sped from the
station. As she stared through the glass window—
glass!—Maire saw that the countryside had changed
from the farm-dotted wilderness of her time. Houses
huddled together, some with cracked walls and shattered doorways. She nudged the fisherman's wife, and
pointed.

"It's from the bombings," the woman said.

The image Maire received was of shattering explosions and red pain. Never had she thought of such atrocities.

The shabby walls were bescrawled, and children played in burnt-out metal shells: dead vehicles. Some streets were barricaded—to defend the neighborhoods, the woman said.

Maire cursed the Sight the Sídhe had given her, for with it she saw that the very land was haunted. Grey wraiths wisped over ancient battlefields; she heard the centuries-old weeping of the wounded and bereft. But another presence dwelt here: From the bloodsoaked land a living creature crept, a beast that fed on hate, that had long outlasted those who'd called it forth. Maire could see it crouched, a red-eyed mist, on barricades; it padded wolflike after groups of children who wielded sticks and played at war. Lean it was, bright-fanged, but no one else saw the thing, unless they were accustomed to its presence.

As Maire stared, the beast met her gaze and snarled. She cringed back from the window. *This is your enemy.* This was the second time her inner voice had spoken. *It will kill you if it can.* Yes, she was fey.

Even surrounded by cold iron, she did not feel safe. Charms were no protection against that beast: It was no denizen of Faerie, subject to its rules. It came from elsewhere. And it saw and knew her.

Belfast clattered and stank. Traffic hooted, and people bustled in dizzying confusion. The hate-beast, Maire knew, paced the grey streets, crawled the cluttered alleys, and peered from the boarded-up buildings.

The fisherman's wife guided Maire down several streets. Marie followed as if in a daze. The crowds, the smells, the profusion of sights were too much. At last they reached a building marked "Belfast City Hospital." Maire was surprised she could read the writing, for the letters and language were foreign.

They walked in the door; Maire's escort paused at a sort of table and handed over the note.

A white-clad woman read it, nodded, and said, "Please to be seated. The doctor will see you presently."

The fisherman's wife guided Maire to a bench, where they waited with several other people. Maire looked about her, puzzled by the strange clothing, the brightly colored parchments on the tables, and the bustle of activity whose purpose she could not fathom.

At last another white-clad woman led them to a private room. Again they waited, until a man entered and asked Maire questions. She answered truthfully all those she understood; many were meaningless, even with her faerie-gift of Understanding. Here, she knew, she was considered daft. She could see it in the man's eyes.

You will find a task, and soon. The voice, again. It was wise and the words held power to compel.

Maire forced her attention back to the present. She walked now down a light-green corridor. Not the glowing green of faerie-halls; these walls were flat and dead. The woman she followed was clad in white. "Nurse," she'd heard her called.

The nurse paused before an iron door—for a brief, bitter moment Maire remembered the golden entry to the banquet hall—and pressed a button. The door swung open. Another white-clad woman held out her hand and smiled.

"You must be Maire ní Donnall, come to stay with us for a time. My name is Margaret. I will show you about the ward. We are safe here. You have nothing to fear, no matter what may have happened outside."

The "dayroom" was grim. Someone had tried to brighten it with pictures, but the windows were screened with wire netting, and the shabby furniture blended with the dun-colored walls.

Maire was introduced to the other patients; eight sat in the room, men and women both. She noticed three bewildered changelings of various ages, two *gealta*—the sort who became violent—a sad-looking young girl, an older man whose blotched face and shaking hands spoke years of drink, and—*that one*.

A man in early maturity sat rigid, his back shielded by the wall. He watched every motion. He had neither the vague look of a changeling, nor the driven intensity of a *gealt*; his scarred and pitted face showed fear, and his eyes were those of the hate-beast.

Maire stood before him, keeping enough distance not to pose a threat. His cheeks were gaunt and black-stubbled; the skin about his eyes was dark. She could not tell, from his hands, what work he did; whatever it might be, he had not done it in some time, nor, from their crippled look, might he again.

He stared at Maire for long, uncomfortable moments, then licked his lips. "Get away or I'll kill you."

Maire retreated a few paces, but no farther. The man glanced about the room, as if to reassure himself. Finally he looked back at Maire. He clenched his crooked fingers, lacing and then untangling them with great care. His hands gleamed with scars.

"Who are you?" His voice was a whisper. "Who sent you to kill me?"

"Kill you, and I a healer?" Maire was insulted. "No quarrel lies between your clan and mine."

He regarded Maire with suspicion. His sunken eyes were pale blue, with a light grey circle around the pupils. The effect was eerie. "Everyone is planning to kill me—nurses, doctors, the other prisoners. It might be the food they've poisoned, or the medicine they force on me, or they'll creep in and strangle me at night—I try not to sleep"—at last the strange eyes blinked—"but I grow so tired." He straightened. "I've not seen you before. Where did you go to school?"

" 'Tis the second time today I've been asked," said Maire, "and it puzzles me as to why any care. My mother trained warriors, my father was a chieftain, and at seven I was fostered to a healer and her husband, the armorer. Taught was I by Colin the Bard, and by my foster-mother. But why should this matter?"

The man looked at her in amazement. "Why, to know what side you're on." He waved a hand, indicating the other patients. "Spies, all spies, waiting for me to give out information. It's only in that hope they keep me alive. But then, perhaps a bomb will take us all," he laughed, "them together with me."

Maire stared. "I do not understand what you say."

The man laughed again. "Well, then you *are* an innocent! Each moment outside, your life is in danger, and in here, as well, though these folk are more subtle in their killing." He glanced around again.

"I'm in no blood-feud," said Maire, "and my kin are long dead."

"As you breathe and walk the city you are in a blood-feud. They hope to wear us down, but our cause is just and we are strong. Ulster will never surrender."

Again in those strange eyes Maire saw the hate-beast. In the man's mind she felt utter sincerity, and a new form of madness. She shook her head and walked away.

An old woman, one of the changelings, sidled close to her. "You're one of *them*, aren't you?"

"One of whom?" said Maire. She'd seen changelings before, the lost, vague ones. Tadhg's foster-brother Fionn had been that way. No one could help them; they were other than human. Now, with the Understanding, she sensed the woman's jumbled thoughts. Fragments of ideas swirled, and the world outside was distorted. The changeling's thoughts were worse than fever-dreams, and in them was no flavor of the Sídhe. Could it be that changelings did not come from faerie-folk? Had they always been human, but flawed?

"One of *them*," the woman repeated, nodding toward the door. "You don't belong here."

Indeed, I belong nowhere at all.

"Yet there's something odd about you, too," the women continued. "I've seen your kind in hospital before. The lost ones, from the wrong world."

Changelings sometimes babbled hidden truth. Might there be others like herself?

The old woman laughed at nothing Maire could see, and darted off to stare at the wall.

Maire tried to rid her mind of changeling-tainted thoughts. Could it be these folk were not substitutes for the Taken? Why would humans be born flawed? Was that what happened to Brigid's child? But Tadhg had been truly Taken, and a changeling had been left in his place. Tadhg had not been strange from birth. Overnight his mind had wandered, and she herself had found where he was prisoned. Then, to have lost him again—she must not think on that, or she would weep.

She looked back to the young man in the corner. He lived in terror, but the folk here in "hospital" seemed kind, not the sort to harm hostages. Perhaps he was held as surety for some agreement, and his people had forsworn themselves.

She approached and again stood before him. "Are you then a hostage, and if so, in what war?"

"I am no hostage. I am a political prisoner." He pointed to a scar on his cheek. His hand lacked the ends of the second and third fingers, and the palm was pink with fresh scar-tissue. "I was doing a small job—they'd just killed two of our boys, and we must retaliate, of course—"

"They?"

"The Catholics. The bloody IRA." He was impatient at the interruption. "I was on my way to plant a small device, but its timer was faulty. It went off early. When they found me I was not dead, so they brought me to hospital and kept me downstairs for a time, with needles and tubes and spy machines. I would let none of the jailers near me, so they sent me up here. These are spies as well, but with the bandages off my face I can watch them." The strange pale eyes narrowed. "Why would you be wanting to know all this? So you might inform on me?"

"No," said Maire, "I find your world strange. Are you certain these folk mean you harm?"

He laughed. "Where could you be from, in this day and age, not to know of the Troubles? It's years it's gone on; it's printed in the papers and shown on telly every night. They're trying to wear us loyal Ulstermen down, with their bombings and terror. What can we do but defend our land? Dirty, overbreeding Catholics, they come up from the Republic to steal our jobs or get on the dole. The shiftless drunkards would snatch Ulster from Britain and make us all take up their filthy Papish ways. But we won't forget we stopped them at the Boyne—"

"I have not understood one word in three," said Maire.

"You must be dafter than you look, then," the man said. "Or would you be Catholic?"

"Not that I know of. What would a Catholic be?" In the man's mind Maire viewed a drunken ignorant lout, an adherent to some bizarre religion led by a villainous "Pope," whose subjects kissed his feet. "No, I think I am not a Catholic."

"You'd know it if you were. Ah, it's been almost three hundred years since our good King Billy whipped them at the Boyne, and it's all those three hundred years they've been plotting and scheming—"

She could not have heard right. "Three hundred *years?*"

"Yes, and before that too, the disloyal scum, always in rebellion against the Crown, as if we hadn't tried our best to civilize them."

Maire tried to imagine a span of three hundred years. How many lifetimes? This story must be a great legend such as the *Táin*, yet its telling held no poetry. "You would be a bard, then, to know the old stories?"

The man snorted. "Ah, we're taught in school to know right from wrong, Protestant from Papish. I'm no bard; I'm a welder at the ship foundry, or was, until my accident. Away with you, the nurse is coming and I don't want her writing down what I say. They'll use it against me for sure. And don't you tell them I've been talking, mind."

Maire wandered to the window. More glass—where did they get it all?—but behind the wire netting it was streaked and dirty. Seen through it, the city sky was grey. She curled her fingers around the wires and looked down as far as she could.

Below her lay a courtyard. The wall enclosing it was topped with fanged wire, and a guard stood at the gate. Vehicles rumbled past on the street outside. She wondered if she would ever get used to them; she must, for they were everywhere.

She had indeed come to a strange and nightmare time; yet though she might be safe in hospital, she wanted to be free—*I have a mission.*

She stepped back into the hallway, walked its length, and tried the handle on the iron door. It did not move; *locked!* But she'd eaten or drunk nothing here, and these folk were not the Sídhe—or were they? They were merely human, no matter that they lived in a time of marvels.

A nurse appeared at her side. "The door is locked, Maire. Come away from there now."

"Would you be so kind as to open it, then? I wish to leave."

"You must stay with us a while, Maire," the nurse said, "until you feel better."

"But I wish to leave *now*." Why should she be held against her will? She was no hostage.

The nurse took her arm. "You cannot leave, Maire." Then, louder: "Margaret! Fifty, liquid, for the new one!"

Maire looked at her. "Please remove your hand."

Another nurse, the one who had smiled and welcomed Maire earlier, appeared with a clear cup of purple liquid. "Drink this," she said, "it will calm you. The doctor thought you might require it."

It reminded Maire of the wine of the Sídhe. She had no wish to stay here. "Thank you. I am not thirsty."

"You need to drink it, Maire." Margaret held the cup close to Maire's face.

"I do not wish to be rude, but no. Thank you." Margaret touched the brim to Maire's lips; with a toss of her head Maire sent it flying. The purple liquid splashed over Margaret's white uniform.

"Orderly!" Two men appeared; after a brief struggle, Maire relaxed. It was no use.

"I will go quietly, but I will not drink your wine."

They escorted her down the hall to a small room; Margaret opened the door. "If you will not take your medication by mouth, you must have it injected."

Maire said nothing, and lay, as directed, facedown. Margaret lifted the back of Maire's skirt and pulled down the strange garment the fisherman's wife had insisted she don. Maire felt cold, then a sharp pain and a spreading ache. She bit the bedclothes, too proud to cry out.

Her dress was rearranged. "You'd best lie quiet for a time, if you're not used to chlorpromazine. It may make you dizzy. We'll be looking in."

Maire lay rigid and outraged until all had left the room and she heard a key turn in the lock. *Yet I have not eaten or drunk anything of theirs by choice.* Her buttock ached, and as she lay considering her plight she realized her mouth had grown dry. She was dizzy, and could not lift her head. *What have they done to me?* She drifted into semiconsciousness.

They woke her for a meal. When she refused, they tried to make her eat. She threw the tray across the room. They came at her again with the stabbing pain. Again she slept, but now she also dreamed.

They may have subdued you, Maire ni Donnall, or subdued your body, but they do not know against whom else they strive. I need you free.

"Who are you?" Maire whispered into the dark. Her lips were chapped, her tongue thick. She received no answer, and drifted off to sleep.

They woke her in the morning, with more offers of purple wine. They also said she should eat breakfast, or at least drink water. She was parched, but she knew what she must do. *Take nothing in this place, or stay forever.*

Her hands shook, now, and the muscles in her neck were stiff. Her eyes refused to focus, and when they helped her up to the toilet she nearly fainted. Margaret came to see her alone, concerned. "You must eat and drink, Maire. Is there anything special I might get you?"

Maire shook her head, and the room spun. This woman was trying to be kind, but could she not understand?

The white-painted walls of the room wavered, as had the walls in the palace of the Sídhe, but no rainbows chased across them. Maire looked at the angle between wall and ceiling. The sun shone through the wire grid, and made patterns like the surface of

Lough Neagh. She drifted, she rocked on gentle waves—

Voices outside the door. "If she refuses to eat she must be forced." A man's voice. "We'll try to reason with her first. She cannot be left this way."

The door was unlocked—well did Maire know the sound by now—and a group of five walked in; Margaret, another woman carrying a clipboard, one of the men who had helped subdue her, and two older men who seemed to be in charge.

"This is Maire ní Donnall," said the woman Maire did not know. "She was picked up swimming in Lough Neagh in the middle of the night, and gave an incoherent story. Dr. O'Farrell of Antrim Town referred her here, as a possible schizophrenia, or acute situational stress reaction. She has refused oral medication, has demanded to leave, and has not eaten or drunk since her admission Friday afternoon."

One of the older men stepped near the bed. "How are you feeling this morning, Maire?"

She turned her face away. Her tongue rasped over dry lips. "I wish to leave. You have no right to keep me here. I am a free woman."

"Do you have any relatives, Maire?" the man persisted.

"Not any more. They are all dead, and Tadhg must have died under the lake, when the palace vanished."

"You refuse to eat or take medication."

"Of course."

"We cannot let you starve yourself. If you will not eat you must be fed."

I will not eat your food! The voice—not Maire's own—reverberated. She sat bolt-upright. *Do you not know who I am? How dare you confine me!*

The man stepped back; Maire saw fear in his face.

Her head swam, and the room moved in jerky flickers. She—not herself, but whatever had hold of her—

commanded the room to be steady. The five people stood frozen. Time stopped.

Whatever they'd given her was forced from her system. She rose and walked toward the door. One of the aides made a slow movement toward her. She stared at his hand; it curled and knotted like that of an ancient cripple. She stepped out into the corridor.

She no longer feared anything. The patients shrank silent against the wall.

Patients. Ah, yes. The part of her that yet was Maire remembered the terrified man in the dayroom who insisted he was a prisoner. He might, after all, be right.

She peered into the room. There he was, crouched in the same corner, watching, always watching. She strode toward him. "If you would leave, I can help you escape." He looked up, cowered, and curled into a ball. She stood looking down at him; he refused to meet her gaze.

The door opened easily, once she willed it. Partway down the staircase she remembered who she was: only Maire ní Donnall. She leaned against the wall and picked at flaking paint. *I forgot invisibility. I need not have crippled that young man; he was doing his job. I could have escaped unseen.* Whatever she'd been, though, was not Maire, and it had powers not granted by the Queen of the Sídhe.

But now she was only Maire. She held her hand before her and willed herself invisible; when she could no longer see her hand, but only the wall and the staircase, she walked down. Out past the guard into the roaring, fume-filled street she stepped; she knew not where she went, but she was free.

CHAPTER SIX

Traffic howled and hooted in soot-black canyons. Sun glinted off windowpanes, and the city stench was eye-watering. Crowds bustled on the grimy sidewalks, into buildings whose purpose Maire could not imagine. Amid the other vehicles rolled an armored car; it carried three soldiers. Passersby stood and regarded it, their mouths sullen. The soldiers—small, undernourished youths—kept a nervous watch. They carried neither bows nor spears, Maire saw, but held what might be weapons.

The voice spoke: *You have come to heal; you will confront the enemy.* But where in all this chaos was the enemy? Surely not these frightened boys.

Beneath the traffic fumes lay the heavy, primitive scent of blood. Maire knew it from the battlefield and sickroom; always it was mingled with the stench of fear. Here, too, she smelled terror, though no one lay wounded.

In her memory that scent spoke ill, and told of pain: a birthing gone wrong, the woman, exhausted on the bed, her forehead damp with sweat, her eyes large with fear, knowing her time had come—too soon! Or the overturned chariot, its horses screaming in mindless terror, knowing only that their legs would not move; the driver, his skull stone-shattered, sprawling nearby. Or the aftermath of battle, where slaughter strewed bodies across fair green fields, and ravens pecked the eyes of those still living. . . .

Maire sensed her ancient enemies, pain and fear. Here she felt them; she felt the hatred, too, soaked into the stones of the buildings. It trickled in the gutters and gibbered from dark corners. It lived, and watched her.

She must leave this sick place. The rushing traffic followed a pattern. She observed a while longer, and when a group of pedestrians started acrosss the road, she followed.

Halfway across the black, oily expanse she heard a snarl and felt hot breath on her neck. She turned but saw only a flicker, a quick crimson shape. Maire turned cold. Had she seen her death?

A vehicle swerved around the corner, heading for the pedestrians. Maire saw the driver's pale, frightened face, saw his hands clutching the wheel. The crowd scattered—all but Maire. Her feet would not move. Again she heard the mocking snarl. Instead of fear she felt fury. *Coward carrion-eater! You dare not face your foe!* She did not speak aloud, but the taunt was heard. She hurled herself to the pavement, out of the way. *Another time.*

The car shrieked to a stop. The right-hand door opened and a man staggered forth.

"You all right, Miss? I don't know what happened—the pedal must have stuck, the brakes wouldn't work, and the wheel jammed. God in heaven, I might have killed you!" His voice shook.

Maire rose. Her knees were bleeding and her hands were raw, but the hate-beast was gone.

"At least we're right by City Hospital, Miss," the man said. "Let me help you inside and we'll see if you've been hurt."

Maire dared not reeenter that building. "I'll be fine," she said. "Not to worry." She backed away.

"But Miss, it's my fault, it's the least I can do. I've no idea what happened—the car was safety-checked not a month ago." He reached out to touch her, as if to assure himself that she was indeed alive. Maire stepped out of reach.

"NO!" She had to leave this place where death— her own death!—prowled the streets. She fled into the nearest alley.

Her dress was torn and her hair was tangled. Homeless, she hid in the back alleys of the city amid squalor and filth. She had not eaten in two days. She rummaged in dustbins for food, though the rancid leavings turned her stomach. Shame burned her. She, a healer and a free woman, reduced to scavenging!

Scraps of litter tumbled past, borne by a chill autumn wind. Was it the wind or fear that raised bumps on her flesh? She knew she was stalked by something neither human nor faerie.

It is the ancient battle, life against destruction. The voice spoke with calm power. Maire shook her head. She crouched amid broken glass and sweepings, listening to the scurry of rats. Dirt she was used to, in farmyards, but the filth of this place reminded her of an untended sickroom, choked with the waste of a helpless patient.

Maire ní Donnall should not huddle like a beggar. She rose, brushed herself off, and realized, with repugnance, that she had not bathed in days.

Somewhere amid the grey, grim city she might find a safe place. Despite everything, some folk must be kind.

Maire wandered through warrens of twisted streets. The thick air choked her. How could anyone live

here? Then, overhead, her eye caught a flash: a wren!
"Wait!"

The bird fluttered to the pavement at her feet.
Maire crouched and spoke. "I am lost, druid-bird." It
regarded her, then took wing. Maire ran among walls
and grey streets, chasing the one thing that reminded
her of home.

She smelled the living green before she saw it. The
area was small, but riotous with growth. Many of the
plants were strange to Maire, though she had made a
study of herbs, bark, and leaves. What were the
bushes with thorny stems and bright, petal-heaped
flowers? She bent to sniff them, and enjoyed their
scent, though they had been cruelly cut and trained.

The very grass was not let to flower and seed, but
was cropped short. She bent to touch the springy surface; it would feel good to walk on. She kicked off her
stiff shoes and wiggled her bare toes in delight. Here
were no stones or nettles, naught but smooth ground-
cover. For a moment she marvelled. But the grass was
sad; it strove to reach the sun, to seed and die, and
was always thwarted. Maire stroked the starved,
stubby stalks in apology.

Amid the grass a pool mirrored the sky. This
was not one of the green-skinned, mud-bottomed pools
that dotted fields and forests. This had been dug. Its
banks were stones set in a hard grey material, and an
iron pipe fed it clear water. No tiny life teemed in
the shallows. She cupped water in her hands to rinse
her face.

Few people strolled the park in the late autumn afternoon. The sun shed golden dots through glowing
leaves. Bright and dark patterns shifted across the
lawn and the pebbled paths. The heavy perfume of
the last flowers, the light whiff of new-cut grass, and
the sleepy scent of trees masked, in part, the city's
alien smells.

Maire sat on a stone bench. It was plain, without

the lacy carvings of the Sídhe, or even the inter-
twined patterns with which Maire's own folk decorated. But the stone was sun-warmed, and for a
moment she felt at peace.

In the distance, Maire saw a woman push a cart;
she heard wheels crunch on gravel, and listened to
the cooing of a child. Up the sun-dappled path
strolled a young man and woman, their hands
clasped. Maire soaked in the sun and smiled. Even
here, in the grey city, life went on.

The couple stopped at a nearby bench. They looked
about, then sat close. Though they whispered, Maire
overheard.

The young woman leaned forward. Her long dark
hair swung in a shining mass. "Michael," she said, "I
fear Mother suspects I'm still seeing you. It isn't so
much that she'd mind, but it's the neighbors, especially that Mrs. O'Shaughnessy—you know when
they caught her Cathleen going with a soldier, her
own mother wielded the scissors—" She shook her
head. "I'd not want my hair shorn and myself tarred
and feathered. And it's not only me I fear for. Think
what they'd do to you!"

"Oh, Rita, you shouldn't worry so much. Your
mother's a decent woman. She wouldn't hurt her own
daughter." Michael was tall and thin. His pale brown
hair straggled across his high forehead, and his light
blue eyes were always moving. He watched the light-
and-shadow interplay as if enemies lurked amid the
trees.

What sort of place was this, where even lovers were
afraid?

"When she learned you were a British soldier,
Mother took on so terribly I had to promise never to
see you again. And that Mrs. O'Shaughnessy misses
nothing." Rita touched Michael's arm. A tree-shadow
moved; she flinched and withdrew her hand.

Michael grasped her by the wrist. "It's only three

months before I'm sent home, Rita. I want to take you with me."

"Back to the London slums, then, among the rats and fleas?" Rita's voice was sharp. She turned her face away. Maire saw tears on her cheeks.

"It won't be the slums again. I'll have my army benefits, I've saved my pay, and I can get a decent job. We don't have to live in London at all, if you'd like."

Rita turned back to Michael. "And what will your friends think of your Northern Irish wife? I've heard stories from those who've travelled in England; as soon as they hear our accent they expect us to have bombs in our handbags. They think we're all daft, instead of most of us!"

"Still, what future have you here, a Catholic girl in Belfast?"

"I have a decent job, unlike most. And I'd be Catholic no longer, if I married you. The Church would condemn me and my mother and father would disown me."

Michael put his arms around her. "Ah, Rita, let's not argue. There's only a little time before I go on duty."

"I'd rather not sit here longer," Rita said. "We might be seen. The museum is open on Saturdays, now; it's more private there."

They rose to go. Maire wondered what their problem was. Did they belong to rival clans? Something flickered nearby. She looked down. A bird hopped toward her, the same wren that had guided her here.

It stopped a few paces away and regarded her with sharp black eyes. "Maire—"

She jumped. Did wrens also speak?

"Maire, follow the young people. Do not let the girl out of your sight."

Maire thought of death and terror on the city

streets. "I wanted to stay here. It is peaceful, and I feel safe."

"There is nowhere safe from what stalks you. You have a mission; do as I say." The wren watched her a moment longer, then took wing.

Maire left the park close behind the young couple. She passed shops and paused to glance inside. So many things for sale! Who could possibly have time to make them all—or use them?

The distance to the museum was not great. The large stone building was set back from the street; as she drew closer to it Maire could hear the dry, shadowed whispers of ancient things. Here dwelt the past; here she might even find something from her own time.

She entered the museum through double glass doors. The guard pawed through Rita's purse and passed a wand over the couple. The device cried out near metal, Maire saw. Michael had to empty his pockets.

Maire herself carried no metal; she'd left her belt-knife in the drifting boat, long ago. The guard checked her, frowned at her shabby clothes, and let her pass.

Maire lagged behind the pair. She did not wish to be observed. Besides, the museum was full of treasures, and she was curious.

She walked past a counter where books were sold. Writing on paper! She paused and wondered if she could read them with her faerie-sight. The script was strange—Maire remembered puzzling over the physician's note—but she could decipher some words. Others made no sense; what was "archaeology"? She hurried to keep the young couple in sight. They stood before a case of ancient gold ornaments. Maire looked at a torc, its massive gold wires twisted, its terminals fashioned into animal heads. Her throat felt constricted, as if clutched by cold dead hands. Barrow-treasure! The King of the Sídhe had placed such a collar about her own neck, and she had worn it gladly—for a time. She touched her throat; yes, it was bare and free. In the case the collar gleamed, undimmed by time. It had been old when Maire was alive—but she was living yet.

When she looked up the young couple had moved on. She passed an exhibit of bronze spearheads, also older than her time. Her own people had used iron. She climbed a flight of stairs, and found Rita and Michael admiring a collection of cut crystal.

Accustomed as Maire had become to glass, the glittering crystal facets dazzled her. Not even the palace of the Sídhe had held such beauty. She stepped closer. Flowing, rounded letters, unlike those on the books downstairs, decorated some of the uncut surfaces. They seemed at first to be another language, but they were only a different style of writing. The words, again, called no images to mind.

Michael and Rita stood at a little distance, near another display case. "Why do all these pieces mention some bloody Orange Lodge?" Michael said. "You'd think there was nothing else on Earth."

Rita laughed. "Well, we are in Belfast, where even art is political. If you admire crystal as artwork you might prefer the National Museum in Dublin."

Michael stepped closer to her. "I'd like it if you'd take me there."

Rita drew back. "And how would I explain to my mother where I was for two entire days, which it would surely be, if we had any time to see the sights at all?"

Michael sighed. "Well, I probably couldn't get leave the same time you did. Every weekend you're off-duty, I work. They think the sooner we get home from Ulster the better, and there's nothing for us

Tommies to do on leave-time anyhow." He looked at his wrist. "Christ, I've got to get back right now!"

"Go, then," said Rita. "It's best we're not seen leaving together." She squeezed his hand and watched him as he left, then lowered her head and sighed. She made a face at the crystal and went on to another room. Maire followed.

Animals crouched in the wall-cases. Maire thought at first they were alive, but they did not move. How could the eyes be so real? Maire recognized many of the birds, and stopped at the sight of a large trout, frozen in mid-leap. Its eyes, though, were those of an ordinary fish, not amber. Then she saw what loomed in the centre of the room.

Was this a haunting from the bog? Dead things should not stand upright. The skeleton towered over her; its huge antler-spread was twice as wide as she was tall.

Rita walked past it with only a casual glance. This must be naught unusual. Maire saw, then, how wires held the skeleton to the ceiling. It did not stand by its own power. *Though stranger things have happened.* She saw, too, where the great bones were connected, and where some missing ribs had been filled in with other material. The bog had once yielded a skull like this. Folk called it a relic of the Horned One, and left it where it lay. This, though, had a body like a deer, but much larger. Could it be the King of the Deer? Or the Horned One himself in animal guise?

She stepped closer and looked up at the skull. It was bog-brown with age; the eye sockets were cavernous. She reached out and touched the smooth, dry bone. "What were you?" She expected no reply, but a weary sorrow flowed to her.

. . . *The bog was cold and wet, the footing treacherous. Mud squelched beneath huge cloven feet, sucked them down until the animal's knees were covered, until struggle as he would, he could not*

*break free. His antler crown, once held aloft in pride
was now a cruel burden. His head was borne down by
its weight until his muzzle touched brackish water,
and his nostrils snuffled it in. In terror he reared his
mighty head one last time, and plunged, but found
no footing. The mire chilled his belly.*

*. . . Dry ground was not far off; there stood the
shining company of hunters, thwarted by the bog.
They bore spears from which the pale sun struck gold
gleams; their faces were white, and their eyes milky
and strange. The beast closed his eyes and lowered
his head in surrender. His muzzle sank beneath the
water.*

Maire drew back her hand. The Horned One had
died a hunted animal. But who were those who
tracked him down? The Sídhe? They were no folk of
Maire's, that she knew; no one in her time had seen
such a beast, nor were there even ancient tales of
them.

Rita was leaving the room, and Maire must follow.
Down curving stairs she went, into the room where
the books awaited buyers, and out the double glass
doors into the fading light.

Rita walked with the easy stride of one used to
foot-travel. When a car carrying soldiers rumbled past
she looked at it, then glanced away.

The trip across town was long. Rita paused from
time to time and picked late flowers, sheltered in cran-
nies. She carried the bouquet in her hand. They
passed houses in varying states of disrepair; gradually
they came to an area where the streets were narrow
and the houses squalid. Coils of fanged wire topped
many of the walls.

Scrawled on almost any surface, the slogans puzzled
Maire: *Up the IRA, Join Provos.* They had something to do with the atmosphere of fear and hatred,
but the meaning of the words eluded her.

A group of yelling urchins rounded a corner; when

she reached the intersection Maire saw them stoning
an armored vehicle. One of them flung a bucket of
paint, then all scattered for cover. Rita stopped and
shook her head, then hurried onward. Maire half-
caught a glimpse of something red and misty slinking
against a grey battered wall. When she looked again
it had vanished. She shivered; she'd seen it before.
She was followed.

Rita hastened now, looking straight ahead. Her
hands were clenched at her sides. The bouquet
dangled. They reached a less shabby neighborhood.
Save for Rita and Maire, the street was deserted.
Maire heard a distant rumble. Rita heard it too, and
stopped.

An armored lorry turned the corner, and everything happened at once. Maire heard a sharp *crack*
and saw sparks fly from the vehicle's metal plating.
The first report was followed by others. From an alley
came men, masked and bearing the same sort of
weapons as the soldiers; they crouched in doorways
and behind dustbins, and opened fire.

Guns. Of a sudden Maire understood what they
were. She fell flat to the pavement a scant second
after Rita.

The armored lorry returned the fire; bullets
screamed against cobblestones, ricocheted off houses,
and shattered window glass. Maire knew if one struck
her she would be hurt, even killed—at such a distance, by such a tiny thing! The masked men fired a
few more rounds, and another armored vehicle came
on the scene.

"Ah, they've called for their mates!" one man
yelled over the din.

The cobblestones were gritty against Maire's cheek.
She raised her head, then ducked as another bullet
whizzed past. She had to get off the street, get indoors
somewhere, out of this madness—

Rita had not moved. Maire raised her head again.

No, Rita was not tensed, prepared to run; she lay still. A thin stream of blood trickled down the gutter. Maire's impulse was to save herself, but she had been trained as a healer. She inched forward, scraping over cobbles and trash, flattening when the fire came too close. The combatants seemed not to care if they struck bystanders.

Maire was level with Rita's ankle now. She must leave the safety of the gutter and crawl up a slight rise toward the centre of the street, so as to come alongside the injured woman. Rita's breathing was weak, but perceptible. Maire saw she'd been struck in the back of the neck; her long black hair was clotted with blood. Beside her, the flowers lay scattered in the gutter. *Gods,* Maire thought, *what can I do?* Here she herself was in mortal risk; but if she left Rita in the street she might bleed to death, or be struck by another bullet. *But I am not to let her out of my sight.*

"Psst! In here!" A door opened a crack, then quickly shut. Maire checked the location, grasped Rita by the ankle, and began to crawl. Her burden was heavy; most difficult was dragging the unconscious body up the curb. The sidewalk seemed as wide as a field. She pushed at the door, and it opened. As fast as possible she boosted Rita up to the stoop, crept inside, and pulled her after. She lay gasping and shaking in the dimness. Finally she noticed a pair of large feet, thick ankles and legs. She propped herself against the wall and looked up at her benefactress.

"I'm Mrs. O'Shaughnessy," the woman said, "and if Rita wasn't out gallivantin' all the time with Lord knows who, she'd know when business was planned, and be indoors where she belonged." The speech was delivered with an air of injured propriety. Maire looked at the speaker in amazement. Her resemblance to Brigid was uncanny.

"She's hurt," she said. "Unconscious. Have you any water?"

Mrs. O'Shaughnessy sniffed. "Of course I have, and what's it to you? It's Rita what works in a hospital, with all her airs and graces." She regarded Maire's clothing with contempt.

Maire rose and brushed herself off. Her knees were shaking. "I should like to examine the injury," she said, in her mildest tone.

"Very well. And as soon as they're done shooting out there I'll help you see her home; it's but next door, after all." She cocked her head. "They'll stop before more reinforcements come; these diversions are only good for a few brief minutes. That Rita always was a one to get in trouble. I said to her mother only yesterday, I did . . ."

Maire followed her into the kitchen, looking back once at the limp body of the young woman. Outside, the sounds of gunfire ceased.

CHAPTER SEVEN

On a quiet street in the outskirts of Dundalk, Tadhg stood before the old woman's cottage. Its clear glass windows were a novelty, but the thatched roof reminded him of home.

"Well, will you be coming in, or standing dumb struck in the street?" The old woman stood holding the door.

"May this house be blessed by fortune." Tadhg stepped across the threshold. House interiors had changed much; the old woman led him toward the back of the house, where he was surprised to find an indoor kitchen. The fire was metal-shielded, unlike the open cookpits of his time. A good change, that: less danger. He inspected the various unfamiliar utensils that hung from the whitewashed walls and cluttered the work surfaces. As he looked about, the woman busied herself preparing food. Tadhg knew something of cookery, and watched her with interest.

At last she set a steaming plate before him: coarse-cut bacon, fried eggs, and bread. Such substantial fare was a far cry from the subtle viands of the Sídhe. He fumbled with unaccustomed implements, but managed to clean his plate.

"Starved you must have been for sure. It pleases me to feed a hungry man. Cruel long years since I cooked for my own, though the boys do come by from time to time." The old woman trailed off and looked at him, her blue eyes young in the wrinkled ruin of her face. "From where did you know those three?" She brushed away tears.

"I did not know them long." Tadhg spread butter on another slice of bread. "I met them but last night, in a Belfast pub, where they were playing. They took a fancy to me—or perhaps to my harp, here. They asked if I'd travel with them to Dublin."

"How, then, were you not killed with them?"

Tadhg shrugged. "Like as not the others failed to notice me." He saw her incredulous look and added, "or they had only planned to kill the three." He could see the corpses yet, flies buzzing round their heads. Suddenly sick, he set down his bread. "You knew their folk," he said, "those they planned to meet here in Dundalk. Can you show me to them? I bear messages, and they and their kin must claim the honor-price, lest the feud go on."

"It's a strange one you are, and odd your way of speech. Where do your people hail from?"

The far past, I fear. Aloud: "From Lough Neagh. Country folk." That much was true.

"You're not much of a talker," the woman said. "Here, have a spot of tea and I'll find you some better clothes than the disaster you're wearing. Scrubbing rags, they look like. Where could you come from, with tatters on your back and a harp in your hand? Well, I've saved my man's garments, packed them away against need. The boys you seek won't be about 'til late, readying their night errands, of which the less I know the better. Come on upstairs and I'll see to clothing you. Despite the food you still look peaked. Up all night, I wouldn't doubt, or sleeping in a ditch. You may as well take a rest while you can."

* * *

Tadhg lay on a soft bed and slept. Twilight was deep when he woke, and he felt ready to face whatever laired for him. He put on the woolen clothing. It smelled sharp, like the crystals it was stored in, yet the garments fit, and the cloth was thick and warm.

Downstairs he found the old woman drowsing by the stove, a striped cat curled on her lap. She sat as if guarding the door. At the sound of his steps she looked up and jumped; the cat fled. She raised a hand to her mouth. "Holy Mary, for a moment I thought it was himself alive again. It's the size, of course, and you've much the same coloring, but to see you standing in the doorway, wearing his clothes—" She stopped. "Well, you'll be wanting to get along. You young ones are always hurried. I'll take you over to the pub and have a pint of stout myself. It's been an evil time."

Tadhg picked up his harp from the corner.

"Must you be taking that?" The old woman's tone was wistful. " 'Twould be safe here. You might lodge with me for a time, I've room enough."

Her loneliness struck at Tadhg; that, and the old messages spoken by the clothes. Long had they wanted a body within, or a touch without. They had last been packed away when this woman was a young widow. Her tears still sprinkled them. Earlier, they had covered a brave man, a man who'd set them aside for a soldier's uniform, a man who never more came home. Tadhg felt the rough tweed cry, felt the shoes yearn for mountain paths. He gentled his voice. "I may need my harp. I dare not leave it behind. Who knows where I must go, or when return?"

The old woman shrugged, set her face into a smile, and led him out into the twilight.

Entering the pub was like stepping into a cave. The brown walls, ceiling, and furniture soaked up all light save that which glinted off bottles and reflected from the sign-cluttered mirror. Whiskey, beer, smoke, and sweat pervaded the air.

Toward the far end of the bar two young men faced half-filled mugs. They were not concentrating on the drink; they and the bartender spoke low. All three looked up as Tadhg and the old woman entered. "Good evening, Missus O'Carroll," said the shorter man. He wore a brimmed leather cap pulled down over his face; the hair that straggled free was black, and his white skin was scarred and pitted. His gaze wandered to Tadhg; he sat up straight and nudged his companion.

"It's an evil day, boys," said the old woman. "You've heard the news?"

Both customers nodded. The second, taller, with light-brown curly hair and freckled skin, said, "Ah, it was a dirty business." He hoisted his glass.

The bartender, a red-faced, paunchy fellow in late middle age, moved down the bar toward the newcomers and began polishing glasses.

The short, dark young man spoke again. "What brings you here this evening, Missus O'Carroll? And who have you brought along?" His voice was polite, but as he looked at Tadhg, his fingers whitened on the edge of the bar.

Mrs. O'Carroll settled onto a barstool. "I'll have a pint of Guinness, Kevin," she said, "as will my young guest here. And I'll be taking it here, not in the snug. I've need to talk with the boys, and they've a need, it seems, to watch the door."

With deliberate ritual the bartender placed a large glass under a spigot and poured brown foamy liquid; he watched the creamy flecks swirl and settle, as if that were his sole concern.

"My young friend here," Mrs. O'Carroll remarked, "claims to be the last to see Padraig Byrne, Thomas O'Brien, and Rory White alive."

With a knife the bartender scraped foam across the top of the glass. Mrs. O'Carroll reached into her pocket and pulled out several coins.

The dark young man slammed a handful of change onto the bar. "Beggin' your pardon, Missus, but I think I owe you a pint—you and your friend. How did you come to meet this one here?" He gestured, still wary, at Tadhg.

"Coming out of church, and long it's been since either of you were seen inside the door." Mrs. O'Carroll sipped her drink.

Tadhg gulped the bitter, filling brew. He felt certain that these were the men he sought, but they did not trust him. Fear tensed their shoulders; at any noise, their faces turned toward the door.

"You were with them last night, then?" the dark young man spoke to Tadhg. "What are you called?"

"Tadhg MacNiall," Tadhg answered civilly, though he thought the other's tone discourteous.

"I am Connor Lynch," the dark man replied, "and this is Liam MacMahon." He indicated his taller companion, who nodded but said nothing. "How came you to be with Padraig, Thomas, and Rory?"

Tadhg told how they had met, and described the ambush.

"Did you recognize the attackers?" Connor asked.

Tadhg shook his head. "They were masked. I might know their voices."

"How came you not to be killed yourself?" It was the first time Liam had spoken. He turned on his barstool and reached out one long leg, as if ready to leap.

Tadhg shrugged. "I may have passed unnoticed in the confusion, or they might not have wished to harm a stranger. Who knows what manner of men kill bards? They must be *gealt*."

The two men looked at him, puzzled. At that moment the door opened, and all faces turned in that direction.

The newcomer surveyed the scene. His back was against the light, and it was difficult to see his features, only that he stood medium tall. He swaggered in, hands in pockets. "It's wonderful progress you're making here, no doubt." He strode to the end of the room and sat, not at the bar, but apart, at a small round table. Unasked, the bartender set a short glass of whiskey before him.

The newcomer sipped, then leaned back. "Well? Three of our comrades dead on the road, and you sit here in the pub, no doubt solving their murders. Tell me: Do you suspect the Guinness or the Jameson's, for all your interrogations? Or have you asked Bushmills? He's the one I favor, since he has the spirit of the North in him." He propped up his feet. "Good day, Mrs. O'Carroll. Were you at church as usual this evening, praying for our sins?"

"It's a deal of prayer you'll be wanting some day, Sean O'Rourke, and glad you'll be then that I remembered you!"

"If you're praying that I be cleansed of my sins, mind you pray also that our land be cleansed of invaders." Sean drained the whiskey; the bartender proffered another, but he waved him aside. "I'll be wanting a clear head for the night's work, and so will these boys. Serve them no more." He nodded toward Tadhg. "Who might this be?"

"I am Tadhg MacNiall, the bard. I saw the murder of your friends and came to find their kin."

Sean O'Rourke sat up. "You were witness to the murders?"

"So I have said. And what manner of men would act in such a way I do not know. My companions told me they had people in Dundalk, but you cannot be they." He had expected better manners; he stooped to pick up his harp.

Sean glanced at Connor and Liam, who sat silent. They shrugged. At last Connor said, "He thinks to identify the culprits from their voices."

Sean pulled out a chair. "Tadhg, seat yourself. We have much to speak of. You come from where?"

Tadhg stood a moment, torn between pride and duty. Then for the third time he told his tale. When he finished, he presented the packet of papers. Sean read it and tucked it away, then looked at Tadhg with more interest. "Would you see the three avenged?"

"That I would," said Tadhg, "for honor demands it."

"Well, you see," said Sean, speaking slowly, " 'tis a mortal blood-feud we are in. If you would help, then come with us tonight."

Sean thought him mad, Tadhg realized, and humored him. Tadhg had not told them all he knew, neither had these men spoken their minds. The smell of blood and violence choked the air.

"Connor, Liam, take him to the house by the back streets. Get him identification and dark clothing. We may be able to use him. Meet me at moonrise." Sean rose to go.

"Ah, he's an innocent," keened Mrs. O'Carroll, "and you'll kill him with your wicked schemes."

"Do you wish your husband had died for nothing? Give respect to a soldier's memory, woman." Sean strode from the pub.

Connor and Liam rose to obey. Tadhg looked at Mrs. O'Carroll. She was hunched over in misery, her fingers tracing crosses on the wet surface of the bar. She mumbled something he could not hear, then mumbled it again. A charm? He picked up his harp and patted her black-shawled shoulder. "Thank you, Mrs. O'Carroll, for your hospitality. May we meet again."

He followed the two out into the darkened street.

* * *

It was full dark, and stars gleamed overhead. Only a night and a day had passed since Tadhg had surfaced from the lake, yet it seemed so long ago. How many years had the stars watched while he dreamed? Stars saw too much, stars were too old. Tadhg did not like their unblinking eyes.

The house to which Connor and Liam led him was a huddling-place, a den. The glass windowpanes were grime-smeared, mildew spotted the indoor woodwork, and cartons and bedrolls littered the dusty corners. Little cooking ever warmed that kitchen, and no laughter had blessed the house in far too long. Its walls stunk of sweat and anger.

Connor fumbled at something, and sunlike brilliance nearly blinded Tadhg. Never had he cared for sunglare, and who would think to find it at night, indoors? He chose a clear spot on the floor and sat.

"Well, now, let's see your papers and decide if you'll pass," said Connor. Liam was rummaging in another room.

"Papers?" He'd heard the request before, but did not, as yet, know what was meant.

Liam reappeared. "I say he's daft, and Sean's a fool for sure."

"You'd never say so to his face," Connor replied. Then, more slowly, to Tadhg, "Papers. Indentification. Your work card."

Tadhg shook his head. "I have none."

"Did you lose them, or—never mind." Connor raised his voice and shouted to the next room. "Liam? Get him some papers." He wiped his brow. "How did you ever manage?"

After a time Liam returned with a rustling packet and handed it to Tadhg. "Put these in your pocket," he said. "When you're asked for identification, hand them over. They give your name as William Francis. You work in the Belfast foundry, and you are Protestant. God help you if you go to the foundry; you've never been near one in your life, I'm sure." He shook his head. "It won't do, Connor." With that he left again.

Tadhg, bewildered, said, "What now? Shall we avenge the slain?"

"Not yet." Connor sounded impatient. Tadhg picked up his harp and strummed. He did not know what to sing.

Time passed. At last the moon shone silver through the streaked glass-panes. "We should leave," Connor said. He had Tadhg don a black coat and handed him a cap; it unrolled into a black face-mask. "Keep this in your pocket, you may need it."

The three stepped forth into moonlight, and the doorlatch clicked behind them. All was quiet. Tadhg held his harp. Connor and Liam bore cloth-wrapped packages that might hold guns. Gunshot for gunshot was only justice, if the blood-feud had progressed this far.

Tadhg wondered whether he felt fear or anticipation.

A vehicle waited in a pool of darkness. Tadhg could discern litttle in the silver-black shadows, but he heard Sean's voice. "'It's about time. Have a lovely rest?"

"Ah, it's not twenty minutes past moonrise." Liam spoke.

"I never said twenty minutes *past*, I said moonrise itself. We've to cross the Border, find our men, and get back home before the word is out." Sean started the engine, and the other three climbed into the car. "You've papers for Tadhg, I hope?"

"We have," said Connor. "He's William Francis for tonight, a fine Protestant welder from Belfast."

Sean chuckled. "That should confuse the constabulary." The car sped down a moon-dappled lane. Tadhg, not yet accustomed to this form of travel, stayed silent, gripping the seat. Something there was in these men's manner—a furtiveness, perhaps—that struck him wrong. Their thoughts dwelt little on honor.

They were halted at the Border checkpoint. "Oh, come now, we *must* get home by morning. We're working the extra shift and could lose our jobs," Sean pleaded. The soldier frowned. Sean held forth his papers, as did Liam, Connor, and Tadhg.

The guard scanned them and handed them back. "Pass, then. You're late, but close enough, I suppose. Next time—"

"We'll allow more leeway. It's their bloody roads, you'd think they'd never heard of the automobile. Perhaps the Pope hasn't blessed it yet. Why, we punctured a tyre on a stone of such size—"

"Go ahead." The guard waved them through.

Once past the checkpoint Sean snarled. "The bastards! All we need do is slander our own land." He tucked his papers away. "I've a notion where we'll find our quarry, and Tadhg here—William, I should say—can identify them, you claim? Three, driving a Morris?"

"So Padraig shouted when he saw them," Tadhg replied. "I was in the back of the van at the time."

"It'll be the MacIvers," said Sean, "for sure. Not on a Friday night will they be at the Orange Lodge; no Temperance Pledge for them. Toasting and boasting they'll be, laughing over what they've done."

Petty. Tadhg thought. *Do they not respect their foes? What honor, then, to slay them?* "Enough. Have we come after vengeance, or prattle?"

Sean drew in his breath and began to speak; Tadhg heard words of outrage stick in his throat. He slammed his foot to the floor, and the car sped forward into darkness.

*   *   *

The place they sought was a country pub, nestled among fields. They drove into the parking area, where cars gleamed in starlight. The only other illumination, save for the moon, was the yellow light from the pub's door and windows. Each time the door opened they heard raucous laughter and song; and in each sound-blast Tadhg listened for familiar voices. Then:

"MacIver, you're drunk!" Cheers greeted the statement.

Another voice shouted, "So are you, MacIver yourself!"

Tadhg cringed. To slay a drunken man was base. Yet he must tell his companions. "Those are the men. I know their voices." He knew at least he doomed no honest folk.

Sean started the engine. The very car Tadhg remembered—Padraig had called it a "Morris"—flashed on its lights and weaved forth. Sean cut ahead of it, then speeded up and turned off onto a small side road. "Out," he ordered. Tadhg seized his harp and stepped into the night; Connor and Liam, carrying cloth-wrapped packages, followed him.

The Morris, yet weaving, rounded a road-bend, its lights shining through the hedgerows. Tadhg had a moment to admire the tracery on the nearest leaf before the guns opened fire.

Bullets spatted and whined across the body of the car. A scream, and the vehicle lurched into the ditch. Three passengers leaped forth; guns stuttered again, and men fell to the roadway. For a moment they lay still.

So be it; they murdered bards. Sean thrust a weapon into Tadhg's hands. "Let's go—we'll leave him holding the gun, him with his Protestant identification!"

Tadhg held the unfamiliar weapon. It killed at a distance, but *how?* On the road, one of the MacIvers rolled over. He had something in his hand—he raised it, took aim. Tadhg heard a bullet whistle overhead, and threw himself to the ground. Behind him, a scream—Sean's voice—cried a warrior's death. Tadhg dropped the heavy iron weapon as if his hands were burned. He reached for his harp and stood.

He struck a few notes. In the darkness things rose from crumbling earth; dry skulls rattled within rusted helmets, and teeth clenched in fleshless jaws. A bard had called the dead to vengeance. The night hushed in horror.

CHAPTER EIGHT

Maire followed Mrs. O'Shaughnessy back to her kitchen. The room was filthy. Food crusted on heaped plates, flies gorged and buzzed, and over all hung a sour stench of decay.

Mismanagement, Maire thought. *Why she permits her servants*—but this was no woman of noble birth. She doubtless had no servants. She was slovenly, then, like Brigid. She even resembled her: The hair was shorter, as was the dress, but—*How could such a woman wield any power?*

Maire saw the woman's glance, as if she dared her to comment. Maire set her face, ignored the smell, and selected the least crusted bowl. She puzzled at the dripping tap until the woman, with an impatient gesture, flicked it open. Water gushed into the bowl. Maire scrubbed and filled it. "Have you any clean cloths?" She tried not to stress *clean*. The woman jerked open a drawer and handed her a towel, shabby but freshly laundered.

"Thank you." Maire carried the bowl to the front room. Rita yet lay on the floor, but now her eyes were open. She raised her head.

"What happened? There was the disturbance on

the street—and who are you?" she said, focusing at last on Maire. She caught sight of Mrs. O'Shaughnessy, and winced.

"Dragged in you were like a sack of potatoes, by this stranger woman," Mrs. O'Shaughnessy proclaimed, "and it's only luck that has you not lying dead in the gutter."

"I am Maire ní Donnall," Maire said, "and I would like to examine your head wound." Rita flinched. "Not to worry. I am a healer." Rita watched her, eyes wide. Maire dipped the cloth into the water and began to sponge away the clotted blood. As she redipped the cloth the water turned red. Wordless, she handed the bowl to Mrs. O'Shaughnessy, who sniffed but shuffled to refill it.

Rita scrutinized Maire. "Didn't I see you in the museum, earlier this afternoon? Have you been following me?" She winced. "Ah, my head holds two thousand hammers wielded by one thousand ambidextrous demons."

Mrs. O'Shaughnessy returned and slammed the water bowl onto the floor. Maire resumed washing the wound.

"It's not as bad as I feared." She probed with careful fingers. "Naught but a cut, though wounds of the scalp bleed greatly. I'd be wanting to stitch it, but I haven't my bag of herbs." She realized, suddenly, that her bag of herbs, and everything she owned, had mouldered long ago: herbs, knives, needles, and sutures. Without them what could she do?

You do not need tools. You have the Power. Maire knew that voice by now, but yet it startled her. Power? To stitch a wound without needles and thread? Even if she did, without her medicines, how would she stop the red swelling that burst stitches and caused scars?

She looked down at Rita's scalp, and the light grew grey. She *saw*: the straight cut, the severed blood vessels, and, beneath skin and muscle, a gleam of bone. *Heal, then, if I have the power.* She watched the tiny blood-tubes join together, watched the skin mend, watched the bleeding stop. Nothing was left but a line of dried blood. She drew back her hand; the wound had healed, and she'd done nothing but will it so.

Rita touched her head; her fingers came away clean. "What did you do?"

Maire was still stunned. "Did I not say I was a healer?"

"Yes, but wherever did you train?" Rita struggled into a sitting posture.

Maire did not answer. She stared at her right hand, then dropped the bloodstained rag into the water and helped Rita to her feet.

Mrs. O'Shaughnessy stood by, wordless. "I'll be showing the young Miss home," Maire said. The large woman bent and picked up the blood-filled bowl; she took it to the kitchen.

Rita's home, next door, was separated from Mrs. O'Shaughnessy's by a thin wall. *How can they live so huddled?* Any sound must carry, and there would be no privacy at all.

Rita opened the front door, leaned against the doorjamb for a moment, then stumbled into the house. A thin, grey-haired woman flung herself against her. "Holy Mary," she cried, "what's happened now? Was it hit you were on the street? You're blood all over, and your dress—"

"The wound is not serious," Maire said, to forestall hysterics. The woman clung to Rita, sobbing. Their faces were similar, but the mother was a good handsbreadth shorter than her daughter. Her dress, knee-length and drab, sagged on a fleshless frame.

Maire looked about the house. She stood in an anteroom similar to that of Mrs. O'Shaughnessy's, but here was a tidy, cleanly place.

This was a woman who worried much, and wept in secret. She had poured out her soul and body, like rainwashed land; naught remained but a rock-hard skeleton.

Maire wondered toward the cause. Grief gripped this house, an old grief by now, but like a sore it galled and was reopened daily.

The mother was fussing over her child—the child bent her taller head, in kindness—and Maire let herself feel the dwelling, and those who had passed time therein.

There had been a young man, his name was John. He wanted to study—healing? Four years older than his sister Rita, she adored him.

Sunlight glittered a lake. Breezes riffled the water. The rowboat rocked on wavelets, and John, all splendidly eighteen, shipped his oars. He tilted his face to the sky.

"Ah, grand it'll be, at college next autumn in London, an' there's no reason you yourself, once you grow up, couldn't join me. There are women in medicine now, after all, and you've the talent, no matter what the Sisters might say about a woman's place. See how you care for the small creatures you bring home. I'll be a great surgeon." He stopped and looked out across the lake. "If my hands are skilled enough. But today, let us catch some trout. Have you been keeping to your studies, little sister?"

At that point Rita scooped a handful of water and watched it shatter in sunlight as it dashed against John's face.

That was the last bright memory. Maire then saw a vase of withered flowers.

She was embarrassed to have scryed their house while the mother and daughter yet reassured each other. She, Maire, had been introduced to neither.

The same thought struck the other folk; Rita's mother looked at the tattered stranger.

Maire spoke first. "It happened, I was passing on the street."

Rita studied her, hard. With the tiniest motion, Maire shook her head, and continued. "So the Miss here was somewhat damaged, and I took it upon myself to see to her welfare. Mrs. O'Shaughnessy"—Rita and her mother winced—"called me to her doorway, I knowing nowhere else to go."

"She'd be watching, for certain," said Rita. "To catch me out in something, if naught else, and violence fascinates her."

"Ah, not to speak so of your neighbors," said Rita's mother. "She's a good soul under it all, as are most of us."

"Such a good soul, after what she did to her very own Cathleen?" Rita pulled her mother from the hallway into the parlor. "It's the likes of her that will cause more death."

The parlor held a plaster mantelpiece, bedecked with painted cards—*gods and goddesses*, Maire thought—and in their centre, a black-framed portrait of John. *John, of the sun-blessed lake and joking talk.* Before his picture, in a glass vase, stood wildflowers: wilted, now. Rita's newest gathering lay outside in the gutter.

Rita glanced again at Maire, puzzled. Maire shook her head, looking toward the mother. Rita nodded and sat, rather harder than necessary. She raised one hand to her forehead.

"Would you be wanting a cup of tea, dear?" her mother asked. Rita nodded; her mother scurried to oblige.

When they were alone Rita leaned forward. "So there's something about you I'm not to mention. What might it be?"

Speak the truth. "It's a strange story, and will take long telling. You, in turn, could teach me much I need to know, for I am not from hereabouts." Maire reflected a moment. "Or from nowabouts, for that matter. What I will say may be difficult to believe. Your time is much different from mine; my story will doubtless sound like the raving of a madwoman."

Rita looked at her, shook her head, and winced. "I've seen a lot of madfolk, and you're not one. I hope you'll stay to tea, and spend the night, at least? I've an extra bed in my room, and you could tell me your story in private."

Rattling crockery announced the mother's approach. Rita raised her voice. "Since I was unconscious, I'll need neurological checks every two hours, and I'd not want to disturb my parents. Maire, if you have no other plans?"

"I'd not be intruding," Maire said, "but if my presence would help—"

The mother entered, bearing a tray with a china pot and cups.

"We should set another place at table, Mother. Maire here can check me during the night, to make certain I've taken no serious harm. She's trained and knows how."

"We really should take you to hospital," the mother began.

"Ah, what I need most is rest."

"You should lie down, then. I'll bring you a tray in your room."

"No need," said Rita. "But I should like to change from these clothes—" She indicated her bloodstained garments.

"I'll help you up the stairs, then." Her mother set down the tea tray.

"No need. Maire can do it. She might want to freshen up a bit herself; I fear her own dress is past salvation."

* * *

Rita was shaky, and stopped on the stairs. "The head is fierce, and I daren't take anything for it." Beads of sweat formed on her upper lip. "Here we are." They were on the second floor: From a long narrow corridor, five doors opened.

"This is my parents' room," Rita indicated the first door, "and next to it is—" She breathed in, "May he rest, poor John. The first door across the hall is mine, and next to it is the W.C., and beyond that, the bath."

"The W.C.?"

Rita looked at her. "You've a different term? The toilet." She frowned a little. "I've a washstand in my room, and you've a story to tell, so let's get on with it." She opened her door.

Aside from four garish wall-patterns and a grotesque painting of a mutilated man, the room was neat. Rita saw Maire looking at the picture and laughed. "Ah, the Sacred Heart. A fair horror, isn't it? Mother hung it there. She'd fret if I took it down, so in Christian charity I let it be. After a while one learns to ignore it."

Maire wondered how.

Rita went to the corner of the room and ran water onto a cloth. She looked in a mirror. Her image was undistorted. *Their mirrors are so clear*. Maire's own, the one Queen Deirdre had given her, dimmed her reflection. The lake had been better, or the pool— longing and sorrow caught her, and she closed her eyes, fighting for control. *Gone and dead, all of it, all of them. And Tadhg—TADHG!*

"I look like something the cat dragged in, no offense, Maire," Rita said. She sponged an area on the back of her neck. "Ouch! I should offer up the pain, Mother would say. For the suffering souls." Maire opened her eyes in time to see Rita turn pale and clutch the edge of the washstand.

"Best you be lying down." Maire guided the other woman to one of the narrow beds. "It's time I told my story, while you lie and rest."

Rita lay on the bed, then, with a sob, curled into a ball. "Michael, Michael," she said, "he'll be daft with terror when he hears of this. He's troubles enough." She curled up tighter and gripped her head. "I never know if I will see him again, day to day—and yet—and yet I don't want to lose him!" Rita uncurled and lay straight, breathing steadily. "Sorry. I have these hysterical outbreaks from time to time. I'll listen now, even if my eyes are shut. One last thing, though. Do you really know about neurological checks?"

"No," said Maire, "but I could learn."

"This is important. I've suffered a head injury, and I was unconscious. I don't know how you stopped the scalp bleeding. I may have a subdural hematoma—a blood clot on the brain—and, if so, it could swell and cause pressure that might kill me."

"I have seen folk die after waking from head wounds," said Maire, "they were bright at first, then they would grow duller, and collapse—"

"Then you know. If you cannot waken me—and you must try every two hours."

"Hours?" Maire was puzzled.

Rita opened her eyes again. "It's a strange story indeed you'll be telling." She struggled onto her elbows. "Do you know about clocks?"

Maire shook her head.

"I'll set the alarm. When the buzzer sounds you try to wake me. If you cannot, get me to hospital—Mother knows where it is. Assuming I do wake, turn on the light and look at my eyes. If the pupils are equal, and react to light—they do now, I've just checked—all is well."

Maire was fascinated. "The eyes are a sign of brain pressure? What then can be done? Are there herbs to cure it?"

"Emergency surgery," Rita said. "But that's the hospital's worry."

"Would they cut a hole in the skull?" Maire wondered how they would then control the mad thrashing sickness that often came—but now was her time to tell, not ask. She was a guest, after all. "I will do as you say, and in the meantime I will tell you how I came here."

Rita closed her eyes again. The clock made a slow steady sound like a heartbeat.

"I lived on the shores of Lough Neagh, when Conn Sléaghéar was King of the Cruthini, and a fine king he was. Do you know of him?"

"No," said Rita. "When was this?"

"I know not how you reckon the years. But it was some small time after a new religion was sent about the land."

"Christianity?" Rita opened her eyes. "That would be fourteen hundred years! You're having me on." She touched her scalp. "And yet there is something strange about you."

Fourteen hundred years? Maire could not imagine such a time. Her world was so far away . . . but she'd promised to tell her tale. She took a deep breath. "I will relate how this came to be. Back in my own time I was fostered to a healer and her husband, and when I grew to be a woman I wed Tadhg, a bard. He wished to be the best." Sorrow welled in her. "On Bealtaine Eve he slept on the faerie mound, and when in the morning I sought him—" She told the rest of her story.

Rita laughed. "That's very good, you know."

Maire sat silent, unsmiling.

"You're not serious, woman? Faeries, in this day and age, and you from ancient times?" Maire nodded. "Your tale is purely daft. Yet something strange has happened." Rita touched her scalp and looked again at her hand. "Perhaps it's but the head wound, and I am confused myself. But if the Sídhe do exist—the ancient ones—" She sat up and pointed to the picture on the wall. "You'll need to know this much: *That* is the god of your 'new religion.' *That* god rends Ireland. For Him the Protestants kill the Catholics and the Catholics kill the Protestants with equal glee, and the Irish fight their brother Irish *and* the English; it's all in His name. *They use Him as an excuse for murder!*"

Maire looked at the picture. It showed a long-haired, brown-bearded man. Save for his suffering countenance, he resembled Tadhg. He wore a red mantle and a white robe not unlike those worn in Maire's time. He had torn open the front of his robe to expose a bleeding heart, thorn-circled and gold-crowned. But real human hearts did not look like that; Maire had seen many. What sort of heart was this, and why did these folk joy to see the life ripped from their god?

A knock clattered on the door. "Himself is home, and tea's on."

CHAPTER NINE

Save for the thrum of Tadhg's harp and the rattle of
bones in rusted armor, the night lay waiting. The
gunshots ceased, and the breeze held its breath.

Dark it was, black dark. Cloud-fingers drew a veil
across the moon, so that none but Tadhg, with his
faerie-sight, could see the dead rise from the earth.
Part of him cried out in horror at what he had done.

But these are bard-slayers. "May their own land devour them, their ancestors accuse them, their own
bloody history strangle them. I, Tadhg MacNiall,
have called you forth."

In the eerie grey of faerie-sight he saw the three
men on the roadway. Two were wounded, and all
three lay paralyzed with fear. Only their eyes moved
to seek the source of the rustling. Mortals, they saw
nothing.

Sean, Tadhg knew, lay dead with a bullet through
his brain. His companions crouched in terror, for
they had heard the footfalls of the dead.

Through the hedgerows they stepped, the fallen
legions, in tattered garb of many centuries. Some
strode in peasant clothes, unarmored; some bore
pikes and spears; some held what once were guns.

Others stood bare-handed, or their bony fingers clutched stones. They rustled like dead autumn leaves, like the chill wind through naked branches, like memories and night-terrors and the first gibbering of madness.

The troop of them stood and turned toward Tadhg. Pale they were, and dark filled their eye sockets. What had he to do with them? *Vengeance,* said the voice. Tadhg spoke: "There lie bard-slayers, men without honor. Send their spirits screaming." Yet his own soul was sick. The ghastly legion faltered. Tadhg drew himself up to his full height and struck another chord upon his harp. "I have the Power, and you are bound to me. Obey!"

His neck bent forward, as if a weight lay on his head, as if—as if—but then the dead moved, and amid their thin, dry rustling he heard the screams: Three voices, once human, now were purest horror and despair.

In the strange grey light Tadhg watched: the three gunmen, gibbering in terror, surrounded by the legion of the dead. Bony fingers scrabbled at clothing, fleshlesss lips whispered obscenities, grave-mould fell into mouths and eyes. No mortal mind could bear such confrontation. In years to come, till blessed darkness claimed them, the three MacIvers would only drool and babble.

But no, it was not enough. *Those men must die.* And the dead themselves cannot take life. Tadhg's hands were the hands of a stranger as he set down his harp and picked up the gun.

And he knew what to do. He aimed toward the three and pulled the trigger. The recoil jerked him back, and the first burst went high. He steadied the weapon, and watched the bullets strike along the road. *Too far to the left.* He corrected his aim and stitched bloody holes across the MacIvers. They lay still.

"It is finished," he called to the risen dead, "and you may go." The ancient warriors stood watching him, but did not move until he picked up his harp. The instrument felt strange in his hands. He played a sleep-command and the dead melted, mistlike, back to earth. He looked at the bodies on the roadway. Had he done that? How, and why? His fingers burned, and the harpstrings were cool.

I should take their heads for trophies. He stepped forward and reached for his sword, but he carried none. His own head yet was heavy, as if borne down by—by something, not a helmet. He tensed his neck; the cloud released the moon.

Silver washed the roadway. The blood on the tar pooled black in the moonlight. As Tadhg turned to his companions he caught sight of his moon-cast shadow: for a moment it seemed that antlers sprouted—*the Horned One?*

Connor and Liam crouched, staring. Tadhg had seen such expressions on wounded animals who had passed beyond fear.

Liam tried to speak. He babbled a few moments and covered his face with his hands, then crossed himself. "Holy Mary Mother of God, Tadhg Mac-Niall, *what are you?*"

"There is no such thing," Conner whined. "I cannot have seen or heard it, I must be mad, there is no such thing, no, no, no—" He began to sob in shuddering torrents. "No, there is no such thing—"

Tadhg was chilled. There *were* such things, he of all men knew, but he was human, merely human, a bard, and never before had he slain. *Never before tonight,* the voice said. *Now you lead the Hunt.*

He had done the honorable thing. Tadhg regarded the horror-struck men. Sean, their leader, lay dead. He needed these two. Mad, they would be useless. "You will forget what you have heard and seen," he said, strumming his harp. "But now you ride with me." He played a melody of forgetting. After a time the two men quieted. They rose, carried Sean's body to the car, and sat in back. Their eyes were closed, and they kept silent.

Tadhg took the driver's seat and set his hands on the wheel. The key was still in place. His feet sought the pedals. For a moment he sat, uncertain; then he *knew*. And he could expect no help from those in the rear. His left foot pressed down, his left hand maneuvered a lever, and he turned the key in the ignition. The engine roared into life.

Tadhg eased out on the clutch and pressed the accelerator. The car moved forward. By the time they reached the main highway its progress was smooth. He enjoyed the feeling of power. It surprised him not at all that he could operate the strange chariot; he was, after all, the Leader of the Hunt. He turned toward Dundalk. He knew a place to cross the Border unobserved.

The Three Bards' honor was avenged, but one of Tadhg's own men had died in that battle, and his thirst for blood was strong. He who had before only sung of warfare lusted now to rend and destroy. But not at this time; there were other things to do.

He stopped at the house. The town lay dark and silent, and silver moonlight washed the cobbled street. "Take him to his kin," Tadhg told the two, "and say what must be said. He died a soldier's death."

"They'll not be wanting to bury him in consecrated ground," said Liam—his voice was low—"for he never went to church since he was grown, and they knew the things he did for our cause. Father Mulvaney speaks against the movement as much as he dares. He's an old man, though, and few listen."

Tadhg opened the car door. "What does consecrated ground matter to me? Or Father Mulvaney, of

whatever religion he be priest? Do what is necessary
to give him a hero's burial. Return this vehicle
whence it came—I know it is not ours—then come back
here."

"Sean has a mother," Connor said, "though she'll
not wish to see us this night, for sure."

"Tell her he fell with honor. She should be glad."
Tadhg slung the gun onto one shoulder, picked up
his harp, and strode into the darkened house. Silent,
it was. He should compose a lament for Sean. He set
down the gun and took the harp onto his lap, but his
fingers felt coarse against the strings. They fumbled,
as if they were skilled instead in other work. He set
the harp down and stared silent into the darkness. He
could not remember who he was. Was he going mad?

Tadhg sat in the cluttered house; Connor and
Liam stood before him. "His mother wept," said Connor.

"Mothers often do." Tadhg glanced about the
room. "This place is the den of hunted animals, not a
barracks for soldiers. Have you no pride?"

Connor and Liam began to straighten the clutter.

"Will he have a hero's burial by the custom of
your folk?"

Liam stopped his work. "His mother will speak
with Father Mulvaney in the morning. There may be
problems."

"See that Sean is honored as his people would
wish," Tadhg said. "We avenge him tomorrow, that
he may rest in his grave. I'd not have him wander the
earth on our account."

Liam shuddered, as if remembering something,
then shook his head. "There's an Orange Lodge not
far across the Border, if they're yet meeting—they may
be too afraid, by now—"

"Enough," said Tadhg. "We ride tomorrow night.

And what was in the papers I brought? The Bards seemed to consider them important."

"A shipment of arms, to land next week in the West. The seaward coast of Achill Island, in County-Mayo-God-Help-Us." Connor seemed to draw strength from the details of business. "Do you know the place?"

"Never have I been there," said Tadhg. "A shipment of arms? From where?"

"It'll be guns from America," said Connor. "We'll stay with Padraig Byrne's family, on their farm. They do not know our business, nor would they approve, but we are friends of their dead son—"

"America?" said Tadhg. "Where might that be?"

Connor and Liam looked at him strangely; neither spoke for a time, then Liam said, "The land to the West."

"Ah," said Tadhg. "Tir na n'Óg." It was good to have support from the Land of the Young. "We will depart, then, after Sean's funeral. Ill 'twould be to leave our comrade before then."

In the morning rumors swept the town, how Sean O'Rourke was dead, and how across the Border the MacIvers had been found bullet-riddled. Liam and Connor, their eyes dark with fear, related this to Tadhg. He nodded. They did not remember, he knew, what had happened in the dark of the moon; all they had left was vague terror and respect. This much was well. Men such as they could not live with the knowledge of what had passed, not yet, and Tadhg needed them to explain this time to him, and the methods of war now used.

He asked questions; they showed him their stock of gelignite—innocent-looking boxes of brown sticks. He watched as Liam wired some and attached the timer. It smelled sharp, like strong drink, with a hint of wet green bog, or mildew. The odor made him dizzy. He was not sure he understood explosives, but the image he received was one of satisfying destruction.

Liam winced as he finished the task. "It's my head again," he said, "perish this stuff."

Connor entered the room. "You should wear gloves, and step out sometimes to breathe."

Liam's face was flushed. "I did wear gloves, you fool, surgical gloves, but they must have torn on the wiring, and I can scarcely help breathing the vapor—" He packed the materials in a box, set it in another room, and said, "I'm off to the pub. I'd thought my gelignite tolerance was still up, but it's been more than a week since I assembled a bomb—ah, my head's pounding as if to burst."

"It's all you need, the drink to fuddle you further," Connor said. "I'll be staying here; there's plans yet to be made for the Mayo trip, and I'm weary from last night." He frowned.

"I'll go with you," said Tadhg. "I've naught to keep me here, and a drink would sit well." He saw his harp on the floor, and paused. He had no need of it.

Liam looked at him in apprehension, but held the door open till he passed through. The two stepped out into the sunlight. The town basked in the warmth. On the surface all was calm.

The pub was dim as usual, cave-dark after the sun-washed street, but nowhere as deserted as it had been the day before. Men crowded the bar and the tables; smoke thickened the air, and Kevin, the bartender, pulled pints of Guinness as fast as he was able, though still with the same elaborate ritual, scraping off the foam with a knife and letting the black liquid rise to the lip of the glass.

Toward the rear of the building, in a separate room connected to the bar by a pass-through, Tadhg heard the voices of women.

A man rose, red-faced and hearty. His chin was stubbled. He wore rubber boots redolent with dung. "Ho, Liam MacMahon, what will you be having this fine day?"

Liam was breathless from the walk; his face was yet flushed. "A Guinness—no, whiskey." The drink was brought, and he tossed the amber liquid down his throat. He gasped and held the glass out; Kevin refilled it.

Tadhg stood quiet. The farmer noticed him. "And what will you be having, stranger, as well?

"Mead."

"Mead? We have none," said Kevin. He looked at Tadhg in surprise.

Tadhg shook his head; it felt light, not from the explosive fumes, but as if an accustomed burden were lifted. "Guinness, then. A pint." He waited, took the heavy glass, and sat down where a place was cleared for him.

The farmer leaned toward Tadhg and Liam. His eyes were bloodshot and his breath was strong. "Strange news of last night." His face was eager.

"Yes," said Liam. "What did you hear?" He drained his glass and held it out for a refill.

"They say yesterday early three of our boys were shot on the road south of Newry, and that last night it seems three of theirs were found dead in much the same area. They said 'murdered,' which of course is their own judgemental term." He elbowed Liam in the ribs. "Eh, boyo, what do you know of it?"

Liam put a hand to his forehead and closed his eyes. "Nothing. Nothing at all."

The farmer elbowed him again. "Have it your way, then." He winked.

Tadhg sat listening, sifting the babble and murmur of voices, the clink of glasses, the shuffle of feet, and said, suddenly, "What of the women in the snug? I hear weeping."

The farmer looked at him. "It's sharp ears you have for sure, for Mrs. O'Rourke is the quiet sort. She's back there now, and her friends with her; they've only just convinced Father Mulvaney to let her Sean be buried in the churchyard. It will be a comfort to her. He's being laid out now, and the funeral is the day past tomorrow, when all the boys will have gathered." His eyes narrowed again. "Four *they* got, and three *we* got. They're still one up—"

A woman came from the back of the place and stood next to him, staring down. She was short and stocky, and wore a shapeless sweater and a draggled skirt. Her hair was covered with a boldly colored scarf. The farmer looked up. "Ah, Pegeen, right you are, it's teatime and I'll be going." He drained his mug and rose to follow her.

The woman glared at Liam, who did not meet her gaze. Tadhg glanced at her and she stood frozen a moment, then turned her face away. She led her man toward the doorway. Neither looked back.

That night, when it was dark, Tadhg had Connor acquire a car, and the three crossed the Border northward to settle Sean's score. Liam was huddled in the back seat, somewhat the worse for drink; the package he had prepared was in Connor's custody. Tadhg would have left Liam behind, but he was their explosives specialist.

It was perfect logic, after all: be struck and strike back; settle the score; avenge the honor of the dead. But the package held death for men Tadhg had never seen, and the night was full of lamentation.

This was a battle, this was war, here was honor-price demanded. *But*—battle . . . He remembered the songs he'd sung before battles, to a company that would not all hear him again. *Which ones would fall,* he used to brood, as he sang of plunder and glory. Laughing Aillil? Young Conaire in his new red mantle? Thoughtful Flann, newly wed and thus in love with life? Or any of the host of others whose bright eyes and too-loud laughter made the only mention of fear? None would admit to his fellows that he dreaded the dawn, but to some extent each did. Tadhg's task was to drown their fears in music, inspire them forth to slay and be slain.

The car swerved. What was he doing here, hurtling through the night in this impossible conveyance, bound who knew where on an errand of death? Tadhg MacNiall, the bard, cried out in horror and revulsion.

But then a voice spoke: *Yours is vengeance, you must lead the Hunt. You have the power and the right.*

Fionn, too, had heard voices. Tadhg knew he was doomed. Unresisting, he drove forward into darkness.

They never spoke, later, of what was done, but the folk who gathered for Sean's funeral knew. Young men arrived from out of town—Liam and Connor greeted them all. Many of them wore dark glasses, though the day was grey and the heavens wept.

They formed an honor guard at the place where Sean's body lay, and six of them lifted his coffin, draped in a flag of green, white, and orange. The rest paced silently after. Behind the grim-faced young men walked Sean's mother, the Widow O'Rourke. She held her head high, her shoulders back, and she stared, dry-eyed and with loathing, at those in the honor guard.

The townsfolk followed, and the street was choked with them. Mostly they walked silent.

Father Mulvaney met them at the churchyard gate. He was old, white-haired, and thin; his hands were brown-spotted and the veins stood out, thick and blue. The procession halted. The priest stood a moment, surveying the crowd, and especially the honor guard, as if he would deny them entrance. He sighed, then, and led them into the church.

Tadhg had never been inside a church, and understood little of the ritual, nor did the statues and pictures hold much meaning. Father Mulvaney said a few words to the congregation, mentioning "forgiveness" and "repentance" and the mercy of God— *which god?* Some of the congregation stirred and muttered when he mentioned "Thou shalt not kill." (*According to whom?* Tadhg thought. *There is always killing.*)

At last the ceremony was almost over. They carried the coffin to the graveyard, folded the flag and gave it to Mrs. O'Rourke, who held it to her. They lowered the box into the fresh-dug grave. Ancient bones lay in the pile of dirt.

Hereabouts were newer dead, Tadhg saw. Some graves were strewn with withered flowers, and most of the tombstones stood upright, with inscriptions that could yet be read. He did not try to speak to the past-folk. He had not brought his harp, and he felt no wish, now, to consult the dead.

Old Mrs. O'Carroll stood to one side, weeping, her head covered by her shawl. Tadhg went over to her. She blinked up at him. "They say you were with Sean when he died. It might be had I not introduced you two he'd be alive today. He was a bit wild, a bit arrogant, and he owned no faith in God, but he was a merry lad and brave."

For a moment Tadhg too felt grief; then something cold and heartless gripped him. "He fell in battle."

Mrs. O'Carroll spat. "He was killed setting an ambush for those who had ambushed Padraig, Thomas, and Rory, the which you told him to lead him on, no doubt. He did not fall in battle. My *husband* fell in battle. Sean died committing murder, and his soul may well be damned." She had stopped crying now. "Then the next night, you three—ah, I know 'twas you, we all know—set the bomb at the Orange Lodge. Brave work, that! A seventy-eight-year-old farmer, and the grocer who supported eight children, and the man who drove the creamery truck—desperate characters, all! You might have taken them in unarmed combat, one at a time. Instead you three brave young men set a bomb on their doorstep! I've no love for the Orange Order, but they are human—*and, God help me, they are Irish too!* What have I now? My husband is dead. My young men are dead."

She stood there, a sad, defiant old woman in a black shawl. Tadhg reached out a hand to touch her. She drew back. "I'll have naught to do with you, deathbringer. You yourself may well lie dead tomorrow, and my heart is past breaking."

Tadhg let his hand fall. A wind rose and whipped through the trees; the funeral was over, and the mourners left the churchyard, many bound for the pub. Mrs. O'Carroll looked up at Tàdhg; the force of the wind increased. She paled. "I thought—for a moment I thought I saw—Holy Mother of God, *what is loosed on the world?*"

She crossed herself and shuffled away.

Tadhg stood looking after her. The sad old women, yes, the mothers and the widows—they never understood. He shook his head; it felt heavy, but then the sensation passed.

Someone tapped him on the shoulder. He turned; it was Connor. "The boys are meeting at the house," he said. "They've questions to ask, especially of you. Best we hurry along."

CHAPTER TEN

The knock sounded again on Rita's door. "We'll be right there, Mother." Rita looked down at herself and grimaced. "I'd best clean up, before I ruin everyone's appetite. You don't look much better. We should hurry, though; it's cruel to keep Father waiting. He'll need to be back at the pub soon." She sat up and winced; her face was pale. "Let's not say much about this afternoon. Father takes on so, and then he'll be remembering what happened to John; he's always blamed himself. Were I you, I'd tell your story to no one else. I'm not sure yet if I believe it myself, but my parents have enough trouble without hearing they're guesting someone from the ancient past." She looked at Maire, shook her head, and winced again. "I've a good deal more to ask you, but that's for later. Now we should make ourselves presentable."

Maire's dress was torn in places, from her two dives to the street. It had already been faded, and was spotted now with blood, her own and Rita's. "I have no other clothes. I was given this," she said. "My own garment is hanging in a fisherman's cottage in Antrim town."

"No matter. You're shorter than I, but I must have something you can put on. Best we soak these stains out right away." Practicalities seemed to revive Rita. She ran cold water into the sink and stripped off her bloodstained dress. Maire did likewise.

"Ah, there's plenty of it." Rita watched the water turn red. She drained the basin and refilled it. "Mother would have hysterics for sure, if she saw that."

They tidied up as best they could. Rita took two clean dresses from the wardrobe. On Maire, Rita's clothing bound across the breast, while the skirt flapped at mid-calf. They went downstairs.

Rita's father sat in the parlour, awaiting tea. He was tallish, red-faced, and heavy. Though he looked tired, he rose when the young women entered the room.

"Welcome home, Father," Rita said. "What sort of day did they give you?"

"Ah, vexing. The police were all over the place this afternoon, asking questions, making the customers nervous."

"What about, now?"

"Oh, it was regarding a group of entertainers. They'd played at the pub the night before. But your mother was saying you saw some trouble today?"

Rita inhaled sharply. "It was nothing, not at all serious. Mother should not have mentioned it, but I do owe a great deal to Maire, here. Father, meet Maire ní Donnall, who does the same work I do. Maire, this is my father, Mac MacCormac, who runs MacCormac's Pub when it isn't running him instead."

"Welcome," said Mr. MacCormac, holding out his hand. "Do you work with Rita in Casualty at the Royal Victoria?"

"No," Maire said, "but we do similar work." She

realized he would not sit down until she did, so she found herself a chair.

MacCormac seated himself heavily. "Nursing's a good profession. My son—" He bit his lip and fumbled in his pocket, took out a small white tube and lit it, inhaling the smoke. The smell was choking, but it seemed to soothe him.

Rita sighed. "Like a fiend, he smokes. He won't give up the cigarettes, tell him as I might—"

"Grant me a little pleasure in this life, girl, it's too soon finished anyhow."

Maire realized she was hearing an old argument. Mrs. MacCormac appeared in the doorway. "Tea," she said, "and long enough you've tarried already."

Before they ate, the family performed a strange ritual: They touched fingers in sequence to forehead, breast, left and right shoulder, clasped their hands, and chanted, "In the name of the Father and of the Son and of the Holy Ghost, amen. Bless us, O Lord, and these Thy gifts which we are about to receive, from Thy bounty, through Christ our Lord, amen." They then repeated the gestures.

The words had no meaning to Maire, save the mention of Christ, of whom she'd heard. Where was the thanking of the cook? Such ways were strange. She picked up a spoon, but Rita nudged her. "Use your fork." She pointed toward a three-pronged instrument.

Conversation, at first, was brief, limited to requests to pass things. Maire observed how they were named, that she might remember: "Potatoes" were new. As hunger-slackened bellies filled, folk began to talk.

"You said the police were at the pub today, Father," Rita said, "asking about musicians? Was there a problem, or were they only being officious?"

"Ah, it was the fellows we'd engaged Thursday night; seems they all got killed homebound on the

Navan road Friday afternoon, and there is some question as to why."

Maire dropped her fork. "Killed? Musicians? Who ever would do such a thing?"

Mac MacCormac stopped, a forkful of food halfway to his mouth. "It's done all the time. Why do they kill anyone? There's no sense in it. These boys, though, the Three Bards, they called themselves, some think they had illegal connections. It may be that's why they were shot. 'Twas deliberate assassination, after all, not like the time they set the bomb in my old pub and got John." His red, fleshy face crumpled and his eyes teared. He set down his fork, took a sip of tea, and went on. "That bomb should have got me. Better a wheezing old publican than a premedical student. But no, I had to ask John to help out for the summer."

"Ah, Father," Rita said, "you should not always be blaming yourself. So you'd just stepped back to the storeroom—these things happen daily, who sees more of them than I? They're mad, all of them." She winced and put a hand to her head, then bent again to her food. Maire noticed that though she made a show of eating, her hand shook and she consumed little. It seemed, as well, that she fumbled with her fork, as if she had trouble seeing.

"We should have moved to the Republic when the Troubles started up again, but the money is better here. It's our home too." Mac lit another cigarette and inhaled deeply. His face reddened and he crashed his fist onto the table. "Damn them, damn all of them, with all their bloody causes!"

"Mac," said his wife, in a soft voice, "we've a guest, and shouting does no good. I know the day's brought back bad memories, but John never did anyone a bit of harm, and he is with the saints, I'm sure."

"Right, Father," Rita said, "the excitement does you no good."

* * *

There was a knock on the door; Rita's mother went to see what it was. "Can't a man enjoy a meal at home in peace?" Mac grumbled.

"Mrs. O'Shaughnessy! Ah, do come in, won't you. We're just finishing tea, but you're welcome, of course." Rita's mother did not sound overjoyed.

Rita snarled. "Meddling old biddy, she's come snooping again, wait and see."

Mrs. O'Shaughnessy walked into the room; her heavy tread shook the floorboards. "Ah, Rita," she said, "I'm glad to see you looking better, after your close call this afternoon." She shot a triumphant glance toward Mac.

"What is this, now, Rita?" Mac said. "What close call? You said it was nothing."

Rita glared at Mrs. O'Shaughnessy. "I'm quite recovered, as you can see. Thank you for your kind concern."

"Ah, if you weren't out traipsin' about with God alone knows who of a Saturday afternoon, you wouldn't be getting in these situations."

"Yes, I'm sure my visit to the museum has caused scandal in the neighborhood," Rita said.

"It all depends, child, on who you go to the museum with." Mrs. O'Shaughnessy's smile showed teeth.

Maire was becoming irritated. This woman brought back memories. "As a matter of fact, she was there with me."

Mrs. O'Shaughnessy smiled again. "Indeed? Somehow I had the impression you were a stranger here. Well, Rita's always taken a liking for strangers. And foreigners." Then, to Rita's mother, "I'll be on my way, dearie. I was only worried about the girl. I can let myself out, thank you." She shuffled out of the room; the family heard the front door slam.

Rita's mother looked at her daughter. "What was that all about?"

Rita was pale. She raised her hand to her head and swayed forward. "I'll help you clear the plates, Mother." When she tried to rise, her knees gave way.

"You should be lying down," said Maire. "I'll help you upstairs."

"Never mind about washing up," Rita's mother said. "Are you sure we shouldn't have the doctor?"

"I'll keep watch," said Maire. "It may be she only needs rest."

Rita's father half-rose from his chair. "You still haven't said what *did* happen," he roared.

"It's all right, Mac," his wife said, "it was only a bit of street business." She sent a frightened look upstairs. Mac lit another cigarette. His hands shook.

Maire put Rita to bed. "My head is fierce, again," Rita said, "and I'm not sure if it's all reaction to Mrs. O'Shaughnessy. I do not feel well." She reached for the clock and fumbled with it. "If I doze, waken me when the buzzer sounds." She closed her eyes and lay quiet a few moments. "I'm sorry about Father. It must have been the police that set him off, and those young musicians being killed. He has no use for either the IRA or the UDA, but his is a Catholic pub, and so some of his clientele—it all brings back bad memories. After John was killed, and the pub destroyed, Father took heavily to drink. One day, though, he stopped cold, borrowed money—though who would lend it to him then I do not know—and opened another pub. He finally earned enough that I might take nurse's training." Rita lay silent a moment. "All the money for John's education was long gone. And this way I can stay in the city. I'm all Mother and Father have left."

"Do you work tomorrow?"

Rita opened her eyes. "Not unless I'm called in. I might be, though. Weekends are the worst on Casualty, and sometimes our staff scarcely know what they're doing. They're dangerous in that condition—battle fatigue, they call it—so Sister will call in a substitute. We grumble, but we go."

"You've a difficult job, it seems." Maire said. "You must have a great deal to tell me. I know my own story must sound purely daft."

"It does, but you seem sane enough. We must talk on this more . . . right now . . . have the lights gone dim?"

"No."

"Oh, then, in that case . . . in . . ." Rita mumbled a few more words, then fell silent. Her breathing slowed.

Maire stepped closer to the bed. "Rita?" There was no response. She shook her shoulder, "Rita?" She shook again, harder. Rita lay inert.

Panic struck. Maire had sat helpless while young Diarmiud—only a boy—died after falling from his chariot. Rita was right when she warned of serious danger.

Pupils. She'd said something about pupils. Maire pulled back Rita's eyelids. On one side, the blue iris had almost disappeared. The pupil stared huge and black as a pool of night.

Maire stood stunned. This was what she'd been warned of. *Heal her,* said a voice not her own. *You have the Power.*

She looked at her hands: strong they were, healer's hands, though for centuries they'd done no useful work. She looked at Rita again: The room's yellow light turned grey, and Maire saw the inside of a human skull. She marvelled at the wrinkled surface, saw the centres for speech, hearing, and sight, noticed the boundaries between the lobes; she saw, too, where blood pooled beneath the bone, inside the shiny envelope, and pressed. As the pool grew the pressure increased, for there was no doorway from the skull.

First stop the bleeding. That much she could do; had she not already done so this afternoon? But that was on the scalp. If only she had understood the problem then—though her hands did nothing, she *willed,* and it was so. She watched the torn arterial walls rejoin, and the blood resume its normal circular path. There yet remained the pooled blood; it still exerted pressure, though the clot would eventually be reabsorbed. Rita was in deep coma, and in Maire's time such falling into sleep meant certain death. She was frightened. Whence came her healing power? Not from the Queen of the Sídhe, for the Queen had said she could not grant the gift of healing—that Maire already had. But Maire had always healed in the ordinary manner, with herbs and charms and minor surgery, and she'd been beset by wrong treatment and hopeless cases.

Her hands lay useless at her sides. She could still visualize Rita's brain. She concentrated on the pool of blood. *Begone. You are not needed here; you cause harm.* The dark clot cleared, then vanished, and with it the grey light. Maire once again saw only Rita's face.

Rita winced, tossed her head, and opened her eyes. "I dozed off; I'm sorry. I must have needed the rest. I feel much better." She looked at Maire. "You're white as a ghost, and you're shaking. Were you that worried?"

Maire looked again at her hands. *What did I do? Who works through me?* She could not tell Rita what had happened, not while she herself could not understand.

"You were saying you had some questions to ask me, and I've certainly much to ask you." Rita touched her head and frowned. "This day has been—strange. What did you want to know?"

Maire asked practical questions about objects and how they worked. Rita answered and explained; she seemed amazed at the depth and extent of Maire's ignorance.

It was while she was demonstrating electric light that she stopped. "Mad though your story is, I am coming to believe it. You *must* come from elsewhere. You are an intelligent woman, yet you have never encountered things we use every day as a matter of course. Even the most isolated fisherman on the Aran Islands—" She shook her head.

"It seems I must now live in your time," said Maire. She was confused by all she had heard—the explanations themselves begged for explanations, and most of the words she did not understand. This world was new, her healing power was new, and she feared it and her inner voice. Was she possessed? "Too much it is for me to grasp. I am tired and confused." She covered her face. "I want to sleep, I am so tired, I cannot cope with any more at all."

Rita patted her on the shoulder. "There's something called 'culture shock,' and if your tale is true, you must have the worst possible case. If you've been a healer, you've lived all your life with difficult things. You are strong, but even strong folk sometimes need to cry. It's the strong ones need it most, I think."

Maire sat on one of the beds, curled up, and sobbed in great racking gulps. After a time she stopped and raised her head. "I am sorry," she said, "I do not usually pity myself."

Rita handed her a washcloth. "Michael says he shakes for a long time after he's been shot at, and he's none the less brave for that. Oh, you can't even have seen shooting before today, and now you're in Belfast!"

Maire washed her face; the cloth was cool against her skin. Rita sat next to her. "You'd better stay with me for a time," Rita said. "It's possible I owe you my life, and whoever you are, from wherever, you need a guide."

"Thank you," Maire said. "I'll gladly guest with you. I am lost and frightened."

"In this time, there is much to fear," said Rita. "I'll have a sad grim story to tell you. It's been bad for us all, but I see the worst of it at work. You wouldn't know, of course: The Royal Victoria Hospital is on Falls Road—that's the Catholic slums—and it's not far from Shankhill, the Protestant slums. So we get most of the riot victims. We've become experts in patching up terror cases. I hate to tell you—it makes no sense. The fine sentiments are lies, and there's wrong on both sides." She rose and paced the room. "God *damn* the IRA and the UDA and the police and the agitators and hatemongers and misguided patriots and religious bigots and all of them that send people to our Casualty Ward. Damn them to the fieriest pit of Hell!" She stopped and looked at the Sacred Heart picture on the wall. "I'm not supposed to say that, Lord, but You know I mean every damn word. If You believe what You preached, You'd save the hottest place in Hell for those who murder in Your name!"

Maire glanced at the grotesque picture. "What exactly is this god supposed to have preached?"

Rita laughed. "Love your enemies, and do good to those that persecute you."

" 'Tis a strange attitude for a god," said Maire, "or for mortals, either. How could you keep your honor and avenge your kin? Would not others take advantage, knowing you would not strike back?"

Rita laughed. "We still seek vengeance, but we call it prettier names. Well, you might not find this world so strange at that."

CHAPTER ELEVEN

The parlor of the Dundalk house was crowded. Some twenty-five lads sat on wooden chairs, leaned against the wall, or crouched on the floor.

Liam looked up, startled, as Connor and Tadhg entered. "James has some questions on the doings Saturday night." He nodded toward the lanky blond man who lounged in the only armchair.

The blond man pointed at Tadhg. "Who might that be?"

"This is Tadhg MacNiall," said Connor. Then, quickly, "He was with us Saturday night, and the night before, when—we lost Sean. Tadhg, this is James Bryson."

"Very well," said James, "I'll be questioning Tadhg later." He spoke to Connor. "The business with the MacIvers was well-handled; it was simple retaliation, and those three were not widely loved. But how, in doing it, you managed to let Sean be shot—*Sean*, one of my most valued men!" James shook his head. "And then, like fools, on the next night instead of choosing a single target you set off a bloody great bomb at an Orange Lodge! Have you lost your senses? Didn't you foresee the publicity? Bleeding little stories about the bereaved, photos of the victims, official expressions of horror? We've lost support. Even our own are turning against us. When I think of the public outcry—you *idiots!*" James rose and paced the room. "I'd be asking whose mad idea it was, but I know you well enough to suspect Liam." He paused; no one spoke. "Ah, it *was* he, then. Sean would never have agreed. He knew how delicate the situation 'is. Even you, Connor, should have known better. I suspect you've a brain buried somewhere in that boulder of a skull. And *you,* whom I do not know"— he whirled to confront Tadhg—"they say you went along. I've a mind to discipline the three of you."

"I did not 'go along,' " said Tadhg. "I led them." Did he say that? But he *had* led them, and led them the night before as well. Gods, what had come over him? Inside him the voice spoke again. *This man's arrogance must not be tolerated.* Tadhg stood tall. "You'll not pass judgement on me, James Bryson. Liam and Connor acted on my orders."

The other men in the room stirred and shuffled. James regarded Tadhg at length. His were the keen eyes of a commander. "You've not sworn our Oath."

"Nor shall I. I swear no oaths. I lead."

James' face did not change. " 'Tis best we speak in private."

"I'll talk with you," said Tadhg.

James led him into the storeroom. The gelignite smell was sharp, like the smoke that had lingered after the Orange Lodge explosion. *Vengeance!* he exulted.

James and Tadhg sat on packing crates. James spoke first. "I take it you're not one of us."

Tadhg fought a manic urge to laugh. *One of them, indeed!* "No, I am not a member of your organization."

"So I've no knowledge of you. You might be an informer. Where are you from?"

"Originally, the Lough Neagh area. Antrim," said Tadhg. "I came to Dundalk recently."

"What would your politics be? Who are your people?"

"My politics are my own, and I have no people." No Maire, no feasts at the court, no home and warmth and *Maire,* nothing but this cold time and whatever wild creature possessed him. Of a sudden the smell of gelignite turned him sick. *Shattered windows; tossed against a windscreen, a hand with a thin wedding band. Fire and blood.* He had come to an evil time, evil ways.

"You turned pale when you said that," James remarked. "Are you afraid?"

Tadhg stood. "I fear nothing."

James looked up at him. "You have tried to seize command. Connor and Liam are only followers. My followers."

Tadhg's head bent forward. It was heavy, weighted down. He spoke: *"I lead now. I know your purpose, and I lead your Wild Hunt!"*

Bryson rose to confront him, but his knees buckled. He collapsed onto the packing crate. He gasped, trying to speak.

"I lead the Hunt," Tadhg repeated. Light glowed and shattered through the windowpane, across the cases of gelignite. Bryson stared at Tadhg. Then, of a sudden, Tadhg's burden lifted. Nothing weighted his head, no—*antlers?*

The room, now, again held only mortals.

James blinked, then cleared his throat. "You led Connor and Liam on that unfortunate errand?"

"I did. Sean had been killed. Honor demanded we collect his blood-price."

James shifted on his crate. "That is not the way. Now we must change our plans for next Saturday, in Belfast—plans of which you doubtless knew nothing, but Liam and Connor did, the fools. More of that later, when we speak with the others."

"We'll be back in time, I hope, from our trip to County Mayo," said Tadhg.

James' face brightened. "You'll need to be, it's some of our armament you'll be collecting. Ah, they told me it was you who delivered that information." He frowned. "Padraig's mother has scant liking for us—Padraig never told her he was a sympathizer, and now she'll be distraught. So many of the women fail to understand. *Have peace,* they whine. But we cannot have peace in a divided Ireland, while British troops pollute our native soil!"

A divided Ireland? Was it not divided, kingdom from kingdom, in my time? But this man seems sincere. "I've noticed the women seem angry, the few I've seen of late." He wondered what Maire would think of his recent activities, and flinched from the thought. She had a tongue on her, a sharp one, and she never feared to use it. "What does your own wife think?"

James shook his head. "She's as daft as the rest of them, but she holds silent, thank God. The children keep her busy, though what she's teaching them I'm not sure. When they play at war in the streets she calls them in and spanks them." He sat quiet a moment, then burst out, "Even my *name* is English! My family hadn't the pride and courage to stay honest O'Morison. Do you know how I feel? Each time I speak or write my own name I feel the British heel on my neck. Well enough, Tadhg MacNiall, you are with us now. Faith, you've already committed yourself."

"I have done that," said Tadhg. He fought nausea. *That I, a bard*—but he was no longer only a bard.

James Bryson held out his hand. Tadhg clasped it. When he took his own away it felt dirty.

"We'll rejoin the others, then," said James. "We've business to discuss, while we're all together."

When James and Tadhg reentered the main room of the house, all faces turned toward them. The room had darkened, and seeing was difficult. "I give you Tadhg MacNiall," James said. "He's joined us now."

A voice spoke from shadow. "Has he taken the Oath?"

"No," said James. "He will not swear."

Another voice: "How can we trust him then? We know nothing of him."

"*I* trust him," said James, "that should suffice."

Many of the young men murmured among themselves, but Connor and Liam remained silent. They stared at Tadhg, as if they remembered something, or thought they did.

"He could be an informer."

"But he was in on the Orange Lodge business."

"If he wants to join us, why will he not take the Oath?"

"James is only human, after all. He might be gulled."

Outlaws all, they were, Tadhg knew, and thus suspicious. Again his head felt heavy. It might be the fumes of the gelignite—he had been sitting atop the case—but it was more as if something weighed on him. His voice boomed: "My word is enough, and I find your chatter insulting." The room hushed. All the young men looked at him. Tadhg stood before the window, silhouetted by light from the street. For a moment their faces showed fear. Then the weight was gone again from his head. In time, James' voice broke the silence.

"Let's get on with business, then, and be done. I'm in dire need of a drink."

* * *

Tadhg learned that the Loyalists had planned a march in Belfast next Saturday to conflict with a Women's March for Peace. There would doubtless be incidents, James said; these could be exploited—or assisted.

"We'll use snipers. Now is not the time for bombs, though such we'd originally planned." He looked with contempt at Liam and Connor. "It's a delicate situation, and the fool women aren't helping. But the Orange crowd will be their usual inflammatory selves. They'll draw the impact from the peace march, after all."

The talk then centred on details: where men would be stationed, and where the television cameras and news reporters would likely be. All were to meet in Belfast on Saturday at an address on Falls Road. Business over, many of the group stepped down the street to the pub, while the rest went their separate ways into the night.

Many of Sean's mourners had already left the pub, but enough stayed that it remained packed and noisy. Tadhg noticed the farmer with whom he'd spoken last Saturday, and nodded to him; he grinned back. Tadhg's companions, especially James, were well known. Folk crowded about them, bought them drinks, and vied for their attention.

But not all. One elderly man nearby raised a glass to his lips, stared at the young men, then set his pint back down. He spoke low; something in his manner made Tadhg listen and screen out the other sounds. Even James Bryson, next to him, seemed not to hear.

To his companion, the old man said, "I'll not be drinking with the likes of them, after what they've done to our IRA. It's heroes we were in 1916 and after. Now they're naught but murdering scoundrel terrorists."

His companion, equally aged, nodded. "I thought

it was best to go with the British Army and save the world from the Hun, but when I heard what you boys did at home—and so few of you—I was shamed to be fighting for the Crown. A pity to miss that week."

"A grand week it was, a grand week, even with Dublin aflame and the General Post Office gutted. We'd *done* it, after all. We could no longer be ignored. So what if we lost, for a time?"

"Ah, I wish I'd been there. But *these*"—the old man indicated the young ones—"they're purely mad. And to think they go by our same proud name! I wonder did the craziness start in the Civil War? Lost their sense of humor, they did. A man has to laugh or go mad—and then the daft business of condemning Brendan Behan to death!"

"In his very absence," his companion reminded him.

The first old man snickered. "To be, as he suggested, executed the same way, if they would be so kind? A laughingstock they were. Better if they'd bought him a pint and swapped stories! I hate to agree with the Prots on anything, but these men are hooligans indeed."

Tadhg listened, fascinated. James was convinced that his cause was right, but the old warriors did not think so. Nor the women.

The women. He thought of Mrs. O'Carroll, how kind she'd been at first, and then how she spat on him at Sean's funeral. Yet her own man had died in a rebellion—or so Tadhg had gathered.

As he sat listening, Mrs. O'Carroll herself came out of the snug. Her eyes were red. She gathered her shawl about her and stopped at Tadhg's table.

James Bryson saw her and rose. "Mrs. O'Carroll, how are you this evening? It's many a fine meal I've enjoyed at your house. Sorry am I about Sean. I know how well you liked the lad. I'll miss him too; he was one of my best men."

Mrs. O'Carroll straightened her back and looked up. "James Bryson, you've eaten your last meal beneath my roof, and that goes for your friends as well. There's enough and too much of all this. It sickens me. Your sort sicken me." She turned to Tadhg. "I'd not normally be asking back a gift, but I require my husband's clothes. You've no right to wear them; it shames his memory. Have your friends get you properly clad—I'm sure you'll feel more at ease in murderers' garb."

Tadhg could not speak. Mrs. O'Carroll went on: "Whatever you are, Tadhg MacNiall, and from wherever you come, you're never any simple harpist from Lough Neagh."

It is true, the saner part of Tadhg agreed. *I am being taken over by that which I cannot name. How can I have done such things?* But he spoke no word.

Mrs. O'Carroll turned and hobbled from the pub.

Tadhg looked after her a long time. James said, "Her husband was killed in the Troubles. The early ones, that is; he was with the old IRA. In his memory, all these years, she's fed and housed us, bandaged our wounds, been almost our mother, and we the sons she never bore. I never thought to see the day she'd send us from her house. And I fear it's not only that she had the drink taken." He put a hand over his eyes. "My wife, Mrs. O'Carroll, my own mother—what is it with the women? Ah, I myself have had too much to drink. No, it's not enough. Kevin! More whiskey!" To Tadhg he said, "No work, thank God, to be done for a time."

Tadhg ordered whiskey too. The drink, when it came, smelled like gelignite.

Tadhg woke in the morning with a dry mouth and a throbbing head. He was used to mead and beer, not spirits; he only vaguely remembered the walk home. Moonlight yet had lit the street; someone had started a song about "The Foggy Dew" that harked back to Easter Week 1916. The references were obscure, but the melody was simple. Then there'd been a song about "The Broad Black Brimmers of the IRA." That one made him think of Mrs. O'Carroll's dead husband. Other songs there'd been as well; it had been a fine night, with good singing.

But today his head hurt. He did not want to rise. At least he'd not bedded down in the room with the gelignite, for which he thanked the gods.

He stumbled first to the water closet and thence to the kitchen, where he heard the sound of voices and the clatter of cooking. The food-smell sickened him.

He leaned in the doorway. James sat in a chair, and one of the others was frying eggs and bacon. The cook handed Tadhg a cup of tea.

"You'll have to be singing us more of the songs you did last night, Tadhg," James said. "With your harp and all, in the Gaelic."

Tadhg did not remember playing his harp. "Of course I shall."

"You look fierce," James said. "Not used to the whiskey?"

"Not really," said Tadhg. "Nor to many other things."

Liam came in, white and shaking, and Connor wandered in soon after, looking glum. "I'll be wanting a cup of tea," he said, "and then we must be off today to Mayo."

Tadhg thought of riding in a car, and felt ill. He wanted no more of all this; he wanted to crawl back to bed, find some peaceful place to hide, and be done with killing. But his inner voice spoke. *You have a mission to perform.* He had come to this time, and must live as these folk did.

"I've seen the papers you brought, regarding the shipment," James said. "Payment's been made in advance, of course. Our friends in Boston are responsible for this particular cargo. It's a wonderful slogan they put next to the money-jars in their pubs: 'Give a dollar and kill a British soldier—best bargain you'll ever buy.'" He looked long at Liam and Connor. "You'll be receiving an arms shipment and doing nothing else, understand? Saturday will be touchy enough. We've no need of trouble before then. Any more foolishness and the police might cancel the marches!"

Tadhg spoke, though his tongue was dry. "We'll do our assigned tasks. We'll take Padraig's things to his parents, pick up the shipment, arrange its delivery, and meet you in Belfast on Saturday." He looked at Connor and Liam. They nodded.

"Fare well in the West," said James, "and while you do your work remember that Cromwell consigned the Irish to Hell or Connaught. The difference is not considerable."

"Hell, at least, is reputed to be warm," Liam's hand shook as he raised a mug of tea to his lips.

"Well, for once we need not consider commandeering a car," said Connor. "We can use Sean's." He shivered; his cup shattered on the floor.

CHAPTER TWELVE

Connor, Liam, and Tadhg gathered Padraig's few belongings and provided Tadhg with rough, dark clothing. He doffed the garments that had belonged to Mrs. O'Carroll's husband. *A brave man that was,* thought Tadhg as he folded the rough tweed. *Ill when his widow cursed me.*

By the time they set off, it was afternoon. Liam, still suffering from alcohol, said he was sick and could not drive. Tadhg himself felt none too well, so Connor took the wheel. "We'll go by the Carrickmacross Road; that's the fastest. We've a deal of ground to cover, over two hundred miles. With our late start I doubt we'll reach the West Coast tonight. Twilight comes early now, and farm folk rise with the sun."

Tadhg rode in the front seat; Liam sprawled listless in the back. "Where precisely are we going?" Tadhg said. "The West Coast, County Mayo is all you've told me." Something there was about his errand he did not like; yet was he not leader here? Ever since he'd seen the Three Bards slain, something alien had gripped him. After Sean's killing, and his own vengeance, darkness drew him to itself. It was something he'd met of old, but could not name: wild wind, storms, and clouds that ate the moon. He shivered, though sun slanted on green hills and haystacks gleamed gold.

"If you wish to see where we're bound, there's a map in the door-pouch," Connor said. The road, though wider than most, still barely allowed room for two cars. It meandered; hedgerows made it impossible to see around corners, and more than once Connor had to swerve to let another car hurtle past. He took one hand from the wheel and pointed across Tadhg's lap. "There."

Tadhg reached into the door-pouch and drew out a folded piece of paper. It was, at first, nothing but blotches of lines and colored areas. He could discern what might be printed words. With his faerie-sight he could read them, though the names meant little. Some sounded like his own language, but the spelling was strange. He folded the map, after several tries, and replaced it.

"Ah, so you don't read maps," Connor said. "I've known many like you. Never mind. The road is sign-posted. I know the way, as does Liam, if he ever recovers from the head on him."

The car sped on down the road. It had to slow at times for cattle or horses. "Wait until we're farther West," said Connor. "About milking time it'll be, and there's nothing for it but to poke along behind the herds. Cows never hurry." He looked at a signpost. "Ah, we're in blessed County Monaghan now, where a good part of our trouble started. This was in Ulster before the Partition, you know."

By now Tadhg knew something of Ulster—they'd called it Ulaídh in his day—but of Partition he knew only that it dealt with the Six and Twenty-six Counties, and the current troubles. "So how was Monaghan wrested from Ulster? Did a stronger king, from Munster, perhaps, raid and capture it?"

Connor laughed. "You're a strange one indeed,

MacNiall," he said, "or else you've a wry sense of humor." His hands gripped the wheel. "Had Ulster not been the most rebellious province of Tudor times, we'd not have the problems we face now. Forever a trouble spot, that is Ulster's curse." He looked at a gauge. "We'll be needing petrol before Carrickmacross. Best we stop next chance."

"And I need a drink," said Liam, from the backseat.

"Damned if I agree," Connor said, "but if 'twill make you better company, then drain a barrel. It's purely useless you are in your present condition. I'll stop at the next likely place."

The printed sign read PETROL; the numbers beneath must indicate cost. Tadhg was beginning to understand money. He watched the attendant insert a nozzle into the side of the car and pour a strong-smelling fluid. Liam disappeared into a nearby pub. Tadhg considered following him, but the thought of drink soured his mouth, so instead he picked up his harp and stepped out behind the station, where a low stone wall soaked up the sun. He swung one leg over and looked out across a field. The hay had been cut and stacked; beyond, past another wall, grass yet waved in the breeze. Save for the stench of petrol and the occasional roar of a car, the scene was peaceful and familiar. He could almost be back in his own time, on a late fall day near Samhain. At the golden end of autumn it was hard to believe that wild winter waited to lash the land.

He struck a chord on his harp. Beneath his fingers the strings rippled as did the breeze-blown grass. But as the notes sounded the breeze hushed. Under the grass, in the soil and in the very rocks, he heard a sleepy murmur, as if something woke.

May I no longer play for pleasure, then? Against his will, his hands sought the strings again and played another chord. The murmuring grew louder and resolved into voices:

"We have lost the battle."

"I am dying."

"Our cause is done, Red Hugh is vanquished, the English now will rule."

One wild voice cried above the rest, "Never while we are remembered will *they* rule in peace!"

Fleshless jaws and clacking ribs laughed. "We have lost. It is over. Best to sleep."

Tadhg stared at the peaceful field. Was no spot of ground unstained with blood?

"Who are you?" cried the wild voice, the loud one. "Who are you, to disturb our slumber?"

"A man of Ulster, like yourselves." Tadhg answered in their own speech. It was neither that of his time nor the English of this era.

"How fared we?" cried the wild one. "All seemed lost. Is there yet hope?"

"Sleep, now," said Tadhg. *Until I call,* he added, in his strange new voice. He played the dreaming melody. After a time the rustles and muttering stopped. The breeze once more rippled the sea of grass, a peaceful blanket the Earth drew over centuries.

Tadhg took his harp and headed back toward the car.

In the car, Tadhg sat silent for a time, then asked Connor, "Who was Red Hugh?"

"Ah, surely you've heard of him," Connor said.

"A bit," said Tadhg. He did not reveal how. "But tell me."

"He was a leader in the great rebellion of 1601. Defeated, of course. Until then the English had stayed mostly out of Ulster, though they'd spread to much of the rest of Ireland. But Ulster had proud leaders in those days, and these leaders swore to oust the English. So fierce was the battle that the English never more did trust Ulster Irishmen. When the Earls fled after their defeat, the English seized the land and gave it to Scotsmen they'd imported for Plantation. Which is why there's so much trouble in Ulster now, the Prots being from Plantation days and yet considering themselves British—ah, if we'd won then, all might have been different."

Tadhg thought of the dry dead voices. "How long ago did you say?"

"Well over three hundred years. Nearer four hundred, now."

Tadhg shivered. So long a time! "So those who settled then—during Plantation, you say?—they and their descendants have lived in Ulster ever since?"

"They have," said Connor, "but we were here first, and the land is ours."

"Are they not Irish-born by now?" said Tadhg. "How long does it take?"

Connor spat out of the open window. "As long as they call themselves British and keep ties with England, they can never be Irish. They will never be Irish until the Six and Twenty-Six Counties are one United Irish Republic. That is why we fight."

Tadhg thought of the legendary cycle of invasions: the Fomorians, the Dédannans, the Milesians. He remembered the dead beneath the dolmen, who had lived long before his own folk walked the land. Always there was war: for cattle, honor, land—it never ceased.

The smell of ancient blood sickened him. Then the voice within him spoke. *Ireland is sword-land. It belongs to the strong. You are strong, now; yours is the battle. What greater joy can there be than to lead the Hunt and feed your spear fresh blood?*

Tadhg grinned, baring his teeth. The car sped on through green and golden countryside.

*   *   *

Through the town of Carrickmacross they travelled, then from County Monaghan to County Cavan, through villages and past lakes which rippled blue in the October breeze. Through Granard and Longford, whose narrow streets wound past ancient buildings. An occasional donkey-cart appeared on the road, though most of the traffic yet was automobiles and lorries.

They came to a bridge. "It's the River Shannon we're crossing now," said Connor, "where it flows into Lough Ree."

Tadhg looked to his left. A reed-rimmed river widened to a lake, larger than any he'd seen since Lough Neagh itself. Did another faerie palace dwell beneath its waters? He saw nothing but reflected sky.

Twilight was falling now. The trip had started late and, over winding roads, had taken hours, though they travelled at speeds impossible in Tadhg's own time.

"Over a hundred miles to go," said Connor, "and I for one am weary. There's small point in arriving at the Byrnes' farm in the middle of the night. We should find a bed-and-breakfast, then start fresh in the morning. Perhaps," he looked back at Liam, "others might help with the driving tomorrow, as well."

"Ah, it's enough of your ragging I've suffered today," said Liam, "and you never the worse for drink in all your life, I suppose. There should be several places in Roscommon, it's a large enough town. The shipment's not due till tomorrow night. You fuss like a biddy."

"Someone must tend to details," Connor said. "Roscommon it will be, then."

"Not Roscommon," said Tadhg.

Connor slammed his fist on the steering wheel. "You're not wanting to drive all night?"

"Not that," said Tadhg, "but it's not to Roscommon we go. Take the Tulsk road instead." *Rathcro-*

gan, said the voice inside him. *You are bid to the palace at Cruachan tonight. There is one who wishes word with you.*

"Tulsk? Man, are you daft? 'Tis miles out of our way, the road is badly marked, and it's not to play tourist we've come. We've serious business in the West."

"I fare tonight to Rathcrogan," Tadhg said, or what commanded him spoke. "You will find a place to stay near Tulsk. Sleep then, and eat, since you require such things. But I will guest at Rathcrogan."

Where stands Cruachan, the ancient palace of the Kings of Connaught. What might they want with me, an Ulsterman? The struggle between his own Ulster and the folk of Connaught was long-famed in song and story. *It is not with folk of this time you will speak tonight, Tadhg MacNiall. As a bard you are protected, and there is one who would hear you.* "Rathcrogan," Tadhg said once again. Connor spoke no word, but turned north on the Tulsk road.

Outside a small, neat white house hung a sign: "B&B." The house stood beside a quiet side road; flowers brightened the fenced garden. Colored stones lined the gravel path that curved to a red-painted door.

Connor pulled the car into the space provided. "I'll see if there's room." He knocked on the door; a woman opened it. She nodded, and he came back to the car. "She has a room for three, with two double beds. She'll give us tea, even though it's late."

Tadhg picked up his harp and his small bundle of clothing and followed the two into the house. The anteroom was small, its floor highly polished; on a table before a wall mirror stood a red-bound book. Connor signed in for the three.

The woman of the house waited as they paid, then said, "Tea can be ready soon, if you wish."

"No need, for my sake," said Tadhg. "I've other things to do." He set his belongings in the indicated room—it was decorated with garish wallpaper and pictures. A washbasin hung in the corner. He picked up his harp. Connor and Liam were arranging their own gear.

"I doubt I'll return tonight," Tadhg said.

"We could have gotten a smaller room, then," said Connor. "Where are you bound? It's several miles to Rathcrogan." He fingered the car-keys in his pocket, loath to surrender them.

"I'll go where I'm going," said Tadhg. "It's a fine night for a walk. I'll be back when you see me. Perhaps for breakfast."

"You can scarcely traipse about the countryside in the dark. You'll get lost, you've never been here before—" Connor fretted.

"I said I fared to Rathcrogan, and it's to Rathcrogan I'm going. Meddle not in what you do not understand." Tadhg left the room. In the hallway he encountered the woman of the house. "A good evening to you, Missus," he said. Of a sudden he felt strange.

She stared at him and crossed herself. "Jesus, Mary, and Joseph."

Tadhg stepped out the front door. He heard it slam and lock behind him.

The dark was grey and pleasant to Tadhg's eyes, and the night was calm. Breeze-billowed clouds caressed the stars. Tadhg set out afoot toward Rathcrogan, and the ancient palace. Part of him feared the legend he sought. But his darker nature was older than legend.

In time he came upon a crossroads. The area was ancient, haunted; here of old had been inaugurated the Kings of Connaught. Not far away many of them lay buried. Atop yon hill had once stood Cruachan, their royal palace.

The very palace of Aillil and Maeve. Long before Tadhg's time had those two lived, and long ago they had striven against the men of Ulster in what began as a cattle-raid and ended in an epic struggle. Tadhg knew the stories in the *TÁIN BÓ CUAILNGE,* as must every bard.

To many dead by now had Tadhg spoken, but all were ordinary folk: It was said Maeve was a goddess. Goddess or mortal, her temper was legendary. She lay buried near here, and it must be she who called him.

Him, a man from another time, a man who lived long after she had perished? Common folk knew nothing of what happened past their deaths. Maeve must yet live on in shadow-form.

Tadhg stopped on the road. He was only human, after all, and an Ulsterman in Connaught. He clutched his harp like a shield. In the darkness grey shapes flickered.

"But it's a bard," said a woman's voice. "Little thought I to see his like again." She laughed. "Yet there is something not mere human on him, after all. He's been touched by Faerie."

"And by more than that," said a man. His voice wavered. "He walks with warriors."

"All the better." The woman crooned: "Come forth, bard, my bardeen. Play for me. Mine is a cold and lonely grave; my husband Aillil wants only sleep, but I would rather roam the night. Play, bard!" Tadhg looked about him in the darkness, but saw nothing.

Wait! Beyond the wall, in the field—his faerie-sight turned the dark landscape lighter grey. He saw a tall woman, clad in a green mantle and an embroidered saffron robe. The jeweled belt at her waist held a sword. Save for the golden circlet on her forehead, her red hair flew unbound. Through her he could see the hill rise dark against the sky.

"You are a man of Ulster." She tossed her head. Her hair glowed.

"I am also a bard. The war between our people is long over, if you indeed are Maeve."

"The woman laughed. "Maeve I was, Maeve I am, and Maeve will never lie alone in her grave. The war is never over. Only the causes are different." She smiled. "Without conflict, life is bland. But what brings you to Cruachan tonight, with naught but your harp? Few harps are seen these days, and none like yours."

"It must have been yourself who called," said Tadhg. "As for the harp, I've lived these many years beneath Lough Neagh, in the company of the Sídhe." He told her how he came to be released.

"Ah? So that proud Queen fares not well? Such a pity. Her King was charming. So here we two are—I, who cannot sleep, and you, who should by rights be long since dead." She sat on the grass; her long hair trailed the ground. "Left you've been with faerie-gifts, else you could not see or hear me. I've few to talk with now; most wish to sleep, even the once-valiant kings."

"They still name girl-children after you."

"I know that. I am of the land, part of history, a part that cannot sleep. But you are not an ordinary bard, not even a bard with faerie-gifts. Something else hovers about you." She looked him full in the face. "And I did not send summons!" Her green eyes glowed. On her white forehead Tadhg saw a red scar. He touched it.

Maeve smiled. "The mark of the stone that killed me. Thrown by an Ulsterman. Ah, fear not, bardeen. I'll not harm you. It's pleased I am with living company. But now you must play."

Tadhg did not move.

Maeve's green eyes became cold, her face haughty. "I command you, play for me!"

Tadhg put down his harp. "I am not yours to command." It was not he who spoke; he feared this flaming-tempered woman who had plunged two provinces into war. But he rose and towered over her; she looked up at him and rose to her knees. "You are no bard," she whispered. "You are He." Her green eyes were wide with fear and excitement. "You ride with the Hunt, you bring violence and rending—" She licked her lips. "The splendid deeds are not yet over. Glad I am I cannot sleep. Take me with you!"

Tadhg's head felt heavy, as if antlers weighed it down. He took a step toward the kneeling Queen. "No. I have other work to do. But you will attend me when I call."

Maeve nodded, "Samhain?"

"Yes," said that-which-was-not-Tadhg. "When I come to rule the year, there will be more to contend with than changing seasons. Forces ride abroad that long have slept."

"I will fight beside you," said Maeve. "It's the hunt and the wild night I always joyed in, not gentle breezes and flowers."

"I need not leave till dawn," Tadhg said. He knelt beside her on the grass.

"Hold me," she cried. Her nails dug into his back—ghost scratches. "Too long has it been, too cold my bed, I cannot sleep for missing life and warmth—" Tadhg silenced her, roughly, with a kiss, and pushed her down upon the grass.

Tadhg woke in the field at dawn. A spider, like a tiny jewel, spun its web across his harpstrings. The completed strands already sparkled with dew.

He was only Tadhg again, cold and tired and confused. No one lay beside him now. The dead slept quiet in their burial-mounds. He did not play his harp; he had no wish to wake them.

Maeve. He shook his head. It cannot have been.

Dead centuries before his time, she was a legend—yet here was her palace, here her burial-place. Here she roamed the night, and came to him. *To him, or to what he was becoming?* At dawn, with dewsoaked clothes, such questions were absurd.

Sleepy, he stumbled back down the road.

When he reached the bed-and-breakfast house, folk were stirring. The smell of food reminded him how long it was since he'd eaten. He tried the front door; it was now unlocked. He heard Liam and Connor speaking in their room. They were awake, then. Tadhg entered. He set his harp on the floor and sat on one of the two rumpled beds.

Liam stared at him. "It's covered with grass-stains you are, and wet and draggled. Where did you spend the night?"

Tadhg said, calmly, "If I told you, you'd not believe me, and you're happier unawares." Liam paled and turned away. Something of the death of the Mac-Ivers still gnawed his memory.

"Well, it's not much use you've had of the bed, but at least you'll get some breakfast," Connor said. "We've still many miles to travel, and 'twould be nice to start early for a change. Whatever you've been up to, Tadhg, you might at least put on fresh clothes. The woman of the house seems frightened enough of you as it is. I thought for a while after you left that she'd turf us out."

"Do I look that badly?" Tadhg stepped over to the mirror. "Yes, I do." He washed his face and borrowed a comb, then changed into dry clothing. Nothing could be done about his shoes—they were the only pair he had, and they borrowed—but he wiped off the worst of the grass.

Connor watched. "You'll not be telling where you went last night?"

"Rathcrogan."

"All night, at Rathcrogan? Speaking to the dead, was it, or dancing with the faeries?"

Tadhg's look turned Connor's face pale. "A jest, of course. Your business is your own."

"Thank you," said Tadhg. "Shall we go to breakfast?"

The journey to Achill was as far again as they'd come the day before. They left the main road at Castlebar and drove along an island-dotted shore until they reached Achill town, where a bridge spanned the narrow sound.

Once on Achill Island itself, the road skirted a high mountain on whose sides sheep grazed. Tadhg gasped at his first sight of the seaward coast: Sheer cliffs alternated with white sandy beaches, and everywhere the water foamed around black rocks.

"It's no sea for strangers," Connor said. "Grace O'Malley, the pirate queen, did well here in Elizabeth's time, bless her, harrying merchant vessels and then sheltering in hidden bays. Laughing all the time, I shouldn't doubt. It's said she was a rare one. We'll be taking a curagh out to receive the shipment. Our brave friends wish to stand well back from shore."

Well might they. Tadhg watched the waves dash against fanged rocks—certain death—and felt cold. He'd never been on the open sea. It was not his element; he would be a trespasser. The car turned off the narrow road onto a track, lurched to the top of a rise, and stopped.

"This is the place," Connor said.

The whitewashed house stood in a small stone-walled barnyard. Chickens pecked the dirt, a cat sunned herself, and a dog roared out to challenge them, then stopped and wagged his tail. Liam patted him on the head.

Tadhg stepped from the car. The air was redolent of cows and hay.

A woman came to the doorway, wiping her hands. Save for her apron, she wore black, and her hair was covered with a black kerchief. Her thin arms were sunburned, and her face was lined. "It's a day too late you are for the funeral." She let her hands hang limp. "But I'll welcome you in Padraig's memory."

"Sorry we are not to have come sooner." Connor did not elaborate the reasons. "We've brought along his things, what little was left. I fear his pipes and accordion were smashed."

"I heard the details," the mother said. "And I'd not be thinking on them, for they pain me sore. You're welcome, and Liam as well. And you, also." She looked at Tadhg.

"I am Tadhg MacNiall, Mrs. Byrne." He did not add, "And I avenged your son," though in his own time he would have handed her the severed heads of the slayers. "I met your son only a short while before—" He let the thought trail off.

"Ah, come inside, for all it's a sunny day there's that wind from the sea, it never stops. Himself is out with the cows, and the children are not yet home from school, though they'll be along soon. Cruel it's been, losing their big brother." She wiped her eyes wih reddened knuckles. "Would you like a cup of tea, or something stronger, perhaps? And you'll be spending the night, of course, as you ever did?" Something of fear crossed her face.

What does she suspect, that she would rather not know?

"Many thanks, Mrs. Byrne, we'd be glad to, though sad the errand that brought us." Connor spoke soothingly. All three followed her into the house.

The parlour was small and dim. Crocheted cloths covered the backs and arms of shabby, faded chairs, and draped scratched wooden tables. Braided rugs scattered the linoleum floor. In the hearth burned a small turf fire; the woman bent and added another chunk. "Sit close, now, you must be chilled after your trip."

Tadhg looked at the walls, where brown-tinted pictures hung. Several of the men looked like Padraig: handsome, pale-eyed, and black-haired, but they wore high stiff collars. Mrs. Byrne saw his glance. "Ah, that's some of the relatives. The Byrne men have a look to them, isn't it the truth? Would you all be wanting tea?"

"That would be fine, Mrs. Byrne," Connor said.

The three sat silent, each with his own thoughts, until the woman returned bearing a tray. "His sister Maureen drove up from Shannon for the funeral," she said, "but she did not stay the night. The last we saw her was Christmas. Never thought we'd be seeing her next at her brother's burial." She turned toward Tadhg. "Maureen works for a car-hire firm at the airport, now, and such fine clothes, such airs and graces you'd never believe. Not that she ever sends home any money, the way Padraig did, not her." She bowed her head. "Padraig was such a good boy; why did the Lord take him? Being murdered is a strange way for the Lord to show favour. Ah, if he'd stayed on the farm with his father! But no, the music had him, and there was no holding him. Even so, he came home when he could. And brought his friends as well, to fill the house with young people. There's only the two smallest left now, Eoin and Ciara, and they already in school. Soon enough they'll be off for further study, and I'll see no more of them either, save on holiday. Time I remember when they all was squabbling like Kilkenny cats and tearing about the house—now it's so quiet, except for the wind." She sipped her tea. "It's a mother's lot to send them forth. But not so soon!" She stood. "Here, I'll show you to your rooms. Decide among yourselves where you wish to sleep, and I'll be tending the kitchen. Himself will soon be home, half-starved I shouldn't doubt, and I think I hear the children already."

The sleeping spaces were a loft and Padraig's old room. Liam and Connor immediately chose the loft. Tadhg knew that neither wished to sleep in Padraig's room, where memories might bring a haunting.

Tadhg shrugged. He had no reason to fear the dead, and had he not avenged Padraig's honor?

"We must be down on the shore at eleven," Connor whispered. "These folk rise early; they should be asleep by then."

"You know the area," Tadhg said, "but if I'm to wander in the dark I'd best see for myself." He hung his clothes in the wardrobe—those he'd worn the night before were still dew-damp from Rathcrogan. Next to them hung garments that mourned their owner. Tadhg touched a thick sweater. Even inanimate things wept. He picked up his harp and went downstairs.

From the kitchen he could hear the clatter of utensils and the voice of a young girl. Ciara must be home from school. He slipped out the front door.

A path led across the field—Tadhg saw sheep in the distance—to a small creek which flowed down to the sea. When he reached its banks he saw that the path led along it. As he walked he looked into the water; the creek tumbled and chuckled for the most part, stony and shallow, but in occasional deep pools the water swirled before rushing seaward. One pool held a dark shape. Silver flashed as a large fish turned. A trout, perhaps? Too late in the season for salmon. He remembered the trout from Lough Neagh. He'd never seen it close up, but Maire claimed it had amber eyes.

Maire! The memory was a blow. He doubled over and called her name. The fish flicked in a circle and was gone.

Maire had come to save him; now she lay drowned, while he wandered this wild land, gripped by something he dared not name. *Maire! Where are you?*

He clutched his harp, the last familiar thing he knew. *Enough weakness.* The voice was cold. He walked onward.

At last he reached a break in the cliffs, and watched the waves foam over rocks below. A small boat, in these waters—water was not his element, it would drag him down! Offshore, two jagged rocks loomed black against the setting sun. Somewhere on the red-and-orange horizon lay Tir na n'Óg, the land of the ever-young. Had Maire reached that place?

The fading light struck gold on his harpstrings. He played a tune—not one to wake the dead, or command the wind, but a simple melody that any bard might play at sunset.

A round black head broke the water, and two large brown eyes watched him. He smiled at the seal and, in jest, sang it a song:

> *Selkie, sing me songs of sea-foam,*
> *Sweeping shoals of silver salmon,*
> *Sing to me, sleek shining swimmer,*
> *Say whether you walk as human!*

The seal stared at him for a long time, unblinking; then it dived and was gone.

This is Achill Island, Tadhg recalled. *Even I, who lived far from here, know that here dwell selkies.* Sunset was a dim orange line, and the air grew chill. Tadhg longed for light, warmth, and human company. He hurried back up the path toward the small yellow glow of the farmhouse window.

CHAPTER THIRTEEN

Maire and Rita talked late into the night. Among other things, Rita told of Belfast security procedures and mandatory curfews. She also explained money, a new concept: Maire's unit of exchange had been the cow. Maire in her turn asked questions about the city and customs of this time, until at last her mind was too numb to assimilate any more, and Rita was exhausted.

"I must sleep," Rita said. "Mother will roust me out for Mass. She thinks there's virtue in going early, and it's nearly dawn."

"I need sleep as well," said Maire. She felt like a child again, fostered in a strange household. Before she knew it she too slept. Her dreams were jumbled.

Sunday was calm. The family attended early Mass. Rita grumbled, for she was tired, but she went. So did Maire, since it was expected. The ceremony was meaningless; she stood and sat and knelt when the others did.

Back home, at a late breakfast, Mac opened the paper and said, "Ah, look! There's been more trouble in South Armagh, as if there wasn't enough."

Rita stopped buttering a scone. "What now, Father? Not that I'm eager to hear, but I may as well."

"You remember those three young musicians killed on the Navan Road, Friday afternoon, in broad daylight?"

"The Three Bards, you said. Yes, I recall. They played well, you mentioned."

"They must have been up to something else besides. But how was I to know? Well, on Friday night three Protestant boys—the MacIver brothers—were killed in nearly the same area." He sipped his tea.

"So much I'd already heard. There's something else?"

"Well, yes. Only last night someone planted a bomb on the steps of an Orange Lodge just our side of the Border. There were several casualties. It's thought to be related to the other incidents—Friday night one of the MacIvers' assailants was shot and killed. No doubt his mates decided to avenge him." He put down the paper. "It's a dirty business. It's not so bad when the terrorists have at each other, but the bombings—"

"All of it's disgusting," said Mrs. MacCormac, "and I'll thank you to discuss it no further at breakfast on the Lord's Day."

They spoke of other things after that. When the meal was over, Rita said, "I'll help you clear the table, Mother, and wash the dishes; then I'll get some rest. Tomorrow I'm back on duty. Ten days straight, this time. You'd think they'd show some pity on the staff." She yawned. "Well, they can't help it, I suppose."

They had just finished carrying utensils out to the kitchen when the telephone rang in the parlor. "I'll get it," Rita said. "Maybe they want Father down at the pub."

Maire could hear half of the conversation.

"Yes, Sister. I understand. That bad, and there's no one else at all? Oh. Gone on holiday. Can't be reached. Yes, I'll be in as soon as I can." She hung up and came back to the kitchen. "Damn and hell!"

"Rita," her mother said, "such language!"

"I wish we didn't *have* a bloody telephone, then they couldn't reach me either."

"Who was it?" Maire asked. Rita had told her about telephones, but she was not certain she believed in them.

"Sister, at the hospital, of course. Today has been one disaster after another, and Marilyn's so exhausted she's walking about like a zombie, and they can't find anyone else to substitute. The other nurses don't have phones, or they're not answering, or they're out of town on holiday—why me?" She headed upstairs. "Time is wasting while I talk. I'd best get ready. They need me at once."

When she came back down, dressed in white, Maire asked. "May I come along and see where you work?"

"I'd love to show you, but tomorrow would be better," Rita said. "Sister says it's utter chaos. I'll be back this evening, assuming the next shift is able to cope." She kissed her mother and told her father good-bye.

After Rita was out the door, Mac said, "I suppose some new bit of nastiness has just happened. Can't they even leave us a quiet Sunday?" He looked down at the paper. "I can't say I like the idea of her going out when there's trouble. I know the hospital is guarded, but she still has to get there and home again."

"She usually has someone walk her home," Rita's mother said, "and if it's truly dangerous she can always sleep over in the nurses' residence."

"Hmf," said Mac. "It's not bad enough she has to take care of the victims, she has to mind she doesn't become one herself. They're all mad." He picked up the paper again.

"I'll help with the dishes," Maire said. If such was the custom of the time, and she a guest in the home, no task was too lowly.

Rita's mother knew where things were kept, so she dried and put away, while Maire washed. "Where did you meet Rita? She never spoke of you before."

"Ah, we've not known each other long. We met, as it were, by accident." Maire rinsed a plate and handed it over.

"I worry so about the girl. She was seeing a British soldier a while back, and that Mrs. O'Shaughnessy next door was making threats—I had to put a stop to it for Rita's own sake, not that the poor Tommies are bad boys, of course, but such things cause trouble. And Michael wasn't Catholic."

"Ah, yes," Maire said. She washed a knife, careful of its sharp blade.

"I'd best get on down to the pub, now," Mac said, from the door of the kitchen. "I'll be home for tea."

The afternoon passed quietly; Rita's mother darned stockings and watched television. Maire tried to watch it as well, but could not follow the story lines, and the flickering images gave her a headache. Rita telephoned at one point to say that the evening shift was also shorthanded, and until they found a substitute she would have to stay; no point in waiting tea.

Maire felt a restless dread. Something was about to happen.

Mac MacCormac came home for tea, as usual; in Rita's absence, conversation was brief. After prayers they ate in silence until Mac said, "Bad doings downtown today, I heard. And the police were by the pub again. It seems there was a fourth man seen leaving with the musicians and only three bodies—"

His wife put a napkin to her lips.

"Sorry. There were things they wondered about, is all. I couldn't help. As I recall, the fourth chap was one of the customers. He got up and sang a bit, then went off with them." He frowned. "I'd hate to think that informers would come to my place."

"Well-enough you know that folk of the *other* sort frequent MacCormac's," said his wife, "and you do nothing to prevent it." She set her lips in a thin line. "When you attract violent people, they bring violence."

"Christ's blood, woman," Mac roared, "I've got to run either a Catholic or a Protestant pub, don't I? It has to be *someplace*. Great fortune and long life I'd have with a Protestant pub on the Shankhill! So men come in to drink and talk—what control have I over what they say? I pull the pints and pour the whiskey, and stop fights when I can. I'm not God, woman!" He coughed into his napkin.

His wife spoke. "I'm sick of it all, Mac, even sicker than I was when John—well, I've decided not to sit helpless any more, no matter what that Mrs. O'Shaughnessy might say. Do you remember Frances Bain?"

"Bain? Ah, we haven't seen either of the Bains in years," Mac said. "Not since it got too dangerous to visit—" He grew thoughtful. "Hard to imagine, now, that we had Protestant friends; they could come to our house and we'd visit theirs, and no one feared travelling after dark. What about Frances, then?"

Mrs. MacCormac set down her fork. "You've heard of the Women's Peace Marches. They're starting up again, a new group, and Frances called me last week. There's one planned next Saturday. I have decided to be in it, marching beside Frances. Protestant and Catholic women together, in public protest against the killing."

"I forbid you to go."

Maire, who had sat silent, clenched her fists. How dare he! *But this time is different.*

Mrs. MacCormac looked down at her plate. "I wish to go." Her voice was weak.

"You cannot." Mac began to rise.

Inside Maire a voice spoke. *This will not be tolerated. She is a free woman.* Aloud, Maire said, "How *dare* you forbid your wife her chosen course of action? She is a free adult. You claim to oppose the killings, yet you wish to keep her silent at home while your daughter wears herself out treating casualties and all you have left of your son is his picture!"

Mac sat down heavily; the chair creaked. He stared at Maire and opened his mouth to speak. Instead his expression turned to awe, then fear. He crossed himself and murmured, "For all Thy blessings, Lord, we give Thee thanks, in the name of the Father and of the Son and of the Holy Ghost, amen." He looked again at Maire, frowned, blinked, and stood up. "Time to go mind the store."

Mrs. MacCormac watched him leave, then turned to Maire. "I know not how you witched him, stranger-woman. But I will be in that march."

At last Rita came home, exhausted. Maire thought, before the key turned in the lock, that she heard two voices outside, a man's and a woman's, but Rita entered alone.

"Hello, Maire," she said. "Don't even *ask*, Mother. It was bad enough living through it once."

"I saved you something to eat."

"I truly think I'm too tired. And to imagine, I must be up and at work tomorrow morning! It's inhuman, I tell you. Maire, if you want to come along tomorrow it's best you get some sleep as well. I must be on duty at seven, and if I'm to show you about I should get there earlier."

"Now that you're home safe, I have only your father to worry about," Mrs. MacCormack said. "I've decided to join the Women's Peace March next Saturday."

Rita stopped dead. "You know Father will never allow it."

"Yes he will. Maire, here, seems to have explained matters to him."

Rita looked at Maire in amazement. "If you can change Father's mind once it's made up, there is little I would believe impossible. Well, I'm working Saturday, so there's no chance I can go. If there's trouble I'll know about it. Do be careful, Mother. I *must* go to bed or I'll fall right over."

Rita's alarm clock sounded at a grim early hour; it was not quite dawn. Rita and Maire rose and dressed in near-silence, then stumbled downstairs to breakfast. Over bacon, eggs, and tea, Rita revived a little.

"Time to go, if we're to get there early," she said. "I do hope it's quiet today. We could all use the rest." She gathered up her purse and a sweater. "I'll see you after work, Mother."

"And I will return in a short while," Maire said.

Some of the neighborhoods through which they walked made Maire nervous. She knew, now, the significance of the painted slogans.

Rita sighed. "I'd like to spank the children who scrawl those signs, children of whatever age." She walked quickly onward.

The Royal Victoria Hospital—so proclaimed the letters over the main doorway—was not one building, but several sprawling red-brick constructions. Courtyards were walled-in and gated, and soldiers stood guard. Rita stopped to greet one. "Good morning, Fred. Is it quiet so far?"

The soldier nodded. He was thin and young, shorter than Michael, his face pitted by adolescent acne.

"Morning, Rita. Who's your friend here?" Though the language was the same, his accent was harsher than the soft local speech.

"Ah, this is Maire ní Donnall, she's come to tour Casualty. She's never seen the Royal. As long as it's quiet, I'll take the chance to show her about."

"Let's hope it stays that way. Yesterday was enough." The soldier's eyes never stopped scanning the street.

Rita nodded to some of the other guards and, through swinging doors, entered the Casualty Ward. A few nondescript folk waited on benches.

Rita stepped toward a window at the back of the room. A woman looked out. She was middle-aged, and wore a black dress, a white apron, and, on her head, a shoulder-length white kerchief. "Rita," she said, "good morning. Sorry about yesterday."

"Ah, well," said Rita, "what else could you do? It seems quiet today, Sister."

"It is that, so far, thank God," the older nurse said. "They took in a 307 a bit earlier, she was injured last week in a blast and woke up hysterical when a lorry backfired. She's under sedation now. Other than that, you'd think we were a normal Casualty service." She laughed. "A 'normal' Casualty service! That's rich!"

"Since I'm early, and it's quiet, I'd like to show my friend around," Rita said. "Sister Shelby, this is Maire ní Donnall, also in the health field. Maire, Sister here is in charge of Casualty Service."

Sister looked at her wrist. "Walking report in fifteen minutes, Rita. Let's hope it stays quiet. We could all use a breathing spell. My pleasure to meet you, Maire."

Rita opened a door at the side of the waiting room and stepped into a white-walled corridor. Directly opposite, another door opened into the staff room. Rita put her purse and wrap into a metal locker, checked to make sure she had her keys, and took a white cap

from a plastic bag. She stood in front of the mirror
and pinned the cap to her head. "Silly things," she
said, "but we're supposed to wear them. Emblem of
rank or some such rot. Well, while we've time, let's
go."

They stepped back into the corridor. Rita pointed.
"There's the office of the surgeon-in-charge; he meets
all the disaster cases and photographs them for the
records. Here's where we store the medications—"
Rita opened a door and looked in; a nurse stopped
counting pills and waved. "Different from what you
were used to, of course."

Maire paused to gather impressions. Not herbs, but
medication refined from herbs, and needles that were
more like thin reeds than sewing implements. They
placed drugs beneath the skin, or into the blood-
stream. She marvelled. Rita walked on down the corridor. Maire followed. "Here are the treatment
rooms, where we do emergency care and ready the patients for surgery if they need it. This is the waiting
room for the families of those who are not expected
to live. Thank God it's empty now." She looked at
her wrist. "It's almost time for report. Down the corridor, there, at the end, is the X-ray room. Ah, of
course, you do not know of X-rays. They're like photographs, only they show the inside of the body,
bones and things."

Like faerie-sight? For this, they have a device?

"Sister won't like me visiting on duty," Rita said.
"While it's quiet I'd best check supplies. If it gets
busy I'll have no time at all."

"Thank you for the tour," Maire said. "I'll be
seeing you at home tonight. I may walk around a
bit." Rita went off into one of the side-rooms, and
Maire retraced the way she had come.

She stood for a time in the waiting room. She
thought she could tell which was the family of the
hysterical woman. They sat, three of them, a man, a

young boy, and an even younger girl; they looked straight ahead at the blank wall. *It's little better shape they are in, themselves.* The boy had a recent cut on his cheek—perhaps no more than a week old, from the amount of healing. The eyes of all three were vacant, like those of changelings. Or of the child who'd fled beneath Lough Neagh.

Behind her, as she left, she heard a crackling sound and a distorted voice: *Code Red, Code Red!* Then, a more human voice—it sounded like that of Sister Shelby—said, "Not this early! And the ambulances are already en route."

Maire walked out onto the street. In the distance, she heard "Whoop-whoop-whoop." It came closer. She stood aside to watch. A white-painted vehicle topped by a flashing blue light screeched into the courtyard. The two men in front leapt out, and flung open the rear doors. Hospital employees rushed toward them.

Maire watched what they carried out. Despite her years of experience, despite all she had seen on the battlefield, she felt sick. She stepped forward. Perhaps her new power—but no. What could she do here? Their drugs were better than her herbs, and even their machines had faerie-sight. She was of no use as a healer. She clenched her fists and turned away.

A park greened the area across the street, but nearby stood a police station, where there was too much noise and action; Maire wanted a quiet place. She walked down Falls Road, past where she would have turned off toward Rita's house, until she came upon a far wider expanse of green, dotted with stones and statues. *A burial-ground.* It suited her mood.

She entered the gate and sat against a tree. Outside on Falls Road cars roared past and the occasional ambulance screamed by with its cargo of pain. But all was quiet among the dead.

Burial customs were different here: statues of winged creatures, headstones carved with incomprehensible statements, transparent domes protecting faded artificial flowers—nowhere did she see a simple Ogham-carved commemorative stone. But these folk too remembered their dead.

Suddenly she laughed aloud. *They should. They spend such effort making more of them.*

Another ambulance passed, and Maire began to shake. She drew her knees up to her chin. Better she had stayed to perish with the Sídhe. Or with Tadhg, whatever had befallen him.

"Self-pity ill becomes you, Maire ní Donnall." She looked up, startled.

It was the wren. "You are an adult woman of noble birth; moreover, you are a healer. You have a task."

"What task?" She scarcely cared.

"As you are needed, you will be told. You have been used once already." The bird hopped away.

"Wait!" Maire called.

The wren flew off. Maire stared after it a long time. *I was told to watch and guard Rita, which I did. I cannot guard her at the hospital; there are armed soldiers whose job that is. But I should wait at her home.* Nonetheless she sat for a time and watched leaves blow among the tombstones. She dreaded her return to the concrete-and-asphalt city. Before she left, she gathered a few flowers. Those in front of John's picture were wilted and had not been replaced.

Maire's walk back to Rita's house was reasonably quiet, though she saw two groups of children—home from school, no doubt, for midday dinner—taunt each other from opposite sides of the street. They carried sticks, but the violence remained verbal; neither group crossed into enemy territory.

Past the worst slum areas, Maire reached Rita's

house and knocked on the door. Mrs. MacCormac opened it. "Ah, Maire, come in," she said. "It's been a time since you walked Rita to work, and I was worried. There was more trouble this morning, it says on telly."

"Sorry I am to worry you. I took a stroll on my own after Rita showed me around." Maire stepped inside and closed the door behind her. The warmth of the house was welcome. "I brought some fresh flowers." She stepped into the parlor and took the vase from the mantel. She carried it to the kitchen, tossed out the wilted flowers, filled the vase with water, and added her newly picked offerings.

Mrs. MacCormac watched. "Rita was to do that Saturday, but—" She turned away.

Again Maire was impatient, waiting through the afternoon. She had a feeling that she dared not leave the house.

Rita came home at last. "I can no longer believe it," she said. "Now they're setting car-bombs to catch men on their way to work. These last few days have been impossible, even for Belfast." She sat down and took off her shoes. "It must stop soon, or there won't be a person left alive in the city."

"Your father will be home early for tea," Mrs. Mac-Cormac said. "One of the men is ill and he must tend bar all evening."

"Poor Father. Is it the curse of the MacCormacs to be healthy and available while our co-workers fall in their tracks? I'd help you make supper, Mother, but if I stand up now I'll collapse."

"Never mind," Maire said, "I can help cook. I should do something to earn my keep."

"Ah, you're a guest and I hate to put you to work," Rita's mother said. "But I must admit you've been a great help. It's like having another daughter at home." She smiled and led the way to the kitchen.

*   *   *

Mac sat at the head of the table and scowled. "I'm purely tired of Barry being sick on Mondays. It's a strange disease, and I think he catches it from a bottle. And I swear if the police come by one more time I'll throw them out myself. They're still looking for the fellow who was last seen with the Three Bards. How am I to know all my customers? He wasn't a regular. He drifted in, they stood him a drink, and he played a song in Gaelic. I didn't understand a word of it, myself. Then he went off with them at closing. They were friendly sorts, those boys, and he seemed lost and bewildered. He was a good harpist, though, with a fine voice.

Maire's teacup rattled on her saucer. "A harpist, you say? Thursday night? How did he look?"

"Ah, nothing special. A bit thin, about my height— say five feet ten. He had the longish hair and beard they all wear nowadays; I think it was light brown. I'm not sure of his eyes, blue perhaps, with that light complexion. He did have a fine old-style harp. I've never seen its like, all carved, and he played it well."

"Did he give any name?"

"I don't recall. They introduced him to the crowd, but I was busy at the time. I think they said he came from Lough Neagh. I found that odd. No town or county, only Lough Neagh."

Maire had managed to raise her cup to her lips. She dropped it; it bounced on the table, but did not break. Tea spilled across the cloth.

"Maire! Are you all right?" Rita spoke. "You're white as a sheet."

"They didn't say Tadhg MacNiall?" Maire whispered. "Might that have been the name?"

"Ah, it's possible," said Mac. "I never remember names. Faces, now, but no names." He took a bite of sausage.

Rita looked at Maire. "Come on upstairs," she said. "You should be lying down."

Maire paced Rita's room. "It's my husband, it must be. I thought him dead, but while I was in the fisherman's cottage in Antrim he must have reached Belfast and met the Three Bards." She stared at the picture on the wall. "But they were all shot."

"Three of them were shot," Rita said. "Only three."

"Where might they have been bound?"

"Who knows? It's thought they were IRA sympathizers, and that's why they were killed. They may have been going to Dundalk."

"Rita, I must find him. He has no idea I'm alive. We were separated under the lake, and I could not find him—the gods alone know what will happen to him in this time!"

"You've very little confidence in your man."

"Well, see how I fared! They thought I was daft and whisked me off to hospital! Had I not fallen in with kind folk—" Maire resumed pacing. "I must find him. Do you think I should start at Dundalk? How would I get there?"

"There's a train."

"But then he might be anywhere between Newry and Dundalk. Perhaps I should seek him on the road."

"It's too far to walk," said Rita.

"I'll manage a ride, then."

"You've no papers."

"I can do without. I need not be seen."

"You truly think this is your husband?" Rita went to her purse.

"It may well be. If it is, and I do not go—he is all I have left."

"I've little money, but it's yours. You need it more than I." Rita opened her wallet and pulled out bills and coins. "Here. £20 and change is all, but you're welcome to it." Maire did not hold out her hand; Rita dropped the money on the bed.

Maire looked at the gaily colored paper, the scattered coins. "I will repay you."

"You already saved my life."

"How may I get to Dundalk by the road?"

"Take the bus. I'll show you the station. Get off at Newry if you wish to begin there. The fare will not be much. But you should not go off alone. You are too new here."

Maire gathered up the money. "I must. Would you do different were Michael lost?"

Rita shook her head. "Go with God. I'll show you to the station and I'll give Mother and Father some excuse. And, Maire—if you cannot find him, or if things go wrong—come back? You have a home here."

Maire hugged her. "I promise." *But first I must find Tadhg, if he is yet alive!*

CHAPTER FOURTEEN

At the Byrnes' farmhouse, tea was taken in silence. Martin, the father, headed the table in shabby tweed jacket and trousers; he had shed his rubber boots for slippers, but his clothing still smelled of cows. Mrs. Byrne was drawn and weary, and even the children said nothing, while they shovelled down fried eggs, soda bread, and black pudding.

Padraig's loss has been a cruel blow, thought Tadhg. *Sad it is to lose a loved one, and he was a man I'd have liked to know better.*

Liam and Connor were tense and subdued. Connor continually checked his watch, and from time to time turned to examine the wallclock. It was only a bit past six.

When the meal was over, Ciara and her mother cleared the table. Martin shuffled to the parlour, settled into a well-worn chair, and lit his pipe, Tadhg, Liam, and Connor followed him. His young son Eoin curled in the corner.

Martin puffed clouds of aromatic smoke. On the walls the portraits of his ancestors looked much as he must have, when young. At last he spoke: "Nasty business. It like to have killed the missus, when she heard. I was the one had to tell her. I thought she'd be frantic, but she just went all-over white and crossed herself." He fussed with his pipe. "Somehow that was worse. Cruel, besides, to know he died without the Last Rites. Such things mean much to her." He looked toward Liam and Connor; his gaze was steady. "It's the manner of his death that puzzles me. Strange, that an innocent musician—three of them, for that matter—should be gunned down in broad daylight on the public roads. Is there any little thing you'd be wanting to tell me?"

Liam fidgeted, but Connor spoke. "Neither Liam nor I were there, so we do not know—" He did not look at Tadhg.

"That's not the question I was asking," Martin said. "And your lack of answer has spoken." He studied his pipe; it had gone out. "Eoin," he said to his son, "you should be working on your lessons, not sitting idle in the corner hearing men's talk. Off with you, now! Your mother will be done in the kitchen. And then you're straight to bed, you know you have early chores—I'll be wanting the sheep moved before school, and you're God's own terror to waken."

Eoin rose. A lock of black hair fell across his forehead. "Yes, Father." His voice was sullen.

"You'll not be coming here again, now Padraig's gone." It was a statement, not a question. Martin stood and switched on the telly; gabble and music filled the silence.

By ten-thirty the household slept. Again Connor checked his watch. "It's time we went. I've electric torches in the car, and we'll want rubber boots as well."

They readied themselves and set forth. The night clamped a black lid on the sky. Save for the torches they would have been blind. Tadhg was glad he had come this way in daylight.

Only the creek's chuckle and the sea-wind's whisper broke silence until they reached the clifftop. Then Tadhg heard the surf boom, and through the darkness glimpsed white water.

"Down below, against the cliff, is Padraig's curagh," Connor whispered. "His father gave it to him, hoping it would keep him home—Padraig did love the little boats. It will be Eoin's now, I suppose. It's the last time we may use it, in any case. Damn Martin for a self-righteous fool!" Connor fairly spat the last words. No one else spoke. They picked their way down the steep path.

Connor's light caught a shiny black beetle-shape: Tadhg recognized the design. *Frail lost thing from another time.* He reached out and touched it, then drew back his hand. "It's not leather!"

Connor looked at him curiously. "Of course not. Tarred canvas. This can't be the first curagh you've seen, man? God, you're a green one—I wish we did not need three oarsmen."

"I never knew much of boats," Tadhg began.

"We'll set you in the middle, then. Heaven forbid you should try to steer!" Connor looked seaward. In the black distance a light blinked. "That would be our signal."

They picked up the oars and set the boat on their heads. Tadhg smelled tar, and fish, and sea-smell, and it was the last that frightened him, for he did not belong here.

Scarcely darker was it now, with the curagh over their heads, than before. They bore it to the water's edge and set it upright. It bobbed on the waves.

"We'll walk it out a bit, then you get in first, Tadhg."

Water rippled against Tadhg's boots, and the odd wave sloshed inside. The other two men steadied the craft as Tadhg clambered aboard; they handed him the oars.

"Mind you don't stick a foot or an oar through the fabric," Connor said.

Tadhg sat utterly still. Whatever possessed him on land cowered here, afraid, leaving him only human. With a practised gesture Liam climbed aboard, his back to the bow; Connor faced the stern. They fitted their oars to the rowing-pegs. Tadhg, watching them, began to do the same. "No," Connor said, "wait until we clear the rocks. The steering's tricky. Later Liam and I will need your strength."

Tadhg's bench was a thin wood plank, and the boat's skeleton was thin wood slats: impossibly frail against the force of those waves. The curagh settled, water hissed a handbreadth below the sides, and they darted backward into the sea.

Liam and Connor had made this run before. They passed almost in reach of a rock—Tadhg heard waves shatter, and spray stung his cheek. Surf roared about him, the boat tossed and wove, as Connor and Liam guided it with silent oar-thrusts. And then the sea grew calmer, the surf-sound was behind them, and Connor said, "Take your oars, now, Tadhg. I'll call the stroke." The curagh skimmed over the darkened sea.

Wood chafed Tadhg's palms, and his shoulder muscles strained. These waves were unlike those on Lough Neagh: They moved in no steady rhythm, but dashed and rippled and shifted.

A light gleamed once across the water. "We're there," Connor said. "We'll draw up on the sea side, we'll need light to load and the less seen from the shore the better—"

Even in the dark, Tadhg saw a deeper blackness loom. They rounded the end and Connor flashed his torch, three-and-two. When he was met by an answering flash, he called out, "In every generation—"

"Must Ireland's blood be shed." The accent was one Tadhg had not heard before. Then, from the darkness, a laugh. "Silly damn business. Connor, Sean, and Padraig, I guess?"

Connor's voice was low. "No. Not Sean or Padraig. You won't have heard?"

"Heard what?"

"Padraig was killed on the road last week, and Sean the next day. Sean was—we all were—doing a small job, and—Liam's come with me."

Silence. "Connor and Liam, then. I saw three men. Who's the new guy?" The voice was edged.

"Tadhg MacNiall. He can be trusted."

"Okay. Let's not take all night. I want to get out of here." A brighter light glared, and Tadhg was near-blinded. "Hi there, Tadhg. I'm Jerry McKenny, from Boston."

"I come from Lough Neagh, myself." Tadhg thought of the deep cold waters beneath him, and shuddered.

"Well, I've got cousins in Antrim. Miserable little dump, isn't it? Come on, let's get you loaded before the Coast Guard comes along. That's all we need."

The curagh rode low in the water. Tadhg would not believe it could hold so much weight. The long wooden boxes were heavy, sharp-cornered, and must be stowed at odd angles, leaving the three men little legroom. The ship was only a murmur in the distance, as they headed back to shore.

"Is Jerry McKenny from Tir na n'Óg?" There'd been little uncanny or blessed about the young man, who cursed and laughed and, at one point, nearly dumped a box on Tadhg's head, when the rope holding it swung wide.

"Boston." Connor spoke between oarstrokes.

"Where would that be?"

"In America. Across this whole wide ocean. Have you never heard an American before? You can always tell them; they speak so loud and fast, and they have a harsh accent."

"The folk of America are sending weapons to Ireland?" Tadhg was puzzled. So there *was* land across the ocean, as the legends said.

"We have many friends in the States among folk of Irish descent. Their ancestors, most of them, left Ireland during the Famine, and grew rich in the New World. They won't come home to fight, but they will give money, of which they have plenty, so they buy guns, and send them for our use."

Tadhg rowed and thought. The Famine. The dead woman in the Dundalk churchyard had cried—

A hand gripped the side of the boat. Tadhg stared into glowing green eyes. He flinched and turned to his companions, but they rowed steadily. This sending was to him alone.

The hand was webbed and clawed, and the eyes were set in a pale face. Save for those eyes, the face might have belonged to a beardless youth. When it spoke, he saw that the mouth held pointed teeth.

"So you venture out onto the sea?" The eyes glowed brighter. "Long have we awaited such a distinguished guest. We'd not have you leaving us so soon."

Other faces appeared now, and other hands grasped the sides of the curagh, but still Tadhg's companions did not see. Tadhg tried to warn them, but could make no sound. Ahead, in the dark, surf snarled on rocks. *The merfolk will push us onto the rocks,* he knew, *and their claws will drag us under, while those teeth—* The surf boomed louder now. Over it he heard Connor shout:

"Veer off!"

"Am I not trying to?" Liam cried. "She will not steer!"

Cold spray dashed into the boat, and one of Tadhg's oars splintered. He felt the shock in his arm and shoulder. As if by instinct, he held out his hand, to ward off—what?

"Christ, we're almost on them!" It was Liam's shout.

In the darkness, Tadhg's hand scraped rough rock. He flinched, but some instinct made him grasp tighter. Solid, the rock was, unlike the shifting ocean. It was part of the land, and on land he was the Master. "Too late! Yours is the sea, but I ride the wind!" In the grey light he saw the merfolk shrink back. From the land roared a mighty gale; it buffeted the curagh, drove it back from the rocks, and then was gone.

"What was, that?" Liam cried. "The wind never blows from the land!"

"Whatever, it saved us. So steer!" This time the craft responded, and darted through the passage until Tadhg felt the bottom scrape sand. First out, he stood in shallow water. The feel of land was welcome.

Connor ventured a light. "She's holed," he said. He pointed; along one side the canvas showed four long slashes.

"What in Hell could have done that?" Liam said. "The rocks?"

Claws, Tadhg thought. He stared out to sea. They were out there, waiting. The sea against the land; the merfolk against that which held him. Cold currents sucked at his ankles. "Let's unload, and quickly. I've had enough of the sea tonight."

The cave was damp and dark. Water swirled through the seaward opening with a sucking sound. On the white sand lay a thick line of kelp. They stacked cases of rifles along the landward wall. "That's well above high water," Connor said, "and to-morrow night we'll get them up the hill to the lorry. In the meantime they should be safe here."

Tadhg looked to where a small cleft in the rock

showed a faint sky-glow. Danger came from the sea. He felt a presence in this black-walled cave. "Are you certain they're set above high tide?"

"Unless there's a storm. In winter, we could not be sure, but it's not until November that the true storms strike, and naught's been forecast. We've used this place before. Come along, now." They edged through the shallow water, out of the cave and onto the beach. Connor ventured a torch-flash, looking for the path, then stopped and cursed.

Beside the beached curagh sat a small bent figure. It straightened as the light struck: dark-haired, white face, tear-stained cheeks. "You wrecked her!" A child's voice, shrill and accusing.

"Eoin!" Connor exclaimed. "What are you doing here?" Tadhg saw his hands clench the heavy torch.

The boy straightened. "Do you think me such a child that I have no idea what you've been about, these many months? All of you coming home with my brother, and creeping out at night—I could hear you quite well, you know—down to the seashore, then stealing back later, boots sandy, trousers damp, and sleeping late next morning? I know your business."

Connor clutched the boy's arm. "And what might that be?"

"I saw you meet the boat. I saw you take the boxes to the cave. You're running guns to the North."

"You'd best forget it." Liam's voice was tense.

"So, you're with the Provos. Do you think me as great a fool as my parents, or my sister? That's why Padraig was shot, I know. Fighting for Ireland. As I shall, when I'm old enough. But you should not have wrecked my curagh. She was Padraig's, and he loved her, and she was to be mine!" He was close to tears again.

"Mother of God, what shall we do with him?" Liam was near panic. "He'll be telling his parents, and they'll set the Gardaí on us—"

"I think not." Connor crouched beside the boy, who looked up defiantly.

"I'll tell no one. Mother and Father are poor patriots, for all they gave us the Gaelic names. They're afraid to fight. I would have helped Padraig, but he'd tell me nothing—thought I was too young. I'm almost thirteen!"

"Then you're nearly a grown man," Connor said, "and old enough to keep a secret."

"You have my word. Nor will I tell Ciara. She's soft in the head, she's only a girl. Tell me, did you get the men who killed Padraig?"

"That we did," said Tadhg. It was the first he'd spoken.

The boy grinned. "Gunned them down, I hope, as they did him?"

"We did," said Tadhg. "Justice was satisfied."

The boy glanced at the curagh and ran a hand over the slashed fabric. "How you could do that on the rocks, and survive—" He yawned. "It must be past one; if I'm caught out this late I'll be thrashed. Will you be coming back to the house now?"

"We will," said Connor. "Our business is finished for tonight."

In Padraig's old room, Tadhg heard sea-wind shake the house, while something scraped the panes. *Windblown branches, nothing more,* he told himself. It could not be that merfolk scrabbled up the cliff, eyes glowing and talons outstretched, to claw their way into his room—but he dared not look out the window. In the wardrobe the clothes mourned for Padraig; his bed was grave-cold, haunted.

Tadhg did not sleep until dawn whitened the sky.

All rose late next morning, and did not have to face Mr. Byrne at breakfast. Mrs. Byrne was busy about the house, and the children were in school. Nothing remained but to wait.

Liam and Connor played endless hands of cards, but Tadhg did not know the game and had little interest in learning. On such a day, to huddle indoors counting scraps of paper—he took his harp and went back to the seashore.

He sat above, on the cliff. The seal lazed near the cave entrance. In sunlight, night-terrors seemed foolish. This was only a seal, and the sea sparkled blue and foamed against white sand; what was there to fear? Again in jest, he spoke: "Greetings, selkie."

It stared at him, its brown eyes almost human, and swam nearer. "Greetings, man. You have the Sight?"

Tadhg nodded, speechless.

"You left something filthy in my cave."

The sun was yet warm on his back, the breeze gentle, and somewhere a bird sang, but Tadhg chilled. A selkie this was indeed: seal in water, human ashore. One of the minor faerie-folk. And on Achill Island some human clans claimed them as ancestors.

"We'll remove our goods from your cave tonight, with no harm done."

The selkie snarled up at him. He was a huge grey seal, and Tadhg was glad to be above on the cliff, rather than below, within reach. "You lie," the selkie said. "Evil will be done. Well I know what those boxes hold, and what use you plan for them. How can you, who have the Sight, deal in death?"

"How can I fail to avenge my friends and my land? Have you folk of the sea no honor, seek you no vengeance?"

"Were we vengeful," the selkie said, "no man would ever dare the waves again. A selkie does no harm unless he must. But my friends the merfolk have no human hearts."

Tadhg winced. The selkie smiled sharp. "So you

have met them? Few live who can make that claim."

Pebbles scattered on the path. Tadhg turned and saw dark-haired Ciara. She looked out to sea, and waved. "I'm only just home from school—"

The selkie vanished underwater. Ciara caught sight of Tadhg. "You must have frightened him!" She thought a moment. "Maybe not. He would never come around when Padraig and his friends were here; he said he did not like their sort. But I heard him talking with you."

"Child, it was only a seal." Tadhg strummed the forgetting song. "Only a large grey seal."

"Only a seal," the girl repeated, as if by rote.

"It's time for tea," he said.

When dusk fell, Tadhg, Liam, and Connor slipped from the house. No one asked where they went.

"Why are the arms delivered here?" asked Tadhg, as they stumbled down the path.

"They're more difficult to trace," Connor said. "Were an American boat caught running guns to the Six Counties, great would be the outcry. But smuggled ashore, and then sent off on a lorry—a lorry also carrying hay or turf or manure, never the same vehicle or driver—they'll pass the Border with ease."

Light had faded, but the western horizon still gleamed pale. Tadhg looked past the rocks, far out to sea, hoping to catch a glimpse of Tir na n'Óg. Between him and infinity stretched naught but empty ocean.

In the cave it was full dark. They sloshed ashore, and Liam stumbled. "Damnation!" He flicked on his torch: Clear water lapped across a rifle.

Connor switched on his torch, as did Tadhg. Scattered in the shallows and across the damp sand lay their precious cargo. Most of the crates had been ripped to boards.

"Oh my God, not salt water," Liam moaned.

"No harm, once we rinse out the sand. They're still coated with Cosmoline. But who could have done this? I'd not have suspected the boy; and he's had little time today. These cases are heavy. 'Twas the work of a grown man." Connor looked at Tadhg. "You visited the shore this afternoon."

Tadhg stared back. "That I did, and what is it to you, that I must account for my coming and my going? It's a civil tongue I'll expect." His voice echoed against rock.

Liam turned pale. "He meant, perhaps you might have seen—"

Connor knelt on the sand floor. "They've been deliberately unwrapped and scattered, but the coating is intact. Whoever did this knew little of armaments."

Tadhg kept silent, but he knew the culprit. He, Connor, and Liam gathered the weapons and replaced them in the unsplintered crates.

"Bloody damn," said Connor, "we'll have to hand-carry most of them. All the more trips up the path. Best we start immediately. When the lorry crew come they can give us some help." He shouldered a few rifles, as did Liam and Tadhg.

The stack of rifles grew beneath the haystack, and they'd muscled two of the last four crates up the path, when lights swept the road. "Drop!" Connor ordered. They crouched behind the stone wall. The light stopped, and Tadhg smelled engine-stink.

"Ho, Connor! Liam!"

"Ah, it's our boys," Liam breathed. "They're not asking after Sean."

Connor stood. "Here." The motor stopped. Two dark-clad men clambered down from the cab. Doors slammed.

"Are you ready?"

"We're not, worse luck, and we're fair perished. Give us a hand, now."

"You were supposed to be ready."

"The bloody crates broke." Connor did not elaborate. "We've been bearing the cargo a few pieces a time up the path, and we're near done for. Give us a hand."

"Someone must stay with the lorry."

"I'll do that," said Liam. "I'm so ruined I doubt I'd manage another trip." He leaned against the cab.

"Lazy bastard. This way." Connor led Tadhg and the two lorry-drivers down the narrow path. When they reached the cave, one of the drivers whistled.

"Fell apart, you said the crates did. Torn apart, I'd say." He shook his head at the scattered boards. "It's a rare tide that would do that." He and Connor lifted a crate and set off into the darkness.

His partner looked at Tadhg. "You're with them, but I do not know your name."

"Tadhg MacNiall. And yours?"

"Brian Murphy." The man gestured to the last remaining crate. "Shall we?" He bent to lift it; Tadhg heard a sound and turned.

Wading toward them from the sea came a tall, fine-featured man. He was unclad, and his golden hair hung to his shoulders. His skin gleamed pearl. For all his fairness, his eyes were deep brown. *Seal's eyes.*

"Worse will befall you, if you foul my cave again." The naked man stepped forward. The lorry-driver dropped his corner of the crate and stared. "You, with the Sight, should be ashamed, Tadhg MacNiall. Were you not once a harpist for the Sídhe?"

Tadhg stood frozen. The lorry-driver reached into his pocket and drew forth a heavy torch. "Whoever you are, you're a dead man!" He leapt forward, his feet splashing in the shallow water. His arm raised once, twice; bone crunched and the selkie gave a strange inhuman cry. Tadhg dropped his torch, and the cave was dark.

The driver swung once more; Tadhg heard the blow connect, and then a splash. A light flashed on; the driver swept it across the water. Nothing could be seen save a thin red curl of blood.

The man wheeled and faced Tadhg. "Fine lot of good you are in a pinch!" He reeked of tobacco, and his hands yet held the torch as a weapon. "If I didn't kill him, there's one now who'll inform on us." He stepped forward swinging the torch.

"Come no farther," said Tadhg. "That one will never inform."

The man stepped closer.

"No farther, I said."

He froze in his tracks, staring at Tadhg. Tadhg reached out and took the torch.

"You are only a messenger. Remember your place." The man's eyes grew huge, and he lifted one corner of the crate.

"Yes. We must rejoin the others."

Tadhg needed all his courage to walk into the water and wade to the beach. When he turned his back to the sea he felt eyes watching him, but on land he was Master.

The lorry sped into the night. Without bidding farewell to the Byrnes, Connor, Liam, and Tadhg took the car and set off toward the northeast. There was a safe-house in Dungannon where they might shelter. A long dark drive it was until they crossed the Border, and then they had another day to wait.

CHAPTER FIFTEEN

Rita showed Maire to the bus station. It was not far from Belfast City Hospital, where a dazed and confused Maire had been taken on her first day in the city. She feared for a moment that a staff member would recognize her and drag her back to the Psychiatric Ward.

Rita helped her purchase a ticket to Newry, explained the denominations of bills and coins, and waited. The bus would leave soon.

"You're sure you want to go?"

Maire stared into the grey concrete bus station. Some of its blast-shattered walls had been patched with plywood. The chill wind flapped plastic sheets across open spaces. People huddled in warm clothing. "I must."

The Newry bus was announced. Maire rose.

"Don't forget to come back if you can."

"I will remember." Maire made her way to the loading platform and climbed aboard.

The blue-plush seat was comfortable, and, after the drafty station, the bus was warm. She leaned back.

* * *

She heard the seat next to her creak, and felt herself crowded by another's bulk. Maire kept her eyes closed. She did not wish to speak with anyone. After a time she slept.

When she awoke her face was sticky and her mouth was dry. She'd dozed most of the time. She rubbed her eyes, yawned, and sat up.

It was late afternoon by now, and the bus was between towns. To the left, a sweep of hills stood gold-dappled in the last light. Maire yawned again and turned toward her seat-mate, a fat middle-aged woman. On the floor in front of her lay a package-crammed string bag; her coat stretched taut across breast and belly, and she wore a garish headcloth. Her face was red.

"Ah, you're awake now," the woman said. "Slept like a champion, all the way from Belfast Station. Where are you bound?"

Maire blinked. Her eyes were gritty. "Newry, for a start. Where are we?"

"We passed through Banbridge some way back; we're not far north of Newry, now. Do you have a family there?"

Maire thought of Tadhg. "No."

"Business, then?" The woman settled in for a chat.

"In a way."

"It'll be dark soon after we reach town. All the shops will be closed. Have you a place to stay?"

"Not yet."

"My sister runs a bed-and-breakfast, you might stop there. She's not fancy, but she's reasonable. I'll show it to you when we get off the bus."

I must stop somewhere, Maire thought, *and it's far too cold to sleep in the open.* "Thank you."

Once they reached town, the woman introduced Maire to her sister—equally bloated but not quite as shabby—and took her leave. Maire wondered where to begin her search.

"I am trying to find someone who may have come through town a few days past," she told the landlady. She described Tadhg.

"Your husband, you say?" The woman looked at Maire's ringless left hand.

"Yes."

"And ran out on you? Ah, let him go, Missus, if they run off like that they're not worth having. Didn't my own do the same, these eight years past, and leave me with the children? Never a sign of him have I seen again, and none of his great friends would give me time of day. But I managed."

"My situation is different." Maire could not explain.

"If you must go looking, you may as well try the pubs, that's where the menfolk congregate. But few there are who'll tell you aught; they're all in it together."

Maire thanked the woman and stepped out onto the dark street. Where to turn? She may have chosen the wrong place to begin her search—but perhaps if she asked— She walked to the nearest brightly lit public house.

"Any luck?" said the landlady as she set Maire's breakfast before her in the morning.

Maire looked down at the limp fried eggs. "No. Not here. But they did say I might try in Dundalk. He was travelling with the Three Bards, who were shot on the road last week."

"Ah," said the landlady, "he was Catholic, then?" She put her hands on her hips.

"No," said Maire. She took a sip of tea. "I do not know how he fell in with them; in some Belfast pub, I'm told."

"Well, those were strange sorts for him to be running about with, mark my words. You're not thinking those three were killed for no reason, are you?"

"I cannot," said Maire, with perfect sincerity, "imagine any reason for their deaths. But then I never knew them, and Tadhg—my husband—cannot have known them long." Maire rose. "I must be on my way."

"And how will you get to Dundalk? Miles, it is. Will you be wanting the bus again?"

"No," said Maire, "I may get a ride, later on."

Without papers, she slipped across the Border invisible. So must Tadhg have done, if he had come this way. For a while she watched the soldiers stop north-bound vehicles. *Had Tadhg walked this very road?* She strained to feel his presence.

A few cars passed. Visible now, she was twice offered rides, but declined. At last the ill-fitting shoes blistered her feet, and her legs were weary. She accepted the next offer.

"Climb right in, then, Miss," the man said, holding open the left front door. "Where are you bound?"

"Dundalk."

"Ah, I go through there myself." He drove onward.

He smelled sour; his hands were dirty and his clothing was caked with grease. His chin bristled with several days' growth of beard. *Why did these men insist on shaving?*

He glanced sideways and saw Maire watching him; his hands caressed the steering wheel. He smiled, reached into a dashboard compartment and pulled out a flask. He tossed back a drink and handed the flask to Maire. "Here, it'll put some warmth in you."

"Thank you." She sipped the fiery liquid; it burned on the way down. She capped the flask and put it back.

"Have you folk in Dundalk?" the man asked. The car swerved, and he forced his eyes back to the road.

"No," she said. "I am looking for my man."

"Ah, are you now? And why should a fine-looking woman such as yourself have to search? Do you not have all you can handle?" he leered.

Despite the whiskey, Maire felt cold, then angry. She saw how he thought of her: a thing to be used. His idea of pleasure had naught to do with what the woman wished.

"Your attitude is offensive." She gauged their relative strength: He was larger, but she could give a good account of herself.

"Ah, don't get on your high horse with me, Miss, you walkin' the road and takin' rides from strangers, and your dress so tight in front it might be painted on, and no ring on your hand—"

"I am wed," said Maire, "though what business that is of yours I fail to see."

The man reached over and put a hand on her knee, then moved it up to her thigh, rumpling her dress. "Ah, you're wantin' a real man, you are, not like my missus. I've got just what you've been cravin'. I know a side road up ahead—"

Maire tried to push his hand away; he insisted. His fingers bruised her thigh. Suddenly she was furious. She spoke in another voice: *Touch me again and I will strike you impotent.*

The car swerved; the man jerked his hand away as if burned. His face turned pale. Slowly he looked at Maire, his eyes wide. "I did not realize—my apologies, Lady."

Maire said nothing. He was silent the rest of the way to Dundalk; he let her off on the outskirts and drove quickly away.

So this was Dundalk. Maire stood on a narrow street. There stood a pub, yonder a church—had Tadhg been here? She walked to the churchyard, toward the city of the dead.

It seemed that here lay a fresh grave: No stone stood at its head, and its flowers were unwilted. The mounded earth itself was dark and moist.

Who had been buried here? Maire sensed violence, but the grave did not speak. *It cannot be Tadhg who lies beneath this soil.*

An old woman shuffled up to the grave, crossed herself, and murmured a prayer. When she had done, she looked at Maire. "Excuse me," Maire said, "but could you tell me whose grave this is?"

"It belongs to Sean O'Rourke," the woman said. "Killed near Newry Friday night, committing murder, God rest his soul, not that Sean would admit he had one." She dabbed her eyes. "You're from out of town?"

"I only now arrived from Belfast," Maire said. "Sean, there—he was killed Friday?"

"Yes. His funeral was yesterday, and I've told his mates to come around my house no more. Did you know him?"

"No, I am a stranger here, seeking my husband."

"Mine lies yonder." The woman pointed to an older portion of the graveyard. "You think you'd find your man here?"

"I might. He and I come from Lough Neagh."

"Lough Neagh? I once met a man from there. He was a stranger too. Ah, let's not stand here blathering, come over to my house. It's not far. We can have some tea and talk out of the wind. Cold it is, almost the end of October."

A cat purred by the stove. The old woman hung her shawl on a hook and brewed some tea. A knock rattled the door; she opened it—Maire could not see who stood outside—and said, "I told you your kind were no longer welcome!"

"Sorry, Mrs. O'Carroll," came a young man's voice, "but James asked me to hand this back to you." A parcel was thrust into the woman's hand; she slammed the door, then stood looking down at what she held.

"It's *his* clothing. I asked for it back. Husband, I did wrong to loan out your tweeds to a murdering rascal, though I did it in good faith. I'll pack them away again."

She shuffled upstairs. When she returned she tossed a crumpled piece of brown paper into the stove. "Tea's ready."

Maire sipped the hot liquid. She'd been far more chilled than she'd realized.

"I'm Widow O'Carroll," the old woman said. "I failed to catch your name?"

"Maire ní Donnall." The tea was good. Maire poured another cup.

"And you've come here looking for your husband?"

"Yes." Maire considered what to say. "He and I lost each other near Lough Neagh. I have reason to think he went first to Belfast, and then headed here. He was last seen in the company of three musicians."

Mrs. O'Carroll set down her cup. "Musicians?"

"They were called the Three Bards. I'm sure he only knew them for a brief time. He doubtless met them because of his harp-playing; he's a bard himself, after all." Maire looked up. "Mrs. O'Carroll! Is anything wrong?"

"His name—it would—it could not be Tadhg MacNiall?"

Maire set her cup down with great care. Her hands shook. "Yes."

"I knew a Tadhg MacNiall, a harpist," said Mrs. O'Carroll. "To think I introduced him to that crowd! He said he carried messages from Padraig, Thomas, and Rory, and must find their friends—so I gave him my own man's clothing and took him to the pub." She covered her wrinkled face with her hands. "Sean was killed that very night, and the following night the Orange Lodge was bombed, and I've had enough, I'll stand no more of it at all." She looked up at Maire. Her face was tear-streaked. "Are you in it also, with your man?"

"In what?" said Maire.

Mrs. O'Carroll told her.

After the catalogue of horrors, Maire sat silent. Finally she said, "None of that sounds like Tadhg. He was always a gentle man. What could have changed him?"

"There is something about him not quite human," said Mrs. O'Carroll. "The day of the funeral he stood in the churchyard like a demon, with antlers and blazing eyes—only for a moment, but that moment was enough."

"That could never be Tadhg." But Maire thought of the Horned One and grew cold. "If I told you our full story you'd never believe me, but we both are lost folk, out of time. He thinks me dead. I, until yesterday, thought the same of him. Your world is so strange—"

"You sound like he did when first he came to town. You'd not be telling me what happened? He would never say."

"We were Taken long ago."

Mrs. O'Carroll shook her head. "Poor things. Either it is true or you believe it true; it matters not. If you must follow your man—though I doubt you'd know him now—I can tell you where he went."

Maire half-rose. *"Where?"*

"I'm certain he and Liam and Connor went to the Byrnes' farm on Achill Island. Up to no good, they are."

"Where is Achill Island?"

"A great distance, across the width of Ireland, more than two hundred miles, girl."

Maire slumped in her chair. "So far?" She had

some idea now of what a "mile" was. Two hundred was a great distance. "How could I get there?"

"They had Sean's car. You might find a ride—"

"I found a ride earlier today. The man was insulting. I'd rather not run that risk again."

"No matter; I can find you honest folk. Old Nicholas should be headed westward tomorrow, and when he reaches his destination he'll have a friend—leave it to me."

"Tomorrow?" Maire was anxious to be on her way.

"That's when Nicholas is delivering hay. Best you get an early start in the morning." Mrs. O'Carroll rose and took her shawl. "You stay here, you've had enough of a time. I'll go over to the pub and find Nicholas." She shuffled to the door. "Taken, were you? If so, that would explain a great deal." She opened the door; chill late-October wind wailed into the kitchen. "I'll return soon. Be at home."

Nicholas' lorry left at dawn and bumped over the roads. Nicholas himself was a quiet elderly man who struggled to keep the vehicle headed in the proper direction, and did not believe in idle talk. When they stopped, Maire helped off-load bales of hay, despite his protests; she might as well help pay for her ride.

Several changes of conveyance later—Nicholas' friends had friends—Maire's back and arms ached from tossing hay bales, hoisting milk cans, and picking up boxes of provisions. A slow trip it was, but she progressed steadily westward.

Daniel, it was, who drove her now into deepening twilight. "We're nearing the McMurphy's farm, now, Missus. That's as far as I go. Old Mahlon McMurphy has a trip tomorrow. You'll be welcome to spend the night with his family, and set off early in the morning. It's a cruel long way, but that's how it is. And thank you for the help." Young he was, and shy.

Maire smiled at him. "Ah, it was no trouble at all. I should make myself useful, should I not?"

The McMurphys welcomed her at the farmhouse—hospitality, at least, had not changed over the ages—and found her a bed in with one of the younger daughters.

"I hope you don't mind," said the woman of the house, "but we've no spare room, and Eileen sleeps soundly. She'll not wake in the night and cry, for all she's only five." She paused. "There's an urgent reason you're going across country? Daniel said something about how Mrs. O'Carroll in Dundalk had set it on the farmers to see you safely to the West Coast."

"That she did," said Maire, "and it is important I arrive soon. My husband may be in danger."

"Ah," said the woman. "Sleep well, I'll wake you early enough to be off with Mahlon."

"Thank you," said Maire. She was so weary she could scarcely stand. How good these folk were to strangers—and how cruel to their own! At least in Ulster; perhaps things were different, here in the Republic. She'd not been asked for papers or searched since she'd crossed the Border. She undressed, crawled between the bedclothes, and fell fast asleep.

The next day was the same long journey. The countryside was green and almost familiar; save for the towns, and the rattling noisy vehicles on the roads, she could well have been in her own time.

Mrs. McMurphy had packed a lunch for her and Mahlon, and she'd had to spend no money since her stay in Newry, so she still had over half the £20 Rita had given her. She was learning the value of money in this time; she must be careful.

Thus it was, when her fourth ride of the day dropped her on the west coast of Achill at twilight, she did not seek lodging in town, but asked, instead, the way to the Byrnes' farm.

From afar Maire saw the light in the farmhouse window, and noticed a car parked in the barnyard, but pride forbade her to seek shelter with the bereaved family. By now it had been dark for hours. The wind from the sea blew chill; it whistled in the stone walls, and in the distance, surf boomed.

She could shelter behind a wall, perhaps huddle in a haystack until morning. Her dress was thin, and she longed for the warm woolen mantle she had abandoned centuries ago. But folk had suffered worse privation.

She walked along the road seeking a break in the walls. A lorry sped past, and she drew aside out of its roar and glare. In the renewed silence she heard chuckling water. A stream flowed under the roadway here, in its hurry to the sea. She paused a moment and heard a loud splash.

"Well-met, Maire ní Donnall!"

She jumped and looked around. The night was empty.

"How soon you forget your friends!" The voice came from the stream. Maire crossed to the seaward side of the road. Through the culvert flowed a shallow creek; she knelt and looked into one of the pools. In the darkness she saw a glowing amber eye. *The trout.* How came it here?

"I have seen your husband, Maire," it said, "and that but lately."

Maire's heart clenched. "He lives? Where?"

"That I cannot reveal. I am under a *geas* until fate be served. But he is alive."

"Is he well?"

"He is uninjured. That is all I may say."

"Where am I to go? How may I find him?"

"For now, you must follow this watercourse to the sea. On the shore you will find one who needs you." The glowing eye vanished. Naught remained but water chuckling over stones.

* * *

One who needs me. Tadhg, perhaps? Maire stumbled over uneven ground. Branches clawed her legs and tore her skirt. Downhill she hurried, toward the salt surf.

At clifftop she paused. Black night stretched unbroken. She could not tell where the sea met the sky, or whether islands lay offshore. She must get down to the beach, she knew, but in this darkness? *You need not be blind.*

Grey faerie-sight revealed a pebbled shore where waves foamed and shattered on sharp rocks. Maire's foot slipped on something slimy; she picked it up and smelled it. Salt, and a tang of disinfectant, such as used at the Royal Victoria. She set it down—some sort of a plant, it must be—and walked to the water's edge. A grey rolling plain stretched to the horizon.

Then she heard breathing, labored and painful. A heavy body scraped over rocks. "Who is there?" *Could it be Tadhg, and he hurt?*

A shining shape crawled from the water and lay at her feet. Man-size, but with a sleek grey-furred body— of course, it must be a seal. Travellers told of such creatures.

She knelt and stroked its head. The beast opened dark eyes and lifted its shattered muzzle.

"Poor thing," Maire said, "you have been cruelly hurt."

It whimpered low in its throat and lurched back toward the sea.

"Wait," Maire said. "Wait—perhaps I can help you!" She waded after it. The water stung her scratched legs.

Waist-high the water reached; she followed the wounded seal around rocks, then into a black-walled cave. White sand covered the floor; Maire saw mantracks, and the marks of dragged objects. But her first thought was for the animal. She knelt on the sand, and the seal struggled out of the water to lay its head on her lap. The muzzle was crushed, as if by a heavy blow; blood blackened the fur, and the strong, fine teeth—curved for catching fish—were shattered and loose. She stroked the sleek head; the creature shuddered. "Poor beast. How did this happen?" The creature closed its eyes.

So fragile, those facial bones. Vessels welled blood, pain throbbed—and there was another pain Maire could not place. She held her hand close to the broken face, for to touch it would cause agony. *Heal, then, by my Power.*

In the strange grey light she saw the fine bones knit, the blood vessels rejoin, the swelling recede. *As I did for Rita.* Sharp, now, were the curved teeth; proudly the creature raised its muzzle, opened its eyes, turned, and sought the sea. Maire heard it splash toward the cave entrance as her faerie-sight faded.

She smiled bitterly. *Expected I a word of thanks from a dumb beast that fears me?* At least she had shelter for the night. She was wet and cold; she moved as far as possible from the water, curled up, and shivered.

Through closed eyelids she saw the green light. She sat up: From seaward swam the seal, towing in its mouth a string of glowing globes. When it reached shallow water it stood and stripped off its skin to become a tall, pearly-skinned man. Maire gasped. A selkie! He set the skin carefully on a rock shelf and carried the glowing globes ashore. Tall he was, slender, fair of skin and hair—all save for his large brown eyes. He sat the globe-lights on the sand.

Maire looked about her: In the green light the black cave-walls sparkled with amethyst and quartz. Even the sand turned to glittering jewels. The selkie took her hand. She rose.

"I thank you, healer. It seems that not all humans touched by fey turn evil, then." He brushed his face with the back of his hand. "But no matter." He took her other hand and looked down at her. "Sea-treasures have I, all you might wish to eat or drink, if you will stay this night and guest with me."

Splendid was his body, firm and strong and young, and his large brown eyes were kind. Maire no longer felt cold. She raised her hand to his face. "Was it humans, then, that hurt you?"

He smiled, but his eyes grew sad. He released her hands and strode to the back of the cave. From a high rock shelf he took down a flagon of green glass and handed it to Maire. She ran a wondering finger over the surface. Glass, indeed, but rough—

"Sea-worn glass," the selkie said. "Long did this lie beneath the waves, guarded by Spanish sailors." Maire shuddered. He smiled. "Oh, I had naught to do with their dying. Years ago it was. The merfolk claim they dragged them down in a storm. The galleons are rotted now, the cannons crumbled, and fish swim between the sailors' ribs. They have no need of wine."

The flask felt cold. Dead men's treasure! But what had Maire to fear from the dead?

"Drink with me," the selkie said, "to forget those who fouled my cave."

Maire unstoppered the flask and raised it to her lips. The wine was sweet and tingled golden in her mouth. "But who—"

"They were murderers, killers of their own kind and of mine. Would that the merfolk had taken them! But one"—he sipped the wine and handed back the flask. "No matter, now. They are gone, and you are here with me."

Maire had a question she must remember. But what cared she for murderers? The cave was blood-warm, the sea beat with her pulse, and the selkie drew her close. "Forget," he said. "Forget the pain with me, and the pain that is yet to come. For I am a man upon the land."

He was warm, and strong, and kind. Maire lay with him. The cave walls sparkled, and the sand was soft.

Cold rising tide lapped Maire's feet. White dawn: The selkie was vanished, his sealskin gone from its shelf, and the green globes beside her glowed pale. She sat up, brushed the sand from her hair, and sought her crumpled dress. The water was chill; she stood and looked about the cave. Remorse struck. She should have asked—should have sought—but she had fallen victim again to the enchantment of Faerie. Then, on the sand, she saw the straight and slanted lines: *Belfast. Weapons.*

It was the old Ogham alphabet, and the words were written in the language of her own time. Then she saw the other marks where crates had been dragged. A few splintered boards yet lay against the wall. Sickness gripped her. *Tadhg was with the murderers.*

She waded into the cold salt sea and washed until she felt cleansed, then made her way ashore and rinsed in the creek. She coiled her long hair, damp, into a knot.

Belfast. Tadhg was travelling to Belfast. She might find him yet. But this was Friday. Saturday was the peace march, and Tadhg travelled with murderers. What use did they plan for the weapons?

As she stumbled up the cliff the sea hissed at her back.

CHAPTER SIXTEEN

In the cold Belfast dawn, Tadhg, Liam, and Connor
knocked on the door of the Falls Road house. Tadhg
remembered the neighborhood, with slogan-scrawled
walls topped with barbed wire. This was where the
Three Bards had stopped before their trip south.

*Join Provos. Ireland divided will never be at peace.
We got six, you got four, Provos knocking at your
door. God damn the Queen.*

Tadhg understood what these meant, now.

The door opened, and they stepped inside.

Maire reached Rita's door at dawn; the cross-coun-
try trip had been exhausting, but she was too tired to
sleep. She'd had no further trouble from men; they
seemed to sense something about her, now, even those
who were not by nature courteous. She knocked; Mrs.
MacCormac opened.

"Maire! Rita said you'd been called away on a
family emergency." Rita's mother was already dressed.
She wore walking shoes. "I fear Rita is still asleep.
She worked last night, and has evening duty today.
Have you had breakfast?"

"I've not eaten in a day," Maire said. She followed

Mrs. MacCormac to the kitchen. "You are still determined to go on the march?"

"I am," she said. "I've had enough." She jabbed at sizzling bacon.

"I'm informed there will be violence."

"I'm not surprised. The Loyalists will be out in force. They'll gather at Girdwood Park and meet us at City Hall. And I shouldn't doubt the IRA will make itself known."

"You could be killed."

"Women can be brave. Our group gathers at Belfast Cemetery; at the Royal Maternity Hospital we will join those who've come down Springfield Road from Woodvale. Together we'll march down Grosvenor Road to City Hall." Mrs. MacCormac scraped the bacon and eggs onto a plate and set the food before Maire. "Tea's in a moment. If women have no right to gather at a cemetery and meet at a lying-in hospital, what rights have we? Time and again we've borne children to be killed; time and again we've escorted our husbands and sons to the graveyard. After all, Ireland is a woman!"

Maire was tired. "I'll join you in the march."

They spoke in whispers in the house on Falls Road. "The Loyalists will gather near County Antrim Prison," said James Bryson. "They'll march, then, collecting support and hangers-on, down Antrim Road to Clifton Street, Donegal, and Royal, to the City Hall. Flashpoint should occur at midtown. That is where we will be stationed." He proceeded to deploy his men. "Tadhg, you are not experienced with arms. You, with your harp, will be a good visual symbol; stand near the television cameras."

"What of the army and the constabulary?" said Connor.

"They tried to forbid the marches, but the women swore to defy them; then the Loyalists demanded their right to march as well. They'll be out in force. Cover yourselves well and expect provocation." James added, "The new M-16's have arrived. Best you spend the next few hours removing the Cosmoline from your weapons."

At the Royal Maternity Hospital the women gathered. They brought their children with them, some still carried in arms or bellies. A small platform had been erected. Maire watched Mrs. MacCormac step toward the microphone. "I've lost a son to terror, and my daughter deals with it daily as a nurse in the Royal's Casualty Ward. Time it is we let the men know we've had enough. Our children must live!"

She was loudly cheered; she stepped down and found Maire. "Never before have I spoken in public," she said. "Was I all right?"

Maire squeezed her hand. "You were perfect," she said. The march began.

They hid in garrets, on rooftops, around the corners of alleys, and waited. Security checks in downtown Belfast could, with care, be evaded.

Tadhg himself crouched behind a dustbin in an alley not far from City Hall. James Bryson had sent him there, and said he'd be called when needed. Tadhg watched the trash blow across cobblestones; everything, even the sky was grey. *But not the grey of faerie-sight.*

At one P.M., the marches were to start. An hour later, they would near each other. Bryson's men waited.

City Hall was surrounded by green; its copper roof was green as well. Across the street from it stood bombed, boarded-up buildings, but the hall itself remained intact.

British Army units ringed it, as did the Ulster police. The marching lines converged, one from the west, one from the north.

Portable television cameras stood near the juncture; the newsmen wore flak vests and helmets.

From the west the women walked; they bore no banners, but carried children in their arms. Maire guided a toddler whose mother had too many to look after. *About the size of my lost son, he'd be.* She held his hand.

Ahead Maire saw British Army lorries, with young frightened soldiers pointing their guns at the crowd. She pulled the toddler close; *only boys themselves, they are.*

Converging at the crossroads she saw the other marchers, orange-bannered and vociferous.

A portly, white-haired woman bedecked with British flags—even the parasol she carried bore the colors—stood at the head of the Loyalist march and spat at the women in the other group. "Traitors!" she said. "You'd be joining the Republic and having our rights taken away, so we could be ground under the Pope's heel. Sluts! Papish whores!"

"I'm as Protestant as you," came a reply, "and a deal more Christian, I'm thinking."

The flag-bedecked one stepped forward. "Keep a civil tongue in your head, tramp!" She pushed; the woman who'd answered her fell to the street. Others stepped forward, angry. "Don't fight," the victim pleaded, from the ground. "They're trying to start an incident; that's their way. Take no notice."

The police stepped forward; the army stood, rifles at the ready. Someone started shoving. More folk fell to the street, and stones flew.

The woman who had fallen was being kicked, now. Maire heard bones crack, and saw blood trickle from her mouth. The police swung their nightsticks. More demonstrators fell. FLASHPOINT!

From somewhere overhead, Maire heard the *snap* of a rifle. A British soldier tumbled.

Rubber bullets ricocheted off buildings into the crowd. A young boy spat teeth. A woman, struck in the eye, gushed blood from an empty socket. Sticks thrashed, stones thudded, and over all Maire heard the occasional *snap* of rifle fire.

Rolling clouds of yellow vapor covered the crowd. The gas stung her eyes and nose. She choked: tears streamed down her face. Coughing, Maire clutched the small child—where had his mother gone?—and stumbled on through madness.

She felt a jolt and looked down. The child's scalp was gashed. Blood ran down his face. He lay stunned. Maire touched the wound, but here, amid hatred, she could summon no healing power.

I must get out of here, I and the child both. That was a rubber bullet, but real bullets are also being used. There are snipers on the rooftops!

She could not see Mrs. MacCormac, who had marched toward the front of the crowd; she must be in the thick of fighting. Maire thought of searching. *But I cannot take the child back in there, and I can scarce abandon him.*

She stumbled backward. A hard object struck the nape of her neck. She turned; a man stood holding a boxlike device, scanning the crowd. A weapon? She'd seen nothing like it before.

"Get out of the way, Missus. You're blocking my television camera." The man wore a helmet and a padded vest.

Television. Maire raged: "You stand by while folk are maimed, women are attacked, and do nothing but watch!" She clutched the bleeding child. "Curse you and your heart of stone. *May you yourself know suffering, and soon!"*

The man filmed her, then turned his camera back to the violence on the street. A surge of the crowd pushed Maire away.

Tadhg, still crouched in the alley, heard Bryson's voice from the rooftop overhead: "It's started now, Tadhg. Get out there in front of the cameras. Stay away from the police, they'll club you for sure."

Blood and screaming on the street. Unarmed women and wounded children. Was this honorable war? Tadhg was ashamed to hold his harp. Excitement took over. That-which-dwelt-in-him made him step forth.

He wanted to strike out. He wished he carried a rifle, even if he were not expert in its use; fury and bloodshed were part of the Hunt.

His harp felt strange in his hands. Something bounced off his head and he felt a sharp pain; he raised his hand to his forehead and drew it back bloodstained. He wiped it away with his sleeve, but blood trickled down his face. A minor injury, only a nuisance. He was angry; how dare they touch the Leader? He raised his harp and sang,

Winter-time and wild winds
Storms that shake and slaughter,
Samhain comes! Now swiftly
Seize the starkest season.

The sky darkened, and a wind rose. A cameraman, fascinated, trained his lens on Tadhg. As the song ended, the man collapsed with a bullet through his throat. His companion picked up the camera and kept filming.

*   *   *

Maire knew not whose the child was—she had not heard the mother's name. Best to take him to Casualty at the Royal, she thought. That's where his mother would start looking, and someone there might know who she was.

Ambulances already screamed down the road; there were those who needed them worse than she, Maire knew. The child's injury was not serious; he was already beginning to stir. It was a certain distance down Grosvenor to the hospital, but Maire was beyond fatigue.

She was met at the door by a nurse—not Rita. "The name, please," she said. She carried a clipboard.

"I'm not sure," Maire said. "He's not mine, I was only minding him during the march—"

"How old? About three?"

"I'd imagine so."

The nurse wrote something in red on the form. "Rubber bullet, looks like. Not a deep cut. Best you take him over to Children's, it's not far, we're going to be very busy here in a few moments. They can stitch him up and hold him until his parents come looking; this happens often enough." She looked up and cocked her head. "Here comes the first load."

"Bryson's hit."

"So is Connor. Stow their guns, anything that might be evidence, and get them down to the ambulance. Innocent bystanders, they were, remember? Innocent bystanders. And time we cleared out of here; the army has our range and the police may be closing in. It wouldn't do if they captured us. We might not survive interrogation."

"Where's MacNiall?"

"Damned if I know. Out there somewhere. Saw him hit, nothing serious, that was some time back. Regroup at the house. And for God's sake stow your weapons! We had nothing to do with it at all, it was the Loyalists' doing. If you see MacNiall, pass the word."

Maire left the child at Children's Hospital and, almost against her will, went back toward the Casualty entrance. The area swarmed with army, police, and ambulances. There was little she might do, but she could not leave. *You will be needed.*

To avoid rousing suspicion—the guards checked everyone—Maire made herself invisible, and stepped into the waiting room.

The room was brightly lit, and crowded. In the corner crouched the red shape that had haunted her since her arrival in this time. *Old enemy, we meet again. Well have you wrought today!* It met her gaze and snarled.

Waiting families glared across the room. "Filthy bastards," a woman said, "you cannot let anything be, you must ruin everything."

From the other side a man answered her. "And who set the bomb, for instance, in the Orange Lodge? And who does the sniping?"

"The IRA, at least," said the woman, "does not bomb pubs."

"Ah, it's in favor of the IRA you are now?" said the man. "So much for your peace march, you and the other softheaded women."

Both rose; Maire thought they might come to blows, when Sister Shelby entered the room. She tapped a man and woman, who had sat silent, on the shoulder; they stood to follow her. At the door, she turned. "If there's any more bickering in here I'll have the army turf the lot of you out, and you can kill each other on the street for all I care. This is a hospital, not a battleground."

The room fell silent. Maire, invisible, followed Sister and the couple. "We've called the priest, Mrs. Rafferty," Sister said. "If you and your husband would be so kind as to wait here"— she indicated the smaller lounge—"you can see her when he's finished."

Mrs. Rafferty sat down, stunned. "She's done for, then," she said. "Jake, we should not have let her go."

"There was no stopping her when her mind was made up, she's like you that way. She was only doing what she thought right." He stepped over to the television and turned it on. "We may as well see what happened. They'll have it on the news."

Maire saw Rita rush past with a tray of syringes.

She heard the door slam open, and a voice spoke with some urgency: "Burn case! The children started throwing petrol bombs!"

A tray dropped; glass shattered, and Maire heard Rita scream: "MICHAEL!"

Tadhg was separated from his companions. His wound was not serious, but he was dazed by the aftermath of violence, and by what had possessed him. He wandered away from the noise and shouting, from the choking gas, to where he might find some quiet.

He still carried his harp; folk on the street looked at him curiously. He wandered at random, until he came to a sign that said MACCORMAC'S PUB. It looked familiar; yes, this was the place he'd come his first night in Belfast, the night he'd met the Three Bards.

He entered; the television was switched on, and all faces were turned toward the screen. The bartender was at the phone in the corner. "You're sure she's not checked into hospital? Well, I can't reach her at home, I've been trying. Tell my daughter to get in touch the minute she knows anything. Thank you." He hung up and stared for a moment at the television screen. "Newscast in a moment," he said, to no one in particular.

Tadhg sat at the bar. The bartender finally noticed

him and frowned a bit. "Nasty gash you've got," he said. "Want to go back and wash it off? Say, you look familiar."

"I've been here once before," said Tadhg. He headed back to tend to his cut. "I'll have a whiskey, when I return."

Maire slipped down the corridor to the entrance. There, on a stretcher, burned and blackened—could it be Michael? So ruined were his features it was hard to tell, and she'd only seen him once. He was escorted by several soldiers, one of whom held his burned hand stiffly before him. "No, don't worry, I can wait," he was saying, "it's my mate here needs help."

Rita, after the first shock, began to cope. "Take him to Treatment 4," she said. A white-coated doctor leaned over the stretcher and flashed a photograph. Michael winced and tried to cover his eyes. "Sorry," said the doctor, "but we need it for the records."

Maire had seen burns, but never had she seen one hurt this badly and survive. His face and arms were charred; the padded flak vest had given some protection to his upper trunk, but not to his lower abdomen and thighs—at least he could feel no pain. That would come later, with healing.

The stretcher was whisked to Treatment Room 4, and the charred bits of Michael's clothing were stripped off. Maire watched, helpless, as a white-coated young doctor inserted a needle into a vein beneath Michael's collarbone. "Start electrolytes," he said, "and we'll want cortisone; he probably breathed flame and seared his lungs. Then let's get him out of here and into Critical Care. Get blood for cross-match, stat." A bustle of activity ensued. Maire, still invisible, stood back out of the way.

Michael was fully conscious. "How bad is it?" he whispered.

"Fifty percent," the doctor said. "We've saved worse."

Maire stepped out into the corridor. Rita was talking with one of the other soldiers. "Kids started throwing petrol bombs," said the soldier with the burned hand. "One landed square on Michael. His flak jacket was about the only thing that didn't burn." He looked down at his hand. "I got this trying to put out the fire, come to think," he said. "It doesn't hurt yet."

"We must see to it," Rita said, "as soon as—"

"Oh, it won't kill me, I can wait. I hate to ask, but—how are his chances?"

Rita shook her head. "Fifty percent burn, mostly third degree. We've saved worse and lost better. At least we have the experience." She laughed; her voice was shrill. "He'll be sent directly to Critical Care; they've been warned already, and can put him in isolation." Another ambulance screamed up. "I must go. Business, you know." Again Rita laughed. Her hands were shaking.

Maire stepped back into the small lounge. The Raffertys had been joined by a better-dressed couple. No words were spoken; both families stared at the television screen.

"Welcome to the six o'clock news," the announcer said. His face was grim. "Top story of the hour is a large-scale riot in downtown Belfast, a clash between the Women's March for Peace and a Loyalist counter-demonstration." His image faded to a broad view of the fighting. "Rooftop-based snipers, placed in advance, helped provoke incidents. Among the scores of casualties was one of our own cameramen. Here is the last footage he took." The screen showed random fighting, milling crowds, and then darkness as someone leaned against the camera lens. In a moment someone leaned against the camera lens. In a moment Maire was startled to see herself: pale-faced, wild-eyed, she clutched a child and cursed. ·

That is not me. That is whatever I am becoming. More fighting scenes, then the camera focused on a young man with a harp.

It looked like Tadhg, but something about him was changed: He stood at ease amid the violence, and seemed to tower, antler-crowned and exulting, over the crowd. The image wheeled crazily and the screen went black. The announcer said, "Our cameraman was pronounced dead at hospital."

"Filthy IRA, I wouldn't doubt," said the well-dressed man. He and his wife stared at the shabbier Raffertys, who sat silent. "It's one of them got our boy, too, I'm sure." The woman looked at her husband and began to weep. "Is it never enough? You're as bad as he is, I know where he got his ideas." The man, embarrassed, stared at the floor. Sister Shelby stood in the doorway, stepped in, and tapped him on the shoulder. "Your son is asking for you," she said. "Best to hurry while he's yet conscious." To the Raffertys she added, "Come along. The priest is finished with her now."

The two couples followed the nurse down the corridor. Between them stalked the hate-beast.

Rita hurried past, duty-bound; Maire could feel waves of pain from her. *She cries for Michael, but cannot pause.*

Michael could not be left to suffer for months, perhaps die. *Use the Power you have. Michael must be saved.*

I cannot heal such an injury.

You have the Power. You have been given a task. Maire followed the signs to the Critical Care Ward.

In the pub, Tadhg stared at the television. There,

the woman holding the child, the one railing at the camera—he set down his whiskey. Some of the liquid slopped onto the bar. *It could not be!* Maire had no child. Their child was dead, and Maire herself lay drowned beneath Lough Neagh. Tears blurred his vision. He blinked and looked again. But something more than his Maire looked forth from the screen. In those eyes He recognized Her.

His inner voice spoke: *Samhain nears, and the struggle for the year will be a hard one, this time. You must fight the Goddess. She is angry, and will not surrender. There will be a great hosting at Tara.*

The human part of Tadhg shivered. He clutched his whiskey glass and drained it. Tara, the legendary seat of the High Kings since the time of the Tuatha Dé Danann—Tara on Samhain, the Feast of the Dead. And he must be there.

He set down his empty glass and called for more.

Maire stood invisible in the Critical Care Ward. About her, folk fought against death. Blood was being replaced—*blood!* There, a machine helped a man breathe, while another traced his heartbeat. Over there, another measured salts in the blood, and here, a nurse stopped pain with a needle. What sort of healer was she in this time? She knew only a few herbs, simple remedies that did not always work; but she also knew when a case was hopeless, and so she would have judged Michael. The best she might have done was brew him soothing decoctions to ease his death.

But now you hold the Power over life. Use it.

The reek of burned flesh led her to Michael. Tubes ran into his nose, fluids dripped into his veins, and he lay curtained off from the other patients. She saw, with cold grey faerie-sight, the burned and ruptured skin cells, the charred fat and muscle beneath them; she saw how his life's fluid was pouring into the damaged flesh. His eyes were open, but he could not see her.

You were but doing your assigned task, Michael, to protect the citizens of this mad city from each other, and from themselves. Such is their gratitude.

Heal him for Rita's sake, and for the land. This is why you were sent.

Burns were different from blood vessels, from clots, from bruises and pressure in the head—Maire saw the shrivelled cells and doubted her own power.

Heal. I command you, be restored.

Slowly, the blackened areas were filled in from the edges by fresh skin; slowly, starting with the muscles and working upward to the surface, the layers of tissue were created anew.

Maire watched until the task was complete, then left the room. She was drained and shaking.

The two families once again sat in the waiting room; both women wept. Maire watched outside the doorway. Between them crouched the hate-beast.

The men glared at each other. At last one spoke. "We lost a daughter tonight," he said.

The beast snarled.

"We lost a son. Shot, he was, by a sniper. One of your boys, no doubt." The other man's voice was bitter.

The beast licked its jaws. It looked at Maire.

I will meet you on Samhain, at Tara, it said silently. *And I will prevail.*

The prosperous-looking woman grasped her husband by the arm. "Have done!" she cried. "Is it never enough? They've lost a daughter, we've lost a son, and yet you keep on. Have you no common humanity?"

The men sat, ashamed. The beast cringed.

I will meet you gladly on Samhain, Maire told it. *One of us will die.*

"Time and enough that this should stop," said Mrs. Rafferty. "Had it stopped yesterday, we'd still have our children. We're Catholic and I suppose you're Protestant. What does that matter? We were all parents."

"You are right," said the other woman. "Nothing else matters." The two men sat stony-faced.

Sister Shelby stood in the doorway for a moment, then cleared her throat. "There are papers you must sign," she said, "and arrangements to be made." They nodded and rose to follow her.

The hate-beast prowled into the corridor. As it passed Maire it snarled. She stared it in the eyes and it slunk off, tail low. *Samhain, at Tara.*

CHAPTER SEVENTEEN

It was early morning when Rita stumbled home. "What with all I couldn't leave until just now. Maire! You're back!" She ran to her friend and hugged her. "And Mother, Father was so worried, he kept ringing up, he thought you were dead for sure."

Her mother shook her head. "The telephone lines were jammed, and I had to see some of the women to hospital, and sort out lost children. I left the fighting as quickly as I could. It was not for a riot that we marched."

"It was dreadful in Casualty. Mi—a friend came in horribly burned; he was taken to Critical Care. But when I went to see—" Rita stared at Maire.

"A young man friend of yours?" her mother said. "Who would that be?"

"Ah, actually he is the father of one of the nurses."

"I should feed you," her mother said.

Rita looked down at herself: Her uniform was smeared with iodine and blood. "I'm filthy and tired. I'd like to get clean and then sleep until I'm due back at work. Maire, would you come upstairs with me?"

Upstairs, Rita closed her door. "Were you at the Royal last night?"

Maire nodded.

"I did not see you."

"I can go unseen when I choose."

Rita paled. "I do not know who or what you are, but were you there when they brought Michael in?"

"I was."

"You saw his burns, then?"

"I did."

"Fifty percent of his body, third degree. Possibly fatal. Yet this morning, after things quieted, I went to visit him. *He was not burned at all.* The Critical Care staff were frantic. They had no explanation."

"I know," said Maire. She no longer felt like herself. "You were more injured last Saturday than you thought, as well. I have been sent to guard you, and, it would seem, Michael."

"You were *sent?* By whom?"

"That I do not know." For a moment Maire felt confused, merely human.

Rita looked at the picture of the Sacred Heart. "What can I believe, any more? Are you a saint?"

"Not in your religion."

"Who, then, have I been guesting?"

"Maire ní Donnall. And the Goddess."

Tadhg wandered the Belfast streets all night. At first light he reached the house on Falls Road. He knocked, and Liam let him in. James Bryson was wounded, he was told; shot in the arm, not serious. Connor had suffered a clean flesh wound, a bullet through the calf of his leg. Neither was in danger.

"I'll rest for a time," said Tadhg. "I'm weary." He found a spot in a corner and pulled stray blankets over him.

He woke to voices.

"Best we clear out of here, scatter for a time, they'll be looking for us—"

"They may do a house-to-house search any moment."

Tadhg sat up. They were ready to flee? "Who among you will join me at Tara on Samhain?"

All fell silent. "*Where?*" said Liam.

"Tara, on Samhain. A great battle will take place, and I must win. It is nearly my time to rule the year."

Murmurs: "He's gone daft."

"Samhain—that's next Tuesday, is it not?"

"He took a hit to the head, yesterday."

"Did you see him on telly? Eerie, it was. Reminded me of something—"

"ENOUGH!" roared Tadhg. He cast off his blankets and stood before them. Drawn by the noise, men had wandered in from other rooms.

The midmorning light vanished, and wind howled through the closed house. Tadhg stood antler-crowned. His eyes blazed, and he wore nothing but a deerskin. "Dare you question the Leader of the Hunt?"

Something scratched at the door. "Open it," Tadhg ordered.

"It might be anyone," Liam said.

"I know who it is. Open it."

Liam complied, and gasped as a red beast-shape slunk through the door. He stood for a moment, his hand still on the knob. "No!" He crossed himself, flung the door wide, and fled into the street.

Connor had limped in from the other room; his trouser-leg was rolled up, and his left calf was bandaged. He leaned against the wall and watched.

"I lead the Wild Hunt," said Tadhg, "my followers ride the winds. Who will ride and fight with me?"

Silence.

"Are you afraid, you men of destruction?" The

beast behind him snarled. He stroked its head.
"WHO RIDES WITH ME?"

James Bryson stepped forward. "I will."

"I cannot believe it," Connor whispered. "Such
things are only legend." He closed his eyes. "But I
remember—the MacIvers—" He opened his eyes again,
and stared: for a moment at Tadhg, then at the beast,
and finally at nothing. He limped back into the other
room. In a moment all heard a muffled explosion.

"Jesus God, women, you're not dressed for Mass
and it's late already." Mac MacCormac came downstairs in his Sunday best. He looked at Rita,
bathrobe-clad, and at his wife; last he looked at
Maire. "I never thought to see *you* alive again,
whoever you are—"

"Best you not ask, Father." Rita's voice was level.

Mac looked at her. "You must have had a busy
night, after those bloody foolish marches. Will you be
going to the later Mass, then?"

"Perhaps. I may not go at all. I'm dreadful weary."
Rita took a deep breath. "There's something you
need to know, Father. Mother, too." She sat and
leaned back. "I am tired of deceit. I never stopped
seeing Michael, despite Mrs. O'Shaughnessy's threats.
But I'll hide no more. I will not be intimidated. It's
that sort of prejudice that feeds the Troubles.
Michael was almost killed last night. A child threw a
petrol bomb. A *child*! What monsters are we raising,
these days?"

Rita's parents stood quiet. Finally her mother
spoke. "Is the boy—is Michael very badly hurt? You
said he was almost killed. Burned, it would be?"

Rita shook her head. "No, he is perfectly well. But
only Maire here can explain; ask her if you dare. I
advise against it."

*   *   *

All save Tadhg and James Bryson had fled the house on Falls Road. Those two sat looking down at Connor's body. The head was shattered; the dead hand yet gripped a pistol. He had sought oblivion the way Fionn had done.

"Connor was always practical-minded," said James. "He found comfort in details. He could not deal with the irrational. Liam doubtless will run to confession and fling himself on the bosom of Holy Mother Church." He laughed. His voice was unsteady. "I sensed something strange about you the first day we met. So be it. I serve Ireland, and Ireland is a land of myth as well as history."

"At Tara the two will meet," said Tadhg. "My time has come."

The MacCormacs stood silent. A knock sounded on the door. Rita opened it. "Mrs. O'Shaughnessy!"

The woman stepped in uninvited. "Tsk, tsk, you'll all be late for the eight o'clock Mass." She looked around the room at the family and addressed Rita's mother. "Strange, I'd swear I saw you on telly last night, at that Women's March for Peace. I must have been wrong, of course. You're not that foolish. I even thought I saw Maire here as well."

"You were not wrong," said Mrs. MacCormac.

"Oh, indeed? I'd have thought you above taking part in such disgraceful doings, marching next to those filthy Prots. I suppose you'd be letting your daughter go with a British soldier, as well?" She smiled. "Or did you know she still sees him? Last week he walked her home. Twice."

"I know what I need to," said Mrs. MacCormac. "What business is it of yours?"

"Some of us don't like our girls going with the soldiers. Things happen to the sort of girls who do. You have such long, pretty hair, Rita. What a shame to see it cut short."

Maire faced her. "You ignorant, bigoted, hate-filled woman. You've never changed. You disgrace your nation and your sex."

Mrs. O'Shaughnessy's jaw clenched. "Says who, and how dare you speak to me that way?"

"I know you of old, and I have more right than any to speak to you, *Brigid*. Well you know who I am. Look at me."

Mrs. O'Shaughnessy stared, then turned pale. "Why do I think I know you—" She blinked. "And why did you call me Brigid? That's not my name. But I remember—" Her eyes narrowed, and her smile was mean. "So it is *you*, Maire ní Donnall, the healer. *You* who would not heal my son, you who called him a changeling. He died, poor thing. You've sought your man down the years, even as I said. Did you ever find him? And had he changed?" She shook her head. "What am I saying? I never had a son, only one daughter, my Cathleen who will no longer speak with me."

Maire spoke: "And you, Brigid; how have *you* fared, over years and lifetimes? Still wed to a shiftless husband, locked in poverty, sloth, and ugliness? No curse is laid without cost."

Mrs. O'Shaughnessy looked at Maire and backed away. "It's not only Maire ní Donnall you are now. Something else, more ancient, dwells in you." She reached the door, began to cross herself, then stopped. "I did not mean it, Goddess. I take back my curse. *I take it back!*" She fled.

For a long moment the room was silent. Then Maire said, "I must be at Tara on Samhain. Rita, you will meet me there, and bring Michael. In the meantime I have tasks to do." She walked from the house.

On Sunday the Ulster Museum stood locked and silent. For Maire the doors swung open, and no alarms broke the stillness. First She paused at the case of ancient gold. A torc, after all, was Her symbol. She had no cause to fear barrow-treasure. She set it about Her neck.

Adorned, She climbed the stairs and stood before the Irish Elk. "Time it is to summon you from sleep."

The great head raised, and wires snapped. She touched the skull. "Waken, now. You live again."

"I live again? *Who calls me back from darkness?*" The skeleton shuddered.

"Your Lady. I would ride you into battle."

"For You I live again." The eyes glowed deep; covering the bones, huge muscles rippled the coarse fur. The beast bent its antlered head and knelt; Maire mounted to its back. On great cloven hooves it stepped off the platform. Its tread echoed through museum halls. Unseen, they set forth into the streets and turned south.

They would stop in Dundalk, at Mrs. O'Carroll's house; it was only fitting that Mother Ireland herself be present at the battle.

CHAPTER EIGHTEEN

The Hill of Tara dozed green in the autumn twilight. Sheep cropped the grass beneath which pagan King Laoghaire, buried upright in his armor, forever faced rebellious Leinster.

Only timesmoothed mounds and earthworks told the days of splendour; the wooden buildings had rejoined the soil. Even the great Banquet Hall was no more, but the ancient Mound of the Hostages still stood defiant outside a modern Christian churchyard.

Below in the valley, cars whispered on the roads.

As twilight deepened, the slight breeze stopped shivering the grass. The air hushed. High overhead a wind hurried clouds across the sky, but at ground level all lay still.

Silent centuries brooded in the ancient seat of the High Kings.

Samhain eve, and all over Ireland the dead arose. They left stone-chambered tombs in the Valley of the Boyne, where one shaft of sunlight struck each Winter Solstice. From the wild waves off the West Coast, the sea's pale harvest of fishermen streamed ashore. Haughty Maeve of Connaught rose from her cold bed at Cruachan, and fared to Tara as she was bid. From royal hilltop tombs and unmarked graves, from battlefields and bogs, the dead walked the night; for on Samhain the doors between the worlds stand open.

In rusted armor and grave-damp finery they fared across fields and through towns. The roads they followed were the roads they knew, not those of modern time. No one who was not fey saw them, and those who thought they might be fey huddled in well-lighted places, behind shuttered windows and locked doors.

From Clontarf, near Dublin, the Irish rose. King Brian Ború had come to lead his men. The Norse dead muttered in their wave-deep dreams; this was not their night to walk.

Brian paused where a ghostly oak-tree grew in the asphalt road. At its base huddled a tortured figure. The king looked down at his slayer. "So I was avenged. Little did it aid me, or Ireland. I was an old man; best I died in battle. If only my dream for Ireland had survived!"

Famine-gaunt wraiths trod the ways from County Cork, where they had perished waiting passage to America; from Dublin a few rebels of 1916 shouldered rusty Mausers.

From all Ireland the dead converged on Tara, for their sleep had been broken by word of a great hosting.

There gathered, also, those remaining folk of Faerie, the little ones who dwell in woods or streams: the wrens, the crows, the ravens. From the coasts came the selkies, in their human shape. Green-eyed merfolk swam up the sacred River Boyne. They hid their fish-cloaks on her banks and squelched web-footed onto land. Hawthorn trees clawed at the moon, and pookahs thundered by on horses' hooves, but all of these were minor beings. The Tuatha Dé

Danann themselves were not seen, though ancient
Tara had, at first, been theirs.

The living folk who gathered felt things flicker past
in the night, whispers and shadows. Four stood on
the hilltop: Rita, Michael, and James Bryson, from
Belfast; and from Dundalk, Mrs. O'Carroll.

At last came the Two who had summoned the hosting: the Horned Hunter, skin-clad, on a steed of
night and storm; at His heels stalked the red and
snarling hate-beast.

Moonclad, astride the giant elk, rode the unarmed
Goddess.

See the pack the Horned One has gathered,
thought the Goddess. *The dead flock always at His
heels, and now the beast, as well. How large it has
grown, this year! I will not give over, this Samhain.
He means to fight. Well, so do I.*

She will not give up the year this time, He thought.
Behind Him snarled the beast. *See Her armies! And
She has brought humans, living ones, with Her.* He
looked at Rita and Michael. *As have I.* His gaze fell
on James Bryson. He shook His antlered head and
urged His mount forward. "I come to claim My right,
My dominion over half the year." Behind Him rustled
the legions of the dead.

The Lady approached Him on Her mount; between the elk's antlers hung the crescent moon, Her
sign. The Hunter gripped His bronze-tipped spear.

She spoke. "The year is not all You wish to claim,
this Samhain." Her voice was silver, sickle-sharp. Behind Her glimmered the hosts of Faerie.

"The wild half of the year is Mine to rule," He
said. Behind Him the hate-beast glowed. Uneasy, His
steed pranced forward.

The elk raised its head and pawed. The Lady laid
a quieting hand on its neck. "Yours to rule the harsh
season, and the storms, and the Hunt. But You are

being ruled; You cannot rule the wildness that eats the land."

"I rule the wildness." His voice mocked. "Shall You have Your way? All will be soft summer, and no death? By right You own but half the year!"

Even the wind high in the clouds held still. The moon vanished, and no vision remained but the dim grey of faerie-sight. Time stopped.

"I have trod the earth as human," She said, "as have You. I have seen through human eyes what plagues the land."

From the dead legions behind the Horned One rose a woman's voice. "The land fares as it always has," Maeve cried. "In war and bloodshed. How else should it be?"

From the same legions a man spoke: "I know you, Maeve of Connaught. Strife and division delighted you, in your day. You took more pleasure in war than in bed. I too fought, but to unite Ireland. Brian of the Tributes they called me. It seems my work did not survive me."

"Ireland is sword-land," said Maeve, "and we are doomed to fight; if not someone else, then each other."

The dead murmured, but so many there were that at first no words might be discerned. Shoulder-to-shoulder they covered the Hill of Tara: the swarthy, skin-clad folk from the burial-mounds jostled the tall fair ones who bore iron. "Invaders," the Old Ones muttered, "you came raiding from the sea and took our land. You drove us West to the last stone forts at cliff-edge. Then we had nowhere left to go, so we died."

"The land is ours by right," the pale ones said, "or was until strangers took it away."

The muttering increased. "Sword-land," said Maeve. "We are destined to slay each other."

"It need not be so." Old King Brian shook his head. His eyes were blue with sorrow.

Behind the Goddess flocked the small ones of Faerie, and, mist-shrouded, the people of the sea: the selkies and the merfolk. A wet-skinned merman bared his pointed teeth. "Why does *She* care if humans fight? They poison the sea and the land."

A mermaid's green eyes glowed; she combed her hair with claws. "Better the days before they were born. How long must we suffer them? Too long already we have stayed our hand." She looked at the huddled band of four humans and stepped forward, talons outstretched.

A selkie barred her way. Tall he was, in his human form, fair-haired and brown-eyed. "So you, a daughter of Manannán, would sink as low as they? The sea should blush for shame." The mermaid bowed her head.

Of the four frozen human figures, one moved: The old woman hobbled forward and drew back her shawl. Ancient she was, her face seamed as was the land, with streams and valleys. She looked at the faerie host and at the legions of the dead, and at the Two who led them. "Sad am I," she said to both, "for crimes done in my name. Sad when my children fall upon their own, and revile each other to gain my favor. Sad, as well, when the children of the land lay curses on the human-born. I am Ireland, and I am weary and sick unto death!" She straightened her bent back: She was young, now, and strong in anger. "So," she said to the Goddess, "You would set the children of the land upon the children of men? And You," to the Hunter, "You would set murderers against their kin?" She pointed to Bryson, and then to the hate-beast. "It is not the war of the seasons or the passions of the human heart that plague me now. It is *that*."

The beast snarled. In the grey light, the other three

humans woke. Michael stood motionless; a moment ago he had been unarmed, but now he wore battle-garb and carried a rifle and grenades.

James Bryson, too, came to life. He turned and spat. "A British soldier, profaning Tara of the Kings!" He reached into his pocket and drew a pistol. Behind the Hunter, the beast growled and licked its fangs.

Rita stepped between the men. Her long hair tumbled about her face and her eyes were wide. She held out her arms. "In the name of God, let be!"

James aimed and cocked his weapon. "Stand off, Miss," he said. At his back the dead rustled and murmured: "Kill the foreigner, the invader!" They pressed forward, staring from empty eye-sockets, their bony fingers clawing the night air.

The host of Faerie stood hushed. The merfolk's eyes glittered, and their smiles showed pointed teeth. Only the selkie stepped forward.

"Stand back, Miss," James said, "for you're in my line of fire." He pulled the trigger.

The selkie knocked his arm aside; the shot went wild, into the ranks of the dead. James staggered, whirled, and fired again. The selkie crumpled, and the merfolk surged forth.

"No," gasped the selkie, "as I am human, spare him."

They threw Bryson to the grass; talons raked his face. Teeth sank into his wrist as they wrested the pistol from him; then they drew back.

Michael was as he had been before: an ordinary man whose woman stood before him, arms outstretched.

A merman held the gun in one webbed hand. "Drown this thing." It passed hand-to-hand, gleaming in the grey light, until it reached one who ran with it down from the Hill of Tara, across the grassy fields to the sacred water of the River Boyne. Mist-shrouded, the merfolk followed, save for one maid who knelt beside the selkie and ruffled his fair hair. "Part-human you may have been," she said, "but yet—" She paused a moment, shook her crested head, and followed her own.

On the wet grass James Bryson curled, his arms across his face. Not far from him, in the moonlight, the body of a great grey seal dissolved to mist.

The hate-beast snarled. Mrs. O'Carroll pointed. "*That* belongs to neither Hunter nor Lady; *that* is what rends my land!"

The beast crouched and sprang at her throat. She threw her arms up to shield her face.

"No!" The cry merged two voices. The Hunter struck His steed. "Back," He cried. "To heel!" The beast continued to savage its victim. The Hunter raised His spear. The Lady's elk lunged forward. The mounts clashed. With a toss of its head, the elk's widespread antlers swept the Hunter to the ground. He lay stunned, still grasping His spear. The hate-beast snarled. "Back," He rasped. It lunged at Him; He spitted it on His spear, then collapsed. The Goddess leapt from Her mount; the Hunter's horse reared, screamed, and trampled the hate-beast under icy hooves.

She knelt beside the fallen Hunter and held His head in Her lap. Bloody, it was, raked and smashed from chin to antlers. *This is not Your enemy. This is your other half. Your enemy lies crushed.*

Antlers? No antlers sprouted from this human brow. It was only a man's head that Maire cradled, a man who lay unmoving, and she, herself—she looked with fear at the host of Faerie and the legions of the dead. *Heal this man, while you retain the Power.*

The face was one she'd often watched in sleep: So young he looked, now. She touched his mangled cheek, traced the line of his mouth. Her hand was work-rough, her nails ragged. She was no one but

Maire ní Donnall, a woman, holding her man Tadhg. He lay bleeding and broken. She fumbled blindly for her bag of herbs, her instruments. *Heal him while you have the Power. Hurry.*

She drew a deep, shaking breath, She needed no tools. "An I yet have the Power, be healed, my man." She *willed* the shattered bones to knit, the flesh to mend, the severed veins and arteries to rejoin, and watched as they obeyed. Light dimmed as Tadhg opened his eyes. Both looked up. Above them, a tall woman bestrode a giant elk. Beside Her, a horned man rode a steed of stormclouds, and brandished a red-tipped spear. Between the Two a red pulp smeared the grass.

"So," said the Goddess, "it is Your time, Hunter, to rule the year. I will reclaim it at Bealtaine."

"So must it ever be," the Hunter said.

Wind rose and howled. Clouds streaked the sky. Rain spattered. The dark rustled, and then the night was empty.

Tadhg and Maire struggled to their feet and stared into each other's eyes. "Maire," Tadhg whispered, "I thought you lost, and dead. I searched the shores of Lough Neagh, and you were not there. We had dealt with Faerie—and then, when I was freed, I dealt with something far older." He shook his head. "Mad, I must have been, for a time. I remember terrible things, nightmare and destruction. I have killed without honor." He stepped back and held out his hands. "Yet I have seen these things and lived."

Maire wanted to cry out to him, but it was old Mrs. O'Carroll who hobbled forward. She laid one hand on Tadhg's shoulder. "Your crimes were not all your own doing." She bent down and picked up a harp. "You may have let this fall." Tadhg took the instrument.

Maire stepped closer and held him again. "Tadhg, oh Tadhg, I too thought you dead. There was that which drove me as well. Another voice spoke in me, another soul wore my body. When I found you again you seemed my enemy; I did not even know you, my husband, my love." She began to shake. "Yet you stand here human, as do I."

Mrs. O'Carroll put her arms about them both. "You are all my children, mortals and Faerie—and gods." Her arms dripped blood from countless wounds.

"Mrs. O'Carroll," Maire cried, "you're hurt!"

The old woman shook her head. "I've been hurt worse and lived. There's those as wonder if anything can kill me."

A figure crawled forward. "It was not for the land, then, I fought," James Bryson said, "but for the beast. Forgive me, Mother Ireland, for the things I did in your name." He stretched himself at her feet.

"Ah, lad, that's enough of that." She leaned down and raised him. "Come, all of you. I know the lady who runs the guest house near here. This has turned into a cold wild night." She looked at Tadhg. "As it should rightly be, this time of year."

A short distance off, Rita and Michael stood, seeing only each other. "Ah, let's get the two young ones in out of the rain, they haven't the sense themselves." She went over and took them by the arm. "Come now, all of you." She herded them toward a distant light and dropped back. Tadhg and Maire stopped as well. "One thing, Tadhg, before we go in. Too many memories can bring sickness, as well you know. You and Maire are no common folk. You've earned your memories, and I have so many a few more are no burden. These others, though—"

So Tadhg played his harp and sang a song of forgetting:

The pain melts in raindrops, no memories wander
The hills and the plains and the shore,

The dead lie undreaming, their sleep is untroubled
By heartbreak, and sorrow, and war.

For no matter what else he was or had been, he was
foremost a bard.

The path led near the Mound of the Hostages.
Rita stopped. "A faerie-mound," she told Michael.
She peered through the iron gate. "Dark as it ever
was. There's nothing to the stories, then."

She, Michael, Mrs. O'Carroll, and James Bryson
walked on ahead. Maire and Tadhg lingered. They
could hear faint music and laughter. Was that a glow
far back around the corner?

"These mounds are only passage-graves," said
Tadhg, "not gateways to Faerie after all, you know."

"Are you sure?" said Maire. The glow brightened,
and before them—inside the iron gate that walled off
the doorway—stood the King and Queen of the
Sídhe, alive again and merry. Each held a golden
goblet.

"Well have you wrought, Tadhg MacNiall," said
the Queen, "or others wrought with you. We live
anew. Would you rejoin us?" She held out her slim
white arms and stepped closer to the grating, then
frowned at the iron.

"And you, Maire ní Donnall, brave as ever," said
the King, "Our feasting continues, and your task is
done. Join the merriment; come back to our palace."
He held his cup closer to the gate. It might pass between the bars, if a human reached for it. "Take this,
and drink good wine."

Maire, afraid, looked at Tadhg. Was the lure
still strong? He regarded the Queen for a long moment, then put his arm around Maire's waist. "No,"
he said. "I have seen your palace, and I would rather
be alive, even in this strange time, with my own wife
beside me."

"And I would rather stay with my man," said Maire. Then she remembered to ask: "What became of the child, the one who fled to your land beneath the lake?"

"He is with us yet," said the Queen. "Since we did not perish, neither did he. We must tell him, now, how the Forces fought—and how they no longer strive against each other. He may wish to return to his own land, now. Something strong calls humans homeward. If a lost young boy knocks on your door some night, he will be as frightened and alone as you once were."

"We will welcome him," said Maire. "But how will he know where to find us?"

"We will tell him. Fare well, both of you," said the Queen.

"Fare you well," the King echoed. "Live out your lives." Both turned to leave.

The Queen looked back and said, "If you think of it in future years, Tadhg—from time to time," her mouth twisted, "until you grow old and die, play your harp near a faerie-mound. 'Twould gladden us."

"I will do that thing," Tadhg said.

Tadhg and Maire watched as the King and Queen of the Sídhe faded into the rock.

"These are only ancient passage-graves after all," Tadhg said, "built by folk who lived long ago."

"But you will play your harp near them from time to time," said Maire.

" 'Tis only kindness for the poor cold phantoms. We can spare it; we are alive, and warm, and glad."

They hurried to catch up with the others. The night was black, and the rain and wind were increasing. Winter, the wild time, had come in its season. Tadhg and Maire should be indoors with human folk.

* * *

The Horned One rode the wind, His host behind Him; He laughed for joy. The Goddess nestled in the earth and slept, till life should spring forth new across the land.

THE SWORD OF SHANNARA

Terry Brooks

Long ago, the world of Shea Ohmsford was torn apart by the wars of ancient Evil. But in the Vale, the half-human, half-elfin Shea now lives in peace — until the mysterious, forbidding figure of Alanon appears, to reveal that the supposedly long dead Warlock Lord lives again, and will destroy the world . . .

Shea, the sole true descendant of Jerle Shannara, must embark upon the elemental quest to find the sword, the only weapon powerful enough to keep the creatures of darkness at bay.

'A marvellous fantasy trip'
Frank Herbert (Author of DUNE)

Futura Publications
Fiction/Fantasy
0 7088 1344 5

THE ELFSTONES OF SHANNARA

Terry Brooks

An epic novel of fantasy and adventure; the long awaited sequel to *THE SWORD OF SHANNARA.*

Ancient, ultimate evil threatened the Elves and the Races of Man. For the Ellcrys, the tree of long-lost Elvin magic, was dying, loosing the spell of Forbidding that locked the hordes of Demons away from Earth. Already the fearsome reaper was free. Only one source had the power to stop it:

And the valiant companions must ride again in an impossible quest.

Futura Publications
Fiction/Fantasy
0 7088 8095 9

SONGMASTER

Orson Scott Card

Mikhal the Terrible, pacifier of the galaxy, has learned of the children trained in the ancient Songhouse of Tew. Only the purest in heart are chosen to be served by one and decades pass before his request for a songbird is answered by the supremely gifted Ansset.

Mikhal's songbird can mould the emotions of his listeners in any form he chooses. But he cannot avoid becoming the tool of others more powerful than himself.

Bereft of his singing voice, he brings tragedy to the universe before returning to the refuge of the Songhouse – an old man with a harsh but precious song to teach.

'a compelling story with a fairy tale appeal'
Publishers Weekly

Futura Publications/An Orbit Book
Fiction/Science Fiction
0 7088 8080 0

THE SNOW QUEEN

Joan D. Vinge

'A FUTURE CLASSIC . . . IT HAS THE WEIGHT AND
TEXTURE OF *DUNE*'
Arthur C. Clarke

Arienrhod. As beautiful as she was ancient, she ruled
Tiamit, whose twin suns circled the Stargate linking
her world with the Empire. Now the Stargate was
closing, heralding the end of Winter rule. But
Arienrhod, faced with ritual sacrifice, has cloned an
heir – her key to immortality and perpetual
dominion. The Snow Queen will defy the laws of the
galaxy for the fountain of youth kept flowing by
genocide and the power of love.

'massive and exciting new novel . . . a triumph'
Publishers Weekly

'a book I wish I'd written . . . a splendid novel'
Anne McCaffrey

'an unusual novel, full of richly woven characters'
Theodore Sturgeon

'a fine tale, a pleasure to read . . . I recommend it
most highly'
Roger Zelazny

Futura Publications/An Orbit Book
Fiction/Science Fiction
0 7088 8075 4

All Futura Books are available at your bookshop or newsagent, or can be ordered from the following address:
Futura Books, Cash Sales Department,
P.O. Box 11, Falmouth, Cornwall.

Please send cheque or postal order (no currency), and allow 45p for postage and packing for the first book plus 20p for the second book and 14p for each additional book ordered up to a maximum charge of £1.63 in U.K.

Customers in Eire and B.F.P.O. please allow 45p for the first book, 20p for the second book plus 14p per copy for the next 7 books, thereafter 8p per book.

Overseas customers please allow 75p for postage and packing for the first book and 21p per copy for each additional book.